D1559853

Johnnie Ray

&

Miss Kilgallen

Bonnie Hearn Hill

&

Larry Hill

CONNETQUOT PUBLIC LIBRARY
760 OCEAN AVENUE
BOHEMIA, NEW YORK 11716
Tel: (631) 567-5079

Copyright © 2002, Bonnie Hearn Hill & Larry Hill

All rights reserved. No part of this book may be used or reproduced, in any manner whatsoever, without the written permission of the Publisher.

Printed in Canada

For information address:
Durban House Publishing Company, Inc.
7502 Greenville Avenue, Suite 500, Dallas, Texas 75231
214.890.4050

Library of Congress Cataloging-in-Publication Data
Bonnie Hearn Hill, 1945 & Larry Hill, 1932

Johnnie Ray & Miss Kilgallen / by Bonnie Hearn Hill & Larry Hill

Library of Congress Catalog Card Number: 00-2002103003

p. cm.

ISBN 1-930754-19-1

First Edition

10 9 8 7 6 5 4 3 2 1

Visit our Web site at
http://www.durbanhouse.com

Book design by:
Strasbourg-MOOF, GmBH

To JR & DK,
and to the **Tuesday Night Writers**,
where it all started.

acknowledgments

We are grateful to the following, who, in various ways, helped our efforts become a novel:

John Lewis, for his graciousness and enthusiasm, and for understanding how it feels to be on the other side of the desk;

Bob Middlemiss, for the red ink and black Lab hair that fine-tuned the manuscript;

Madeline, for making the book a reflection of the times;

Larry Paquette, for moral support and proofreading;

Bridget Bulger, for giving us the Irish America magazine that started our game of "What If";

The Johnnie Ray International Fan Club, for keeping the music and the legend alive;

The SouthWest Writers, for the encouragement and the cash award.

Special thanks to Paddy Calistro, Angel City Press, for the referral to Laura Dail, and to Laura Dail, for being Laura Dail.

Johnnie Ray

&

Miss Kilgallen

PART ONE

Walking My Baby Back Home

one

Johnnie

New York's a cold bitch. She's especially bitter this February of 1956 when I stumble hungover into CBS Studios. I'm trying to find my way through a maze of halls into *What's My Line*, this panel of stiff-necked New York assholes playing their parlor game. Most uppity member of this select group? Dorothy Kilgallen. Little purse-mouthed bitch's been bum-kicking me in her column like I'm a Sing-Sing escapee.

At a crossroads, I bump into Jimmy Witherspoon, who's as lost as I am.

"Johnnie Ray," he says. "Hear you been tearing 'em up, man, since the Flame Showbar, Detroit City."

I almost ask him to say *Detroit City* again in that way he's got. "Happenin', Spoon?"

He grips my hand, pulls me close, wraps me up in his dark suit. His embrace is tough and tender. He smells like sweet danger. "The Flame," he says, looking off like the hall's a train or he's waiting for one. "We tossed you to the crowd in that black 'n' tan."

I grin. "Threw out the honky with the wire going into his head."

He measures my blue suit up, down. "Where y'all headed?"

"*What's My Line*," I say, feeling a snare of apprehension. "I'm the mystery guest."

1

He slaps my palm. "You the mystery, all right." And he's gone, circling a finger above his great head.

Standing in front of what I hope is the right door, I regret not asking him about why he's here tonight. His rich voice remains in the space, sound waves for all time. That kind of echo, Jesus—that would be enough for me.

Few minutes later I'm warned by the guy in make-up, "Watch out for Kilgallen. She's liable to ask you your brand of rubbers."

I act shocked. "Thought they wore blindfolds."

Behind me, a scoff. "Dorothy can see through hers."

Waiting in the wings for the call from John Daly to sign the blackboard, I see a young doughnut runner in a bright yellow shirt talking with the swish who did my make-up. The gofer sleepy-eyes me, turns covertly to others, hides a canary-eating grin with a hand.

What the hell? I got a minute. Passing harried glances, I go stand in front of Yellowshirt, lay a close- up on him. He sweats.

I adjust my hearing aid meticulously, then move my hand and center my index finger on the cleft of his mouth. I hold it against the dry indentation, hush-hush position.

"Careful," I say softly. "I read lips, man."

 # Dorothy

It was all Sinatra's fault.

Dorothy sat in darkness behind the satin mask as the guessing game took place around her. Blindfolded in public. Jesus, a metaphor for her life. She felt the studio audience's vibrations race against her own pulse. Were people across the country checking out her profile, pointing at their televisions, snickering at her image? She squared her shoulders, feeling the rustle of her taffeta wrap.

"Will our mystery guest sign in, please." John Daly's stuffy tone made the memorized command sound spontaneous.

She tried to concentrate. In her mind, she heard only Sinatra, pictured him in his latest Las Vegas engagement. "Dotty Kilgallen couldn't be here tonight," he'd been quoted. "She's out trying to buy a new chin."

God, had she missed her cue from Daly? Down the line to her left, Bennett Cerf asked something that caused the audience to titter. Then Arlene Frances jumped in, her melodic voice enthusiastic.

"Are you in show business then?"

"Yes," the mystery guest replied, voice disguised. Behind her blinders, Dorothy focused her thoughts. Was the voice male? Female? Fred Allen took his turn, and it was back to her too soon. Jesus, she had to react this time.

"An entertainer?" The camera was probably lingering on her mouth. She tried to smile, make her face less stiff.

"Yes."

"That's four down, six to go," Daly said.

"An actor?" Cerf asked.

"Sometimes."

"Five down, five to go."

Arlene's turn. "Singer?"

"Yes."

A singer like Sinatra. She straightened her shoulders. Jesus, it couldn't be Sinatra. No, but from the audience's reaction, as big or bigger. God, had Allen asked his question? She cursed the darkness, felt a moment of panic, tried to smile. Ask something, she screamed silently to herself.

Bennett Cerf was next, then Arlene, in hot pursuit again, Daly letting her go now. Gold records? Yes. Top Ten? Yes. Hits? Yes. Yes, yes, yes. "Female singer?" asked Arlene, getting a laugh before she pounced.

"No."

Dorothy felt dull, vacuous. Who was the mystery guest? His voice struck a chord. She'd heard its rusted edges before. Hadn't she liked it? An image of a man, tall and blond, hovered beyond her blindfold.

Victory bristled in Arlene's voice. "Could you be," she asked smugly, "the young man who made crying a national institution?"

Applause surged. Arlene went no further. Damn her. Dorothy needed only a moment more to get sharp, would have had it had Daly proceeded in proper order.

"Panel, you may now remove your blindfolds," he said, giving all the glory to Arlene, as if he'd planned the course of questioning from the beginning.

Dorothy removed her mask, blinked into the light, exhibited her smile as she would a piece of jewelry. She stared ahead as if still blindfolded.

Applause continued as Daly introduced the guest. "Ladies and gentlemen, let's welcome Mr. Johnnie Ray."

In the bedlam, Dorothy allowed herself one quick look past the other three panelists to the young man smiling directly at her.

Dorothy slammed the door behind her. Her dressing room with its irritating, omnipresent clock closed around her. Marie greeted her, holding out a tumbler of vodka and ice.

"Figured you could use this," she said.

"And how." After primping her, Marie always watched the show from the wings, and the sympathy in her expression left no doubt that she'd done so tonight. Dorothy clutched the glass. "What a debacle."

"Remember," Marie said. "You have more right guesses than all of them combined."

The vodka was warm, friendly. Dorothy began to relax. Marie fluttered about her, tiny but sure-handed. Dorothy faced herself in the narrow mirror, saw the reflection of unopened fan letters on the table. She picked one up, let it drop.

"Don't bother setting these out for me."

"You've always enjoyed them."

"Not anymore," Dorothy said. She spread her hands and leaned against the table. "This goddamned dress. I feel trussed as a turkey."

"It's the boning."

Dorothy frowned into the mirror. "Whose idea was it to wear evening gowns every week?"

"Yours, honey."

"You'd know, Marie."

"Been with you from the start," she said. "Now, let me unzip you."

Dorothy felt the woman's fingers tend to her. "I'm foolish allowing the show to upset me." The evening was, however, tarnished. P.J. Clarke's wouldn't be the same, nor would the Copa. People would know she'd been bested by Arlene—those not already tittering about Sinatra's running barrage against her. The sensation of Marie's touch against her back lifted her spirit. "Press your thumbs there."

"Here?"

"I had a masseuse put pressure there last week," she said. "Tears ran down my cheeks. Forty-four years old, Marie, and it was the first time anyone had ever done that."

"I'm about the same age as you, honey, and I only wish I was in your shape."

"Blarney," Dorothy said. "What did you think of our mystery guest?"

"I think it's true what they say about him having a metal plate in his head."

Dorothy wagged her finger at Marie's image in the mirror. "You're reading Sheilah Graham again."

"Am not. I only read you. He's nervy showing up here after you took him apart in your column."

"I've seen him perform. I should have guessed his identity."

"If he didn't sound so much like a woman you might have." Marie ended her sentence with a gasp.

Dorothy turned from the mirror. Marie's arms flapped away from her. "Oh, excuse me, Mr. Ray," she stammered. "I was just leaving."

Johnnie Ray politely moved aside, allowing her to pass. He stood tall, his blue suit almost tropical away from the set's harsh lights. He stepped toward her, loose-gaited. His body seemed to be trying to flee itself. Energy snapped from him. The hearing aid in his left ear upset the symmetry of his angular face. He appeared more raw, untamed than out in the studio. In the small room, Dorothy backed away.

He glanced at the school-room type clock above her, then surveyed the tidy liquor display. "I got time for a drink," he said, "if you're buying."

She picked up her cocktail. His voice sounded raspy, a bit unsettling. "I'd prefer not to contribute to your delinquency."

Brushing past her, he helped himself to a drink. "Why not? Your readers dig it."

She sipped the last of her drink. The ice burned her tongue. "I admitted I liked *Please Mr. Sun*." God, what was wrong with her voice?

"Big of you."

Dorothy felt an urge for a cigarette but made herself stand rigid. "I saw your act at the Copa. I meant every word in my column."

"That I'm Endsville?"

"Exactly."

"Shit, that was 1952." He tossed his head back as he drank. She watched his throat move. He returned to the liquor, poured another and held up the bottle. "You?"

"Why not? It's been a dreadful night."

The splash of vodka into her glass sounded luxurious in the tight space.

"Look," he said. "I don't want a war."

"Nor do I," she said. "One public enemy is enough."

"Sinatra?"

"Who else?" She was finding her voice again, feeling stronger.

"Some say you asked for it."

So. His appraisal of her feud with Sinatra matched the way most of New York felt about it. "I'm a journalist," she said." I don't answer to him or anyone else."

He chuckled. The slight space between his front teeth made him look even younger than, what? Twenty-nine, twenty-eight? The hostility in his eyes paled. "You pissed off a man don't no one piss off."

"I wrote the truth. I didn't ridicule him personally, and I didn't do it on stage at the Copa, for Christ's sake."

"Don't let it get to you." He drank, lowered his voice. "You got too much class."

She smiled, the first honest smile in a long time, she thought. Perhaps, in spite of his youth, his fame, his armor of arrogance, he was wiser than on first impression.

"Thank you," she said.

"Sinatra shouldn't be knocking anyone's looks," he added. "He's not blessed with a strong profile himself."

"He's blessed with a strong one below the belt," she said, immediately regretting it.

His drink paused at his lips. He looked her up and down, as if searching for something secret she might be hiding. "How would you know?"

"That's my understanding," she replied, carefully. "Everyone's heard the rumors."

"He ain't as blessed as some of us."

"Oh, spare me," she said.

"According to Ava, that is."

So the stories about him and Ava Gardner were true. Sheilah Graham was right again. That bothered her more than this young man's boasting. This entire encounter with him was a bother, come to think of it. She'd suffered enough indignity for one evening.

"I said stop it." She glanced up at the clock. "It's late. We've given those on the other side of that door ample time for conjecture."

He smiled past her shoulder. "Haven't had time to conjecture that."

Turning abruptly, she stared into the mirror. Her naked back, even her garter belt, the tops of her stockings—he'd had a clear view of all the entire time. She whirled back to face him.

"You son of a bitch."

The animated smile didn't leave his face. He reached into his jacket and took out the battery pack for his hearing aid. With a flourish, he switched it off. Without another word, he sauntered from the room, closing the door firmly behind him.

"You son of a bitch," she repeated, shouting this time, in spite of herself.

two

 Johnnie

Friday, broad daylight. I'm still picturing Kilgallen's ass dimples while I sprint from the stage door to Morrie's Caddy. Fans buying early tickets for tonight's show have spotted me and are in squealing pursuit.

I dive into the waiting sedan's back seat. "Hit it, Morrie."

Fists pelt the Caddy's roof. Faces splotch against its windows. Tires crunch ice.

Checking to see if I'm in one piece, I let my mind wander to those low, roving hills back home. I'm hanging onto our Holstein Dinah's tail. My feet are up on her flanks. She's clomping along behind Rover, my shepherd mix. I'm probably thinking life always will be this complete, this full of freedom. My sister Elma watches. She figures after witnessing many such rides, that I'm too charmed to be on board should ol' Dinah decide to shit.

I've suffered awful indignities since, however, striking out from the Willamette Valley in Oregon, the stands of cedar, cypress and ash, the one-room schoolhouse. Dinah. Rover. Goddamn, place a blade of grass between my teeth and I'm exactly what Morrie Lane would have me be.

"Hit it, Morrie," I yell again at the back of his balding plate.

"Like a bird, man," he says.

My devoted fans, mostly kids, drop from the moving car like bees do a hive when you jostle it with a long stick. I turn to see their figures in the gray afternoon.

"Like an owl," I say. "Jesus, watch it."

Morrie spins the wheel like a great sea captain lost in a storm. "Call me owl again, you fucking radical, I spill you out, let 'em cut you to ribbons."

I jerk my topcoat around so I can examine it. Shit, they're using razors again. My coat's in shreds. "Lucky they didn't take a kidney," I say.

Morrie finds a groove in the traffic. "Where's his majesty going? What's in the sack? Dope?"

The bag of platters I snatched backstage has been slashed, but the recordings seem to be intact.

"Look through those coke bottles and stay in the right lane," I say. "Got me a birthday party gig, East Sixty Eighth and Park."

Morrie bounces. My earnings have made him round. "You're dangerous. I ain't staying to chaperone you, some posh penthouse, for Chrissake."

"Wow. How'll we act, no owl to hoot?" I spot a tavern I know, decide I better line my stomach. Besides, I'm a little antsy. The Voice of Broadway did end our first meeting by calling me a son of a bitch. But then she also phoned my record company to request these platters for her daughter's sweet sixteen party. Maybe I just like being sworn at by classy women, or maybe I'm right, and The Voice of Broadway kind of dug me as much as I dug her. Either way, I know what I need right now. "Stop up at this corner," I say.

Morrie is bobbing, trying to catch me in the rearview. "You fucking criminal. It's past noon." Playing the concerned manager now, the old song-plugger, "We got a show in three hours."

"Four hours. And I'm hip. Still need something in my tummy. Got to have my breakfast."

"Breakfast? You should be arrested." Morrie's found the tavern through his thick glasses. "Where? This ginmill?"

"Sure." I have to laugh at the guy. I love him is the sad truth. "They serve cold beer and hard-boiled eggs, don't they?"

Then I hear the shriek of brakes and after a long second, I'm thrown damn near up in front with Morrie. Another minute and I know it ain't too bad. A New York rear-ender is all, our sedan trying it doggie-style with some little Studebaker ahead of us.

Studebaker guy jumps out. So do I, and I look back once to see Morrie slowly ease out his side, squint up at the buildings like some rube his first time in Manhattan.

One more minute and I'm drinking breakfast, thinking about the lady.

 Dorothy

At Dorothy's insistence, the dining room in the Sixty Eighth Street address had remained without a clock for years. Dick at first found her aversion charming. Years passed and so did the charm. Finally, he demanded that she explain her problem with clocks. "They tick," she had told him.

He pointed out that they also kept her from being late, to which she replied that she wasn't the one who missed appointments. As with most of their conversations, this one had drifted into polite sniping. Dorothy since had ignored a defiantly ugly pendulum piece on the wall of their bedroom, which after her move to the fifth floor was in truth Dick's alone. Another timepiece, a bell jar, appeared in the dining room a few weeks later.

It rested today as always on a buffet behind them. As they prepared for their daily radio show early that morning, Dorothy was conscious of its soft whirring. Sitting at the dining room table, the WOR microphone before her, she watched Dick settle across from her. His business suit lacked its hard edges. His actor's good looks had grown mealy from heavy drinking.

As usual this morning, he could be counted on to be on time, but that was about all. No doubt she'd have to carry the show again, And she would, by god. Their lifestyle depended on it.

The director signaled. The tow-headed technician watched as nervous as if it were his first time.

Dick responded on cue. "Good morning, darling," he said in his rich baritone. "It's time for Dorothy and Dick. My, this is great orange juice."

"It's Juicy Gem, our favorite," she responded with exaggerated enthusiasm. "Would you like some toast?"

He clinked two champagne glasses, gave her an evil wink. "No, darling, but I'd like to toast you." Again he rang the crystal. "Eleven years of Dorothy and Dick. Can you believe it?"

Eleven years. "We've certainly had a marvelous time. Met wonderful people along the way."

"Interesting ones, wouldn't you say?"

Now what? "Yes."

"Your mystery guest Sunday night on *What's My Line*, for instance."

She hadn't expected that one. "Yes?"

"The Prince of Wails."

"You must mean Johnnie Ray."

"The Nabob of Sob."

She jerked her head up, catching nothing but Dick's placid smirk. "Mr. Ray is a talented performer."

"The guy with the rubber face and squirt-gun eyes."

Enough. "There is an indefinable something in Johnnie Ray's voice," she said. "An articulation of his loneliness."

"But Sweetie, Elvis is the one with art in his pelvis. 'ticulation too."

Jesus Christ. She bit back her anger. Maybe their banter today approached the sparkle of years past. She promised herself to hold their bickering to a pace the listeners might enjoy. Right now the show was all-important. If their audience moved away, so would Juicy Gem and the rest of the sponsors who contributed to their sixty-thousand whatever yearly reward for conversing with each other every morning.

Straightening her shoulders, she continued to talk into the mike, forcing a smile, as if the world could see.

Knowing the birthday party would swim in teen-age pastel, Dorothy changed into a black dress. A courier had picked up her column, and she was starting to relax before guests arrived. Over a cup of coffee, she watched Dick devour Eggs Benedict at the table they'd broadcast from earlier.

"Really, Dick. Eggs Benedict in the afternoon?" she asked.

He sat as still as a discarded movie showcard while Julian poured him champagne. Julian held the bottle above an empty glass and raised his brow at her. She shook her head, then watched with distaste as he refilled Dick's glass.

Watching him cut into hollandaise-drenched Canadian bacon, she reminded herself as long as they kept the show and their family together, all would be tolerable.

After Julian was out of earshot, she said, "I could have done without the Johnnie Ray dig."

"Just trying to breathe life into the show, darling." He put down his fork, reached for the champagne. "Besides, you've harmed the guy more in print than anything I said."

"Perhaps." It was true, of course, but Johnnie had said he didn't want a war, and in spite of the oath with which she'd ended their meeting, neither did she. "But that doesn't matter now. We've declared a truce."

He cocked an eyebrow ever so slightly. "Since when?"

"Since last night." The coffee and conversation made her pulse pound. She glanced at the bell jar. "Are you going to miss the party?"

"Afraid so," he said. "I'll be back late. I'm meeting with some people about the club."

For an actor, he was a poor liar, or maybe he just didn't care enough to make the role he played at home believable. Looking into his eyes was like trying to gauge the depth of a glassy pond.

"I know how late your meetings run," she said.

"Money people," he put in. "Must quell the nasty rumor I'm Mr. Dorothy Kilgallen."

She pushed away from the table. Tired, she thought, already bushed, and the evening hadn't started.

"Gosh," she said. "You mean being the voice of Boston Blackie isn't enough for you?"

"Don't knock it. Blackie's bought us both a drink now and again."

"So has *Breakfast with Dorothy and Dick*." Circling the table, she stood behind him. "Try to be back at a civilized hour. We've much to go over for tomorrow's show. It's been flat lately."

"Not so today," he said with a self-satisfied smile.

"I'm sure we owe that to you."

"Now that you mention it."

"But what about tomorrow?" *After you've had a few more bottles of that,* she added silently.

"Tomorrow will take care of itself if you'll just relax." He held up a finger. "Quit giving Sinatra the satisfaction of getting your goat. Our listeners hear it in your voice."

"Nonsense." She glared down, watched his head shake slowly left to right.

"Okay, okay." He heaved a dramatic sigh. "So we get a few letters addressed to the Chinless Wonder."

Hearing the expression from his lips almost dropped her. She felt as if she were caving in, the pain within her chest real enough to make her bite her lip to keep from crying out. "Dick," she said in a small rush of breath.

His head moved faster, side to side. "A few letters," he said. "Not like the TV show. A dozen is all, not hundreds, not thousands, for Christ's sake. But it's driving you crazy. You've played right into the little mobster's greasy hands."

"Please." Her legs wobbled. She leaned against the table and picked up the champagne bottle.

"You don't sound natural anymore," Dick continued.

A quick turn of her hand, and the remaining champagne fell away from the neck of the bottle, fizzing like a brook in his graying hair.

"At least," she said, "I sound sober."

As he left the table, wet head and all, he shouted, "Hubba-hubba, darling. Hubba-hubba."

In his sputtering words, she heard a thin, sad echo of gaiety from their yesterdays.

 Johnnie

The five-story townhouse is on East Sixty-eighth, between Madison and Park—final neighborhood on the Monopoly board. I tell the cabby to drop me, then count out his fee and tip from the bar change in my suit pocket.

He goes, "Thanks, pal." I show him my Hollywood choppers. His eyes get big. "Hey, ain't you the *Cry* guy?"

I dash for the steps. The air is ashy, cold against my throat, and I worry as usual about my pipes. An Uncle Tom butler answers my ring, cools on me like he's bored to death. I take a swipe at the egg crumbs and salt on my upper lip, gather platters and shredded coat to my chest.

"Johnnie Ray to see Dorothy Kilgallen," I tell the suede. Without the cotton top, he could be Eddie "Cleanhead" Vinson, raucous alto out of Houston, damn fine blues voice of his own.

"Is she expecting you?"

"Tell her I'm an errand boy running over some records she requested for her daughter's birthday bash."

This gets me a ride up an elevator that groans from the stress. Vinson ushers me down a hall that reflects our walk off every surface. Cold, man.

Doors open into a bright parlor. Lots of jail bait swish around in rustling taffeta. Young boys stand in stiff poses, afraid to flare their acne. Two teen-aged sheiks send me dark stares. A white Steinway baby grand sits in the center of the action. Lid agape.

Before I see her, I know she's near. The honest-to-god delight in her voice rings in my hearing aid. She says something to the butler, then takes my sack of record albums.

"I had no idea you'd come in person," she says.

She is in simple black, kind of a *noir* look with her dark hair, Betty Boop eyes. Her skin is alabaster but soft looking. She stands, more confident on her own turf, a hip chick, sending little sex waves, different than in the CBS Green Room, rank fan mail strewn on her dressing table, and don't ever tell me about rank fan mail.

I head straight for the Steinway. The kids are in shock, my name on their whispers. I try the keys, and it's in tune enough for me. "Ready to raise a little hell?" I ask, rather loudly. Kilgallen looks small and pale among these animals. She sends me a brave smile.

I give them a crash course in boogie woogie, and don't tell me about boogie woogie. Then I settle down and go into Satchmo. Always had him down pat. Give them Louie and Teagarden on *St. James Infirmary*, by God, a duet, but shit I doubt they know that. I feel I'm dragging them down, so I give them a snatch of Edith Piaf to punish them more, then figure hell why not, since I invented the motherfucker, I stand and give 'em Elvis, complete with bumps and grinds.

"My favorite," shouts the daughter.

Later I chat with the brats, watch them dance to my records. Kilgallen brings me a spiked punch, and for some reason, I don't ask her to dance, though I know it's what she'd like. Finally it's time I got to go.

"Showtime downtown," I say.

"I'll drive you," she says. "After your kindness, it's the least I can do."

Kindness or no kindness, women like her don't play chauffeur to guys like me. I got nothing to add to that, so I just stand there. Then I think of some smart-ass answers but stay buttoned up. She looks at me with those huge, soft eyes, and I can't help it. I reach out and touch her bare shoulder, then her cheek with the backs of my fingers.

"I'd like that an awful lot," I say.

three

 Dorothy

In the weeks following the party, she found herself phoning home more frequently. "Just checking in," she'd say to Julian, sensing in the silence before he spoke the impropriety of her behavior.

Johnnie had said he'd call, and she knew he would, although she still wasn't certain why. He was impressed by her power, she knew. As she waited for the message that would surely come, she collected anecdotes for him. She'd tell him about her spontaneous dance with Bobby Short at Eartha Kitt's opening at the Plaza, her coverage of Grace Kelly's wedding the month before.

At times she tried reminding herself that she was a journalist, not just New York's first woman Broadway columnist. *Lindbergh kidnapping. Sheppard murder.* She counted the stories like beads. She didn't need any distractions, she told herself, not even a friendship or whatever it was with this boy. She resolved to do nothing, no sweet note of thanks, no more innocent calls to his record company. If she presented a passive front, then she wouldn't be disappointed, wouldn't be humiliated.

She'd never been the type to kid herself. Even when, years before, she had hoped against hope that Tyrone Power would marry her, a solid part of her had known better and steeled her softer self against the truth. She felt no such protection now, only the pleasant glow of anticipation. Johnnie had said he would call. A month after the party, to the day, he did just that.

They agreed to see *An Affair to Remember*, Johnnie's idea. She told him about her misunderstanding with Vic Damone, who sang the title song, and how they were now great pals. It seemed important that he understand that not everyone she wrote about hated her.

Although she and Dick had long since pursued other interests, she felt almost clandestine as she dressed for her movie date. Silly. She had many male friends. Was ermine too much for a movie? Well, they would surely stop somewhere after. What about a hat, that cute black cloche that went with her Art Deco shoes? No, hats were for dowagers. Better to brush out her hair and let the wind take care of the rest. Did she need more perfume? At least on her wrists, and don't forget the backs of her knees. What did her father say to thwart any comparison to her and other woman journalists? "Feminine to her fingertips." And for tonight, at least, to her toes.

In the end, she decided to tuck the folded cloche into her purse, just in case she needed it after all. For once she was grateful that Dick had left the house before her. Julian barely looked up as he summoned a cab for her and bade her goodnight.

The glaring New York cold made her grateful for the ermine and the knit dress beneath it. The rest of her apprehension vanished when she spotted Johnnie's face. He waited for her outside P.J. Clarke's, standing under the flashing Michelob sign in a black topcoat and suit. As she stepped from the cab, he took both of her hands in his. "Would you look at that?" he said, as if boasting to someone else about her.

They crushed against each other in the padded seats of the theater. He smelled of lime aftershave that complemented rather than covered his own brisk, outdoor scent. He turned, and she felt his breath on her cheek.

"You smell gorgeous. Want a drink?"

"Here?"

He shushed her softly as the credits began. In that frenetic way of his, he reached into his jacket and came out with a leather-covered flask.

She looked from one side of the row of seats to the other, wondering what the penalty for such an act might be, how Sheilah Graham might report it in her column. To hell with Sheilah. This was a rare night, one she might never repeat, and she intended to enjoy it.

She tilted and swallowed, thinking of prohibition, speakeasies, underage kids huddled at football games. The liquor carried that same illicit pleasure in its soft burn. She handed the flask back to him and settled back to watch the film.

So busy was she being a journalist, that Dorothy seldom lost herself in any performance. This film, this night was an exception. This was no *Marty*, no *Streetcar*. It was a bona fide love story, and she couldn't remember the last time she'd seen one of those.

She fought to keep the tears from her eyes, a task that grew more difficult each time she took her turn at the flask. Beside her, she heard a loud sniff. She turned. Johnnie blew into his handkerchief. The dim light from the screen illuminated his face, shiny with tears. She touched his wet cheek, finding it unexpectedly soft, almost delicate. He placed his palm over her hand, squeezed it, then pressed it against his lips. She turned back to the film wordlessly, and they sat like that, sobbing in earnest now, cheek to cheek, drunker than two people should be in a theater, her fingers pressed to his lips.

Outside on the street, she clung to his arm, leaning into him as they walked. "What an absolutely marvelous film," she said. "I'm going to plug it in my column."

People in all manner of dress hurried down the sidewalk toward their own destinations. They didn't notice them, didn't care. Johnnie Ray, she thought. She was walking with Johnnie Ray, his arm around her, and no one noticed.

"That'll be the day, Dorothy Kilgallen plugging a love story," he said.

"No, I'm serious." She inhaled the thin, giddy air, trying to catch her breath. "It's a boon, I'll say, to those of us who are getting tired of pictures about dope addicts, alcoholics, unattractive butchers and men who sleep in their underwear."

He took another swallow from the flask, the scent of vodka lingering in the cold air like perfume. "I'll drink to that, although I liked *Marty*. Cried all the way through it."

Without removing his right arm from around her waist, he threw the flask into the air, catching it before it crashed to the gray sidewalk.

"I believe that," she said. "You're impetuous, you know, and very, very sentimental. I always thought you faked the tears on stage."

His arm tightened around her. "I don't fake anything."

"Wish I could say that."

She expected a laugh in return, a smile, at least. She got nothing but a lingering, unreadable look. Well, she could play the stare-down game too. Better to meet his gaze this way than to let him focus too long on her now infamous profile.

In a moment, he chuckled softly and turned away. "I love to walk," he said. "You?"

"A waste of valuable time," she replied, grateful for conversation once more.

"We head north long enough, we'll reach Central Park."

It sounded like an invitation. Above them, nearly full, the moon glowed. She remembered the hoedown beat and corny lyrics of a terrible song he'd once recorded. "Didn't you sing something about walking home, other than the obvious one, that is?"

"A duet with Doris, God bless her. *Let's Walk That-A-Way*. Don't judge either of us by it."

With every step, her feet were further shredded by the frivolous shoes in which she'd never walked farther than the distance between a maitre d' and the best seat in the house. "Well, don't get any ideas about trekking through the park tonight. I never have, and I don't intend to start now."

"What kind of New Yorker are you?"

"One without sore feet."

He laughed and slid his hand to her elbow as they crossed the street. "Someday I'll pick you up, you put on a pair of pants, and we'll stroll the park."

"You'll see me in hell before you see me in slacks." Her voice brushed over the word, stopping short of a slur.

"You okay?" he asked.

She shrugged and tried for a bright smile. She longed for a warm room, a cold drink, some time to reflect on this odd night, this man. "A little high, I'm afraid."

"This is the time I get started."

A challenge. She took it. "I'm Irish. I can keep up."

He nodded approval and steered her through the couples crowding the street. "Then follow me, girl. I want you to hear a cat who's a friend of mine."

"Anyone I know?"

"Count Basie." He said it almost shyly.

Now he was the one trying to impress her, but she was having too much fun to care. At least everyone at the Copa would be as drunk as they. And if they weren't, if she showed up in Sheilah's piss-poor excuse for a column, it was better than what they'd been printing about her lately. Much better.

She grinned up at the glowing moon and hurried to keep up with him, her fragile heels clicking on the sidewalk.

"I'd love to see the Count with you," she said.

 Johnnie

When we're dropped at the Copa, I'm charged. Harmonics thousands of years old ring in my good ear. Brilliant lights duel the black sky as we glide under the marquee. Inside, a new hatcheck girl takes Kilgallen's ermine, my topcoat. I scare up Umberto, and we're threaded through the crowd. I hold Kilgallen's hand wondering who's pulling whom. Heads turn, do doubletakes, mostly because of me at first, then her, the fact that we're obviously together, *an item* as Kilgallen herself would report it.

I fade back, let her pass, watch her ahead of me, smooth power in her carriage. Her ass is nice. She's sure of herself. The 600-capacity house switches glances from me to her. Basie's band rocks the room by its subterranean balls, swaying its ten-foot palms.

She slides into a crimson banquette. I'm following when she stops me with her hand, says something about dear friends. And here they are, a couple crossing the sunken dance floor. From her four hundred, not mine. It's written all over this pair.

She presents them. "Clara" and "Roland" is all I hear as Basie pushes the beat. The woman's fortyish like Kilgallen, only her curves have flattened. Rollie is fat, with a round face full of barracuda teeth.

This asshole has plans. He ignores my hand, sniffs the air dramatically. "Jesus," he says. "Something stinks in here."

I come back like my writers are Lum and Abner. "Funny, I don't smell anything."

Rollie flashes his sharp teeth. "If you'd take that thing out of your ear and stick it in your nose, you could smell it," he says, an ugly dissonance against Basie's driving beat.

Kilgallen pops up Irish angry if I've ever seen it. Clara tries to apologize. Rollie flings a right cross. I duck, come up smiling. I see in this fucker every heckler who's pitched me a bitch in every joint from Detroit City to Sydney.

Umberto steps in like a ref. Clara helps. Kilgallen bristles. I play the whole scene like a journeyman. "Fuck him," I tell those within earshot, sending a thumbs-up to Basie.

A server brings us a bottle in a bucket of ice, presents the booze for my inspection. "Your brand, Mr. Ray."

I smile at Kilgallen. "Hope it ain't grape."

"Potato," he says, pouring us vodka, straight up.

The Count breaks. After the applause, Kilgallen begins an apology for her friend's behavior.

I hold up a hand. "No need," I tell her. "I get that stuff all the time."

Her eyes grow moist, shine like in the movie earlier. "Yes, I guess you do."

"I've always been the weird kid," I add from Lum and Abner again. "Even before the blanket toss."

Of course this brings, "Blanket toss?"

I point to my hearing aid. "I was twelve. Landed on my head when someone dropped his corner of the blanket."

Her hands fish through her purse. She lights a cigarette then finds a pen and begins taking notes on a Copa napkin.

Shit. "Don't do that," I say.

The pen and bunched napkin fly into her purse. "Sorry," she says. "Force of habit."

"Reet."

"From now on, everything is off the record."

"Then I might tell you my awful secret."

She waves away smoke, watches me. I know she won't ask. I reach for her hand. "I'm really not from Dallas, Texas."

She gives me a relaxed look. "No?"

"I'm from Dallas, Oregon."

"You sly bastard," she says, changing her eyes again. "Next you'll be on *I've Got a Secret*."

We drink hard. She's sharp. I light a filter, try to act cool, feel the booze. I wonder how long she'll eat my cornpone, tell me interesting things in her cocksure fashion.

24

Basie returns. When I see his vocalist dawdle, grin at me like he don't mean it, I'm stormed with a rush of adrenalin. Shit, I know what's coming, hear Morrie in the back of my mind. "No! Last time we step on contracts in that room, Costello's goons lock me in the walk-in reefer!"

"See a friend of mine out there tonight," Basie growls into his mike.

Here it comes. Morrie's screeching, "No, no, no." Kilgallen brightens under a spotlight.

"I been jammin' with the Count now and then," I let her know.

"Ladies and Gents," Basie says. "Let's hear it for the incomparable Mr. Johnnie Ray." Basie's drummer lays down a soft roll. "Get up here and acknowledge your fans, man."

Now the applause is deafening, and don't ask me about deaf.

"For God's sake, Johnnie," Kilgallen says. "Do something."

I tremble like a rabbit, try to scoot out of the booth, stumble. I get back my composure, going up to Basie.

On stage I give the vocalist, new cat Basie's been working with, a palms-up gesture.

"I'm cool with it," he says.

To Basie I whisper, "I'm awfully fucking drunk, man."

"Ain't you the cat never drives sober?" He jabs my stomach with a huge fist. "Give 'em the Mary Jane song, then *Whiskey and Gin.*"

"Mary Jane?"

"The boo song, marijuana," Basie says, irritated.

I shake my head up and down, grab the stage mike, wait for his soft intro. Most of the band's been on this with us before, and they chip in.

So I get hold of myself and give them *Sweet Lotus Blossom,* more like Lady Day than the weird kid. Basie digs it. The crowd ain't so sure.

When I finish, the mob's not exactly rioting. I turn to Basie. "They want some blood and thunder, Count."

Basie nods, intros *Whiskey and Gin*. I start it torchy and then let it go, find a refuge in it. Hate to say it like this, but I become fascinated with my ability to drive the moment mad. The crowd, even Basie's musicians feel it.

I gratify most, offend some. I peak the vocal, jumping off the stage, kissing both Clara and Rollie, who are shrieking now with the rest. I finish up in front of the mike, having wrung the song dry.

Throwing Basie a hand, I fiddle with my hearing aid, grovel my way to the booth. Standing, Kilgallen applauds me, her small hands in a frenzy. There's something in the proud way she holds her head, a grandeur that like punches my chest. I gasp. Sweat drops from my brow into my eyes.

She puts her arms around me, cradles me to her nice-sized tits like I belong to her alone.

four

Dorothy

On the street once more, they stood facing each other. She felt girlish, a teen-ager trying to make conversation before her date kissed her at the door, or didn't.

"You were wonderful," she said. "Better than your records, better even than the night I saw you open here. You sounded like Billie Holiday on *Sweet Lotus Blossom.*"

He rubbed his cheeks, rosy from the cold and the vodka. "Lady Day taught it to me. It's about loco weed, as we used to call it back home."

"You didn't write it then?" She was chattering, couldn't help it. Keep him talking and maybe he wouldn't notice that the evening was over.

"No," he said, but someday I'll sing you one of my songs, maybe later tonight."

"Tonight?" Not even her deliberately flat voice could make it a question.

He touched her cheek, reached for her arm. "Come on," he said.

His bachelor flat, at Fifty-fifth and Broadway, looked like a brownstone flophouse. They stumbled up the narrow stairs as if they came home this way together every night. *Oh Jesus*, thought the sane side of herself. *What am I doing?* They'd cuddled in the red leather booth, clung. But they hadn't even kissed. Now here she was, trudging up the stairs beside him, smiling as he stroked her arm. He didn't seem to notice her hesitation. Humming a few bars of *Walking My Baby Back Home*, he fumbled with his free hand for his keys.

"It's a dump," he said, unlocking the door. "I'll move if you hate it."

The interior of his apartment carried the chilly scent of a bar after too many ashtrays have been emptied, too many glasses rinsed. Neon from the signs outside washed the wall with fuchia light, illuminating a Chesterfield and imposing oak coffee table. Judging from the shadows taking shape before her, everything in the room was massive. Could he tell how uncomfortable she felt in these unfamiliar surroundings? Did he too feel odd, exposed, offering up his home for her scrutiny? She pulled the fur close around her and maneuvered around something that appeared to be an overstuffed ottoman.

"Where's the lamp?" she asked.

"Up ahead. Can I take your coat?"

"Let's find the lamp first." She couldn't give up the fur, not yet.

Just then, she heard a menacing growl and saw the shape of a huge dog as it descended upon her. "Mother of God," she gasped, clutching the fur once more.

"Don't worry." Johnnie wrestled to control the dog, a Doberman. "Sabrina's a sweetheart."

Dorothy stepped back into the ottoman and felt the heel of her shoe crumble beneath her. "Damn," she said, struggling to regain her balance as pain cracked through her ankle. "My shoe."

"Take them off. I'll buy you new ones," he said, reaching out in the flashing light. "Here, give me your hand. Show Sabrina you're not afraid."

"But I am. My Underwood relies on all ten fingers." Slowly, she put her hand out, let him take it. The dog responded with a sloppy sandpaper kiss. "Ick. Her tongue's wet."

"Most tongues are." The dog settled at his feet. "Careful up ahead here," he said, leading her deeper into the shadows. "Morrie might be flaked out on the divan."

"Morrie?" she repeated. "Another dog?"

"An owl, my manager. Morrie, if you're in here, give us a hoot."

Dorothy could hear her own shallow breathing. No answer. They were alone. He took off his topcoat and tossed it in the empty chair, the jacket and bow tie following. He wasn't at all awkward, she realized. He just had his own rhythm, and it wasn't like anyone else's. Pain shot through her ankle again. She leaned against him and removed what was left of the offending shoe and its counterpart. Her eyes were used to the dark and the neon-washed wall by now.

He looked down at her, smiling. "You're short."

"Shoeless," she said.

He cocked an eyebrow, studying her with a fey smile. "Well, that's okay." He led her to the ottoman and sat down. "Here," he said, motioning to her foot. She lifted it, and he took it into his hands. "You have cute feet."

"They're ugly." No one, drunk or sober, had ever called her feet cute before. No one had ever noticed. "My second toe is too long."

He pressed his fingers into her arch, a light pressure that radiated the length of her legs.

"Jesus." She tried to pull away.

"Beautiful feet," he murmured, pressing his lips against her hose.

"No." She pulled harder. He was moving too fast. She needed a minute, a drink "They're dirty, sweaty."

"Good."

She felt his tongue against the sensitive skin of her instep and gasped. "Johnnie, please. This is the first—I mean, I've never done..."

29

Her voice trailed off as his fingers closed around her toes. "Didn't figure you had."

He rose from the ottoman and leaned down, sliding his hands into her coat and slowly pulled her into a kiss. The sound of their quick breaths filled the room, their mouths coming together and apart. Pressing her body against his, Dorothy wrapped her arms around his neck. It was time, she thought, to take off her coat.

They didn't bother to pull down the carefully tucked bedspread, didn't pause to discuss what they were doing. He threw her ermine on the bed and stripped the dress from her. The safety net of alcohol melted away with her gown.

"I'm scared," she mouthed against his naked shoulder.

"I live scared." In the new language they'd learned to speak, it made perfect sense.

They eased onto the bed. Neon bathed the wall and tinted their flesh—his spectacular body, her breasts—purple and green. She heard his intake of breath as he pulled the last lacy scrap of fabric from her. "You're beautiful."

"Johnnie, wait."

"It's okay." He snaked down alongside her on the bed, kissing her as he went. Dorothy tried to twist away from him, to pull him onto her, but he held her firmly.

"What are you doing?" she whispered.

"Taking my time," he said.

"Still scared?" Johnnie stretched out his long arm and handed her the cigarette. She lay nude on the satin lining of the ermine. His head still rested against her ankle.

"Not really."

"How do they hide that body of yours on television?"

She snuggled closer to him. He had no idea what he'd done for her. She'd been cheated her whole life, and she hadn't even known it, hadn't even realized that it wasn't her fault. "God, you're different," she said.

His eyes changed. He looked less vulnerable as he took the cigarette from her. "As in weird?"

"No, that's not what I meant."

"Morrie's had me checked by doctors," he said with a laugh. "'Til most people see me they figure I'm black, I'm a girl, I'm some goddamned hermaphrodite."

She took the cigarette back, inhaled deeply, sighed. "I never thought that, but Johnnie, I had no idea."

He gave her a lazy smile. "What?"

"You know. You must."

"Tell me."

"Do you know how old I am?"

"I don't give a damn," he said.

"Forty-four. I'm forty-four, and I've never really, I mean that's the first time I ever—"

"Came?"

"Yes."

He slid his hand along the bare flesh of her leg. "Want to try for an encore?"

 Johnnie

Debonair in nothing but suit pants and suspenders, I watch Dorothy raid my ice box.

"Your fridge is a disaster," she says, waifish in my robe, naked and showered under it.

The gee-but-it's-great tizzy of another erection thrills me. I approach her from the rear, poke her globes as they flex under soft terrycloth.

Her smile is a raspberry splotch on her alarmingly pale face. "Keep that monster away from me. My hangover is terminal."

I fetch pillskies from a cabinet, cold beer from the box. She don't hesitate, throws them back. She holds the sides of her head and stares at me, reminding me of my sister when we were kids and she wanted to skip school. This moves me past the counter out into the living room, where I step over Samantha, and turn table photos Dorothy's way.

"Hazel and Elmer," I say, "Mom and Dad. This one's my sister Elma and me."

"Nice."

"Hardscrabble farmhouse behind us," I say, jumping Samantha again to make a fuss straightening gold record plaques on the wall. I put early Ellington on the turntable and hear Dorothy sigh deeply. Sabrina yawns under me. I feel her tongue licking my bare toes.

I hear the soft fall of cloth. Dorothy's red toenails come up next to my big feet.

Startled, I murmur, "Jesus, Dotty."

Sun slants in, stripes her body with light. I look at her, can't believe she's a mother of three. I wonder briefly about those kids, her husband. She's got a lot on the line. Tears well in my eyes, spill down my cheeks.

"That's okay," she says, running her slender fingers through my hair.

"You're the only one here with plenty to lose," I tell her, really meaning it.

"Or gain," she says.

I just stand, listening to Duke's band, wishing I could explain to her who is gaining and who is losing.

"Ellington," she says, and the name sounds like a lover's word against my better ear. "You jam with him too?"

"I have," I say. The smell of her rises, sweet and frondy, hint of foreign soap or lotion, something never here before.

"Any records in store with him or Basie?"

"Hope so."

"Who would stop them?"

"Morrie," I say. "Him and the beard's determined I stay with bubble gum stuff."

"The beard?" She takes a step back. Her hands hang at her sides. Her nipples have hardened.

"Mitch Miller," I say.

She pinches her nose, either about Mitch's music or about Samantha, who's out like a light across the room.

I throw a thumb at the plaques on the wall behind me. "Got me those."

She steps closer, wraps the fingers of her left hand around my suspender, unzips my pants with her right. Her grip is gentle on my cock as she pulls it out and sinks to the rug on her knees.

Her little Lifesaver mouth stretches to take me. Her enormous eyes are wet and streaked with red under high arched brows. I shudder and put a hand out against the wall. I want to watch her lips as they move over my crown, but her gaze pleads with my eyes not to linger.

After a short time, she takes her lips away, breathless. Her cheeks are crimson, tiny pointed chin trembling. "Don't know how," she mutters softly.

"You're doing fine," I say.

I'm telling her something else, something low and gushy when I hear Samantha shake her ears. Beyond Dorothy's flawless forehead, dark coffee-colored curls, I see my front door knob turning, and I think, shit, wasn't it locked?

Moving fast, I get my privates put away and throw terrycloth around Dorothy—all this nearly in time.

It's Morrie. With him, garbed in jungle skins and a blond-streaked wig, is Miss Cornshucks. It's her all right, black skin shiny. Both look frightful in the window's curtained light.

Cornshucks dashes past Dorothy and bear-hugs me. "Wow," she says, pressing her pelvis against me. "You do remember me."

Breaking away, I stutter a greeting then turn to Dorothy, who clutches my robe around her. "Dorothy Kilgallen," I say, throwing out an arm. "Meet my manager Morrie Lane. And this is Miss Cornshucks," I add, trying to recall if she had ever given more name than that. "We go way back to The Flame Bar in Detroit."

"Way back," Cornshucks echoes. Her grin shows more gold than I remember.

Dorothy places fingers to her temple, and I can almost feel the hangover raging inside her skull. "How do you do?"

"I do what I can," Cornshucks shouts, placing her fists on her hourglass hips. She looks pounds heavier than when we gigged together.

Morrie beams at Dorothy as if she's royalty. He's dressed in a sidewalk-sale blue suit, screeching at me, something about the Copa last night, about the Mafia.

"They'll cut your tongue out with their greasy hands," he whoops.

Dorothy becomes a white blur as she kicks my robe out in front of her shapely legs, strides into my bedroom, slams the door.

"What's her line?" Morrie says, hee-hawing his own wisecrack.

Samantha untangles herself and decides that Cornshucks' cat spots and stripes need a good ass kicking. Cornshucks leaps into Morrie's arms. They begin an outrageous tribal dance to Ellington, who's really cooking now on *Take the A Train*.

Add to all this the beating of my fists against my bedroom door. "Dorothy, please, for Christ's sake. Open it, would you?"

Dorothy pops out, last night's fancy garb a mess on her. Her mouth is moving like it's full of razor blades. "I thought you said this was your apartment," she says.

I follow her past Astaire and Ginger, past Samantha, who breaks her rhythm to offer a consoling Doberman expression. In the hall, I grab a fistful of the ermine she's gathered around her like some kind of armor. "Jesus, Dorothy, wait up," I plead. "We haven't had breakfast."

"Have it with the owl and the pussycat," she says.

34

Her dark blue eyes are beautiful in the dim hallway. I start to break down. "Goddammit," I sob, "You mean something to me."

"Goddammit," she screams right back. "You mean something to me."

Turning on her broken shoe, she almost goes down. A black, floppy hat I don't remember from last night is angled on her dark hair. As I watch her march away, I'm crying for her dignity as much as she is.

five

Dorothy

The Black Room had always been a refuge of sorts, like a church. Dorothy caved against the back of the settee, watching the candlelight flicker around Billie Holiday's stretched-thin voice. *Lover man, where can you be?* Before her, on a cocktail table shaped like a drum, sat an untouched drink. The soft wash of rain on the window panes only made her feel more alone.

She needed a church tonight, a refuge. She'd allowed herself to be humiliated, a graver sin than the other she'd committed. She still felt every step of that sharp, broken walk down the hall of Johnnie's apartment building.

But he'd chased her, he'd wept. Her attempts at rationalization didn't console her. Johnnie Ray would weep at a change in weather.

He had said she meant something to him. How could she believe him, sleeping with another man's wife, shaking her out like laundry in the morning. Then ushering in those people, that woman.

"Lonely?"

She jumped at the sound of Dick's voice. He leered from the doorway.

"Damn it. Can't you announce yourself?"

He moved closer. "Thought that's what I was doing, darling." His bloated face made his teeth look smaller and shrunken. "You're spending too much time here. Julian says you're not taking visitors or calls from anyone, not even Jack Kennedy."

He settled on the other end of the settee, sending a sharp scent of alcohol toward her.

"Aren't you starting a little early?"

He drew back as if struck, nearly felling a candlestick on the table behind him. "I never take a drink before five-thirty. You know that."

"And you never rise before four, do you?"

"Hubba hubba, darling. I'd watch the sarcasm if I were you."

He thought if he repeated the term enough times, he could make it part of the lexicon. She was sick of it, sick period. "I'm not trying to be sarcastic," she said. "I just need some time to myself."

"As do I, darling." Dick all but preened. Even in candlelight his once-handsome face lay flat and gray. "I'll be late tonight."

"Of course."

"Very late. We're putting the last touches on the club, moving in the piano. Maybe your friend will sit in some night."

Her temples throbbed. "My friend?"

"The Prince of Wails. I'm inviting various entertainers to drop by, do a few tunes. Cheap labor and all. So now that you and the prince are pals—"

"I'll mention it if I talk to him," she said.

"I hope you will. Considering the condition of his career, he ought to welcome any opportunity to perform."

"Last I heard, he wasn't begging for singing jobs." She heard the satisfied clink of ice and knew at once the reason he'd sought her out. "I don't care if you spend the night at your club or anywhere else. You needn't pick a fight to justify it."

The ice rattled again. He rose from the couch as if trying to muster dignity. "I didn't say I was staying out all night. But there is a small apartment above the club, and ifyou're going to be so testy—"

"Just be here by seven for the show," she said. "And be careful. People do talk, even about us."

He stopped at the door. "Yes, darling, they do."

Billie's song had ended. Except for the rain, the room was silent. Dorothy put on Johnnie's record, missing him more than ever. Perhaps she should have taken his phone calls. He couldn't help it if those people showed up at his apartment on that particular morning. She'd been mortified at the time, but now, Jesus. She turned up the phonograph letting his voice blare through her.

"Don't Blame Me," he sang.

Jesus, Johnnie. Johnnie Ray.

They had something, they did, and she was letting it slip away.

For a second, she thought she heard the doorbell. No. The courier had already come for her column, and nobody ever dropped by unannounced. She rushed to the phonograph, nevertheless, lifted the needle. The bell chimed again, clearer this time.

Johnnie. He'd come, and now Julian would turn him away. She rushed to the stairs in her stocking feet. No time for shoes. No time to wait for the elevator. As she ran down the carpeted hallway, she could see Julian, shaking his head, making a commotion.

"No," she shouted. "Wait."

"Mrs. Kollmar," Julian began. "Please."

"No. I've changed my mind. I—" Before her stood two strangers wearing the innocuous clothing of delivery men. Between them was a large object, a piece of furniture.

"I don't understand," she said to Julian. "Is it something Dick ordered?"

"No, ma'am." Julian moved in front of the object. "Leave here at once," he said to the men, "and take that with you."

"What is going on?"

She used the public Dorothy voice, glaring at the men. One looked down. The other smirked.

"It's a gift." He paused between each word for effect. "From Mr. Sinatra."

She moved around Julian and started to speak, but when she saw what the men had delivered, her voice died in her throat. It was a tombstone with only two words on it. *Dorothy Kilgallen.*

Dorothy tried to hug warmth into her body as she watched the cab's windshield wipers. Neon drenched the wet street. The cabdriver asked if he should wait, knowing that she didn't belong to this neighborhood, nor it to her.

"No," Dorothy said. "I'll be staying."

Trying to duck the rain, she ran up the slick stairs. Johnnie would understand about everything. He'd dismiss Sinatra's sick gesture for what it was and keep her warm all night. Yes, all night. She'd stay all night if he asked her.

Dorothy rang the bell, pounded on the door. On the other side, a dog barked. Sabrina. She'd let her lick her this time. She wasn't a bad dog, really. She heard the lock click, and the door opened. Before her stood the black woman. She wore the same robe Dorothy had, and her head was almost shaved, covered in soft fuzz. With one hand, she restrained the growling Sabrina. In the other, she held the gold-streaked wig she'd been wearing the day they met.

"Oh." Dorothy couldn't move, could barely even speak.

"Don't look so scared." The woman shook the wig. "It don't bite." Then glancing down at Sabrina, "Neither does she, unless you make her real mad."

Dorothy forced a tight smile and tried to regain her composure. "Forgive me for intruding. Something happened, and I just jumped in a cab without thinking."

"Well, come on in," she said in a proprietary tone.

A chill set over Dorothy, driving away her earlier panic. She needed to get out of there, before Johnnie came to the door. "No thanks. I shouldn't have come."

"He ain't here, if that's what you're worried about."

Dorothy sighed relief. He wasn't here, not with this woman. "Then why?"

"I have a gig in Harlem. He's out in Hollywood recording. Said I could flake out here."

"Yes, of course." The public Dorothy reappeared, pulling herself up to full height beside this giant-sized woman.

Cornshucks shrugged. "Why don't you help me get this dog inside and come on in? You look like a lady could use a friend."

The words touched her. She felt a tear creep down her cheek. She reached out to pat Sabrina's head. "I could use a drink."

Cornshucks chortled, snapping the mood. "Me too. Let's go in and raid the booze cupboard. Then you can phone up Johnnie. I got the number."

"I could never call Johnnie," she said. "Never."

"So don't." She handed Dorothy her wig. "You take this and let me get Sabrina under control. And don't worry about calling Johnnie. I'll do it for you."

six

 Johnnie

I wake up parched, head splitting, on a short divan, and there's that awful moment it takes to get oriented. I must be in California, because there's Mister Sun coming through the blinds like sliced cheese. Cologne that ain't mine and the smell of chlorine tangle in my nose along with the reek of Camel butts and beer cans.

I raise my torso like a corpse from its coffin. Few feet away, the bed looks so tight you could bounce a quarter off it. An Army uniform hangs neatly on the bathroom's doorknob. I must have insisted my old pal Ding Wakefield take the bed, and remember now that I'd offered him my wardrobe for a lunch date today.

Wonder if he's hurting as bad as I am.

My wristwatch says two-thirty. It's guaranteed waterproof, but I shake it, stare at the numbers. Jesus, I got a session date at four.

My scraped knee looks up at me. My boxer shorts are damp, and I recall skinny-dipping with the Dinger, but I don't panic. Bathing suits are like outlawed here after dark.

A key scratches at the door. The Dinger, coming back? No, it's Morrie Lane, wheezing, panting his way rudely into the room. How does this fucker find keys to my every whereabouts?

Coughing, he waves his straw fedora in front of him. "Holy god, this shit hole should be fumigated." He rattles the blinds. Outside, bird of paradise plants stoop like grotesque Peeping Toms.

I shield my sore eyes again. "Yikes."

"It's called daylight," he says. Watches as I struggle upright, looks hard at the bed, the hanging uniform. "Where's the sailor?"

"Adjust your telescopes," I say, throwing a snappy salute. "That's Army issue. Summer khakis."

"Fuck, what is the guy?" Morrie's inspecting the decorations, the silver bars. "A hero?"

"Yeah, from my hometown."

"Tell him Korea is a done deal, he should get out." He spots a towel on the floor. "Holy god. Blood."

I step out of my shorts, point to my knee as I head for the bathroom. "Swim party last night."

Under the shower, my thoughts drift. Wakefield had proved a swell guy. He'd asked questions right off, his curiosity about my life since school strictly innocent. Over drinks at Ciro's, I'd told him, "Right now I'm wigged over a lady back in New York."

Dorothy is heavy on my mind as I towel off. Staggering out of the steam, I sob for solace. "Kilgallen keeps refusing my calls."

On the divan, Morrie rants behind yesterday's Hollywood Reporter. "She's got too much brains."

So much for solace.

While I dress, Morrie yanks my chain about the session.

"Wish it was Columbia's studio on East 30th," I say. "The vaulted ceilings, those great acoustics."

"Well, it ain't," Morrie says, peering like a bullfrog over the paper. "It's radio recorders in Fag City."

"How you talk."

"Speed it up."

"You let me sleep once in a while, I'd be sharper."

"When you do find a bed," he growls, "you should be certified, the acts you commit."

42

"Against whom?"

"Against God."

This gets my back up. I throw on a shantung sports coat. "I want a vacation."

"You wouldn't know one if I hand it to you on a gold record."

"I need time to compose."

"You know I've insisted you take off to write more songs," he hollers. "You fart me off like I'm fried liver."

"You're always booking me."

"Only way to keep you out of jail."

I move into his myopic view. "Try to find me over here. You ain't working on another movie deal?"

"God forbid," he sputters, jumping up as if in some ancient vaudeville drill. "You only get a couple grand for showing up on the set."

I love his little dance, think of something that might lower his blood pressure. "On the set of *Show Business* last year, I overhear Ethel Merman telling Marilyn Monroe a story about two old maids."

Morrie yawns, rolls his magnified eyes.

"One old maid asks the other does she remember the minuet. Other old maid says, 'Hell, I can't even remember the ones I fucked.'"

"She told Marilyn Monroe that?" His hands are fisted on his hips like a school marm's. "Bet Marilyn didn't laugh."

"Didn't even get it," I console him.

Thinking about Marilyn, that quality of hers that makes even a diehard like Morrie need to believe in her innocence, always makes me a little sad about the state of the world in general and the state of my world in particular. I adjust dark shades and hearing aid, stride forward like I was born Sunset and Vine.

Surprisingly, Morrie lags behind. "Give me a good session today, Johnnie, we'll leave for New York tomorrow."

"Solid," I say, shooting him a grin. "I'll rest back there, get into shape."

"You'll drink, fuck your brains out."

"Won't either. I'll have Dorothy."

He lifts his heavy brow. "So?"

"She's different, man."

"How?"

Forcing myself to ignore the fact that she has refused to speak to me since she limped out of my apartment that morning, I tell him what I know to be true. "Wants to give me something for nothing in return."

Looking like he's about to cry at the state of the world, he waddles ahead of me on the ochre-splashed walk. The air smells like citrus and coconut oil from the starlets basking poolside. I put a hand on his shoulder, point back at the room.

"Errol Flynn shot his wad in there," I inform him. "that very fucking room. You missed the plaque on the wall."

"So did Ernest Hemingway," he says. "Let's hope they did it with a couple of broads and not with each other."

Watching him assume a bodyguard's lead, I can't get over how old he looks compared to the earlier days. I look up at the marvelous sky. How does a town so full of beauty and youth mark you up so bad?

Looking back once, Morrie holds both arms out in a beholding gesture. "Garden of fucking Allah," he says." God save us."

I give him an amen.

I remember Radio Studio from a few days back, Mitch Miller telling me to go home after a couple of takes, first song out of the chute, I look for our engineer Frank Laico, but he's not at this gig. Mitch sneaks up on me as I'm looking things over.

I go for a smile that almost breaks my face. "What's happening, Beard?"

He looks like he could explain Einstein's theory to you in two languages, says, "We're going to make a hit today, kid. Put you back up to Number One."

My eyes wander. Ray Conniff and his boys are a bright sight, sending me waves. This is good. I love a bolero beat he's worked on for me.

Miller notices my appreciation. "Pour your heart out for him, Johnnie."

We start out with *In This Candlelight*, and my voice is gliding nicely on last night's wickedness. Next is *Weaker than Wise*, Miller going for a laugh, saying it's the story of my life. I back him down, lay it out full of sugar. Then we swing into *If I Had You*.

Three on the menu, so good you can taste them. We're all happy at the break. Musicians are jive- assing. Back-up singers are joshing, acting cool.

Conniff wipes my face with a purple hanky from his lapel pocket. "You really do let it go, don't you, man?"

I get cocky, look for Miller. "How am I doin', Beard?"

From my spot at the mike, he gives me his best Mitch Miller glare. He rubs his goatee against my mike. It sounds like marching Prussians on a rough road.

"Pretend this is a woman's pussy," he says, amplified, and rubs his beard into the volts again. "Get up here and go down on *Just Walking in the Rain*."

Ambling toward my spot, I vow to give my best. I see Ding Wakefield on the sidelines with what must be his girlfriend. Miller's crudity has reddened her as it has other females present in the studio. Shit, it's turned Morrie Lane blue. For the first time all week, I'm glad Dorothy is not here with me after all.

I grab the mike. "Welcome to Tinseltown," I say, thinking Jesus, am I ever gonna get out of this town?

Everything is a blur after the session. Wakefield and his gal drive me back to the hotel. We pop beers in my room, pour them over ice, toast the times. His girl has a nice smile, tells me she's never had such an exciting trip.

"Jeez, you're a great singer," she beams.

I say my ah shucks, lay the clothes on the Dinger. "They're from my sports line," I tell him. Keep 'em." What I don't tell him is I got a million of 'em. They ain't selling like they used to.

When they leave, I crash on top of the bed in kind of a coma. I see colors of ungodly intensity, hear sounds like huge cymbals falling from a great distance, ringing as they spin like coins in my head.

Ringing.

Jesus, the phone.

Probably catch it on its last scream, because I have to say hello twice.

"Bout to give up on you, Bones." The voice is a dark, vampy rasp, the voice, the woman, who got me in dutch with Dorothy in the first fucking place.

"That you, Cornshucks?"

"It's the Shucker, sugar. How you doin'?"

"Getting by. Where are you?"

"The apple, baby, still at your place. Got a gal here wants to talk to you."

"Oh man, I ain't got time for games."

But she's already put the phone down, talking to someone else. After a silence I hear a tiny "Hello," that clipped speech like she's afraid to let it out.

"What? Who is this?" I can't believe it's her.

"Johnnie?" she says again.

My throat closes up on me. "Dorothy?"

"Yes." I hear a nervous cough, muffled by a hand over the phone. She's calling me, actually calling me. I want to howl, but I can barely speak.

"My voice is gone," I say. "Gave it up today."

Silence. Then, "It's raining here in Manhattan."

"Reach out and grab some," I say, feeling the strength of my voice once more. "Hold onto it 'til I get there."

seven

Dorothy

In November of 1957, Johnnie offered to sit in at Dick's club. She wasn't sure if he were trying to help or just curious. He was clearly uncomfortable with her marriage and seldom mentioned her husband or children, as if doing so would will them away. When the children returned home for the holidays, she spent more time with them, which she knew didn't please him either.

"Not trying to mend fences with your husband, are you?" he'd asked one night, when she'd had to cut dinner with him short.

In spite of the teasing tone, she could see the confusion in his eyes. Once he got a good look at Dick staggering behind the bar of the club, pawing every woman in sight, he wouldn't be worried about any reconciliation, children or no children.

Before they left for the club, they met under the Michelob sign at P.J. Clarke's and ordered vodka tonics. Hard to believe that a little more than a year ago, she had watched with apprehension from a cab as Johnnie waited for her under this same sign for their movie date. She could still feel the ache of that moment, worrying about the propriety of her fur, wondering if they'd have time for a drink.

In less than a week, the smoky autumn had faded into the bleak neutrals of winter. They drank tonics anyway, clinking their tall glasses, smoking cigarettes.

Roland and two of her other men friends had insisted on joining them. She hoped they would try to get along with Johnnie this time. They always somehow managed to convey their disdain, and Johnnie's friends were no better to her. Except for Miss Cornshucks, the hangers-on around him, especially Morrie, considered her the evil older woman.

Johnnie had promised to be on his best behavior that day and he was, greeting Roland like an old buddy. His act didn't impress Roland and the others, and she silently steamed while they ignored him. Hell, the man traveled all over the world; he could certainly conduct a conversation. Out of desperation, she had resorted to straight vodka and gossip about Jack Kennedy, who brazenly walked in with a woman not his wife. Anything, even whispering about a friend, was preferable to watching the man she loved being patronized.

Dorothy leaned against Johnnie as they waited for a cab. Roland stood on the other side of her, beefy in his khaki fogcutter. "So," he said, narrowing his eyes at Johnnie as if taking aim. "Got any new records planned?"

"I sure hope so. I might be doing another movie. My manager thinks it's good for my image."

Polite murmurs all around, as *Jailhouse Rock* on the jukebox drove home the point. "Oh yes. The music business is so unpredictable these days. You ever think about doing another musical?"

Johnnie nodded. "If the right one comes along."

"You see Peter Pan?"

"No, I never really have liked Shakespeare a whole lot."

Roland and the others exchanged quick, noncommittal glances. Dorothy busied herself digging for a cigarette to keep from laughing.

The men took the first cab, she and Johnnie the second. She loved the intimacy of weaving through the congested streets tucked next to him. She slid her hand into his, snuggling closer. "You were wonderful, darling. That Shakespeare line was the best."

The mischievous glint in his eyes could mean anything, everything. "But I really *don't* like Shakespeare," he said.

Hours later. Days. Who knew? Piano music and Johnnie's voice, one of the songs he wanted on the new record Morrie hadn't been able to nail down for him. *All of Me*. God. How did she get on this piano bench, bunched up next to him, her head on his shoulder?

She glanced down at his long fingers on the keys, then up into his face, a smiling blur. The smattering of applause startled her. *The club*. They were still at Dick's club, of course, although she couldn't remember getting there. God, she hadn't passed out, had she?

She lifted her head, washed the hangover taste away with the rest of a tumbler of vodka on the piano. "Lovely," she said, testing her voice.

The Left Bank was closing. Must be close to two. She'd lost a chunk of the night. The help milled about, no one paying much attention any longer to Johnnie and her, now that the music had stopped. Only Rafael, the singer who had relinquished his piano to them and continued lounging against it, acknowledged their existence.

"Encore," he pleaded. "One more, J.R."

He didn't attempt to hide the adoration in his voice. All the pretty boys, they all loved her Johnnie.

"Not tonight, man." Johnnie turned his attention to her. "Had enough?"

"Never." Her black bra strap had slipped over her shoulder. She tried to push it up. "Have we eaten?"

"Not since the chili at P.J. Clarke's. Mr. K's been harping about it all night, says you need to for your anemia."

"Dick should talk." She gave the stubborn strap a solid yank. Tacky, adjusting one's underwear in public. She slid gingerly from the piano bench, seeking out the floor with uncertain feet. Oh great, she had her shoes off again. God knows what they had done right here in front of Dick and his staff.

Rafael left his perch at the piano, and in moments was at her side. "Freshen that for you?" he asked, touching the empty glass.

His voice was soft, friendly, his eyes dark in the dim room. Only his defiantly shaven head differentiated him from all the other young hopefuls sitting at pianos in borderline clubs all over town to earn enough to pursue singing careers during the day. That smooth, tan slope of his head gave him a masculine look that belied his delicate hands and slender, pianist fingers.

She gave him the public-Dorothy smile, the prim one she used when asking if she might examine the label of one's jacket when guessing an occupation on *What's My Line.* "How very thoughtful of you."

Let him serve her. He'd soon see Johnnie was a lost cause, and if he was as amusing as he appeared, he could possibly join their entourage tonight. Nothing wrong with having two attractive men at her side.

"Want a nightcap before we go home?" she asked Johnnie.

"I'm game if you are." He rose from the bench and turned to Rafael, who had somehow in this unreal world of the after-hours club, become their bartender. "One for my baby and one for the road, right honey?"

"All the way," she said. Life was good when they could joke about Sinatra lyrics. Life was good, period. Though a little blurred around the edges at the moment.

Roland wove his way to the piano. Light reflected from the fleshy planes of his face, making him look grotesquely porcine.

"Dick's locking up," he said. "We can take this party upstairs."

Meaning, of course, Dick's third-floor apartment, where he sometimes stayed after a late night of doing whatever he did in this place. She'd set foot in it only once.

Johnnie draped a possessive arm across her shoulder. "That'll be the day, Rollie."

"I was addressing Dorothy."

Roland's teeth were too white and predatory, too small for his large face and features. Why had she never noticed that? Why had she never noticed how unpleasant he could make even the most polite statement?

"No thank you," she said in her television voice. "We'll just finish our drinks and let ourselves out."

"Well." Roland's helpless shrug finished the statement, and he wandered away, shoulders stooped with the weight of the evening.

Breathing was an effort in the small room. She longed for the narrow, firm mattress of Johnnie's bed, the cool wash of pink neon over her flesh.

"Let's finish this and go home," she told Johnnie.

He pulled her closer. "Well, all reet."

Rafael returned with a fresh drink. "Had to make it myself," he said. "Bartender's stoned out of his skull."

Dorothy took hers carefully in both hands, sipped.

The very act made her feel better. They could always go home, and they would. The night didn't have to end yet. Morning would arrive soon enough.

She sank back down on the piano bench. "Join us?" she asked Rafael.

"I don't want to intrude." He eyed Johnnie, who was still standing beside the bench.

"Your choice, man." He nodded in the direction of a nearby cocktail table. "Take a load off. Ain't none of us going to finish this night sober."

Not even their lovemaking lifted her above the heaviness of the night. Dorothy woke too early, on her right side, head throbbing with a movie-reel memory of them on the bed, the floor, in the shower. Jesus, what had they been trying to prove?

"I think we had a little too much to drink." Johnnie's raspy voice, behind her, punctuated the statement. His lips brushed her shoulder, cool against her fevered skin.

She moaned in pain. "Why are we even awake? It's barely dawn."

"Maybe we didn't get enough."

She felt the spongy pressure thickening against the small of her back and pressed against it, an involuntary gesture that brought his lips against her flesh once more.

"Turn over. I want to kiss you."

"Don't. I taste like sin."

"I like sin, don't you?"

The pressure on her back became demanding, damp. His fingers slid along her torso, found her breast, her nipples. Jesus, it was starting again. She ought to tell him to leave her alone, let her sleep. But she couldn't sleep anyway. At least she could distract the pain of the hangover, prolong it for a while.

She rolled over into his arms. In the dim light, he could be a teenager. She ran her fingers over his smooth face, bewildered as she always was, at how youthful and untouched he looked in the morning, even after the most decadent of nights.

"I love sin," she said, and for the moment, it was as true as anything she'd said all evening.

Johnnie

It's after the holidays. I'm wishing I'd spent more time with my folks and Sis, introduced them to Dorothy. Some things just can't work out the way you hope. I haven't caught up with Dotty since New Year's Eve, and damn, today's my thirtieth birthday. Cornshucks has come up to my apartment out of the snow, and we're having a taste when my drummer, Babe Pascoe, knocks on my door. As I start to open it, I tell Cornshucks to finish her drink.

"We're going bowling," I say.

She gives me a look that goes so far back to the Delta it's untraceable.

Down on Broadway, we slide into the back seat of Babe's Fairlane, join Morrie Lane. Morrie looks at Cornshucks like he's FBI.

"The Shucker goes with us," I say, "or I don't bowl a frame."

Morrie shrugs. Up front, my accountant, Saul Rosen, instructs Babe how to get to the bowling alley. Snow falls silently.

"Babe," I say. "Christsake, turn on your wipers."

It develops Saul don't know bowling from lacrosse. Morrie and Babe keep using the wrong lanes. A skinny-necked pin-setter pops out down the lane, waves a tatooed arm. "You're on the wrong alley."

"They in the gutter," screams Cornshucks.

For the fifth time, the bowling gestapo asks can I *please* control the colored lady. She's the only one not in a Johnnie Ray sport shirt. Her pink pedal pushers are so tight they're a dark fuchia where she's divided. The noise is killing both my good and bad ears. I'm thinking there's a motive behind this venture, but what?

Saul Rosen claps his hands, yanks his pants up Yiddish-style to show his shlong. "Way to pick up that spare," he congratulates Cornshucks. He's keeping score. Why do I know it'll cost me later?

Cornshucks writes me a note on the scorepad. It is projected on a screen above us. Her printing is unknown hieroglyphics, but a school kid can make out where she's betting a blow job next frame.

I sing her some Lady Day. "Love will make you gamble and stay out *all* night long."

She comes back with some whiskey tenor. "Treat me right, baby, and I'll stay *home* every day."

People in nearby lanes stop their deliveries, act stunned, like our song has caused them hernias. My voice is husky and wild today. God, I'd like to let it out of its cage. Babe Pascoe forms an "okay" circle with thumb and finger.

"Crazy," he says.

In the bar above the alleys, we're joined by Saul Rosen's son-in-law. Right away I smell fish. This kid in his Brooks Brothers makes my publicist look like a virgin when it comes to hustle.

Morrie stands in our booth, raises his glass at what he thinks is me. "We didn't forget your birthday, Johnnie."

Shit. The whole gang sings the song. I bawl like a baby.

"Give him his present," Morrie tells his son-in-law. Saul beams. Babe and Cornshucks are still scatting "Happy Birthday." I'm smelling carp from the East Side.

Son-in-law hands me a leatherette folder. "It's a prospectus," he says.

"Thought that's what the doctor sticks up your ass," I say for laughs.

I give the contents of the folder a proper gander. Most of it's Saul's work: Numbers, projections, business shit. I spread out what they want me to see.

"Looks like something out of Buck Rogers," I say.

"Keep looking, Johnnie." Saul grins. "We got the best illustrator to paint the rendering, finest graphic artist to design your logotype. See the sign in front of the building?"

"Johnnie's Bowl 'N Bite," I read aloud. "I get the bowl. Where's the bite?"

"It's a bowling-dash-delicatessen," Saul goes on. "Combination-type place."

"You can see by this jernt," Morrie says, "how television has resurrected the sport from the Pollacks."

This place is filling up. Early evening, and the alleys are thundering.

"We start a chain," son-in-law yells into my hearing aid. "It's called franchising."

"Place you can bowl a few lines," Morrie shouts above the roaring echoes. "Then relax with some lox and bagels."

"Say what?" Cornshucks jumps up. Her enormous teeth shine gold and ivory. "Can't hear you over here."

Babe Pascoe brushes the table top, his hands laying out a soft, soundless rhythm. He's chewing gum Krupa's way, staring at the bar signs like they spell good times.

"I gotta' get out of here," I say, but no one is hearing me.

Babe Pascoe saves me for his last drop off, and he takes me to his favorite tavern, place called Tabby's on 52nd. People are shaking snow, ducking in out of the swirling rush hour. It's night, but the sky has that odd cast like it's really solid white.

Babe buys me a birthday shooter, introduces me around. I start looking for a phone. I'd give my left one to get hold of Dorothy.

"This is your year, Johnnie," Babe says. "Morrie's got us lined up for a world tour."

"Gives me nightmares," I say.

Two broads walk in smelling like French perfume and winter. They adjust their furs, flick their hair. I catch them smiling at me and give them my all-knowing look. They both raise their eyebrows like how do I know they're together—really together?

In no time, Babe is telling them a story how over in London at the Dorchester I end up naked, pounding on the door to Paul Douglas's room.

"You were nude?" one dish asks.

"Buck-assed," I admit, although any memory I have of that night has been enhanced by fiction.

"Paul Douglas, the actor," other one says, then out of the side of her mouth, "You were interested in him?"

"You ever see Paul?" I ask.

"Not in real life."

"You take the biggest bear in the woods. He fucks the wild witch of the north, you got your Paul Douglas."

They crack up. I move off to find a phone. I think I spy, in the tavern's doorway, Liz Montgomery and Gig Young. Maybe I'm drunk or hallucinating, because they look right at me, dance back onto the sidewalk.

Then I see Dotty. Jesus, it's her, and my eyes fill up. I feel for a moment like I'm flying through space.

Next to me now, she throws her arms around me. "Happy Birthday, darling," she whispers.

I bury my face in her dark hair, look past her out on the street. It was Liz and Gig. They and others, her friends, my friends, are jumping in and out of a bus, laughing, drinks in their fists.

"Get in your shuttle, Johnnie," Dorothy says. Liz Montgomery grabs one arm, Yul Brynner the other. I look back at Babe. He waves like he's done his job getting me here.

"First stop, the Colony," says Yul. I remove his porkpie, kiss his smooth plate.

"Then Le Pavilion," someone says.

Dorothy has my face in her hands. "Then the St. Regis, the best for last. All your favorite places."

I don't tell her they're her favorite places, not mine. I'm too happy. I can tell she's waiting for my reaction. I pause on the shuttle's step-up, receive a cocktail from an outstretched hand.

"Take me to the heart of the night," I say, and I can see her smile in the falling snow.

PART TWO

All of Me

eight

 ## Dorothy

The Voice of Broadway, November 3.

Whatever's happened to 1957? In a few short months, we've embraced West Side Story, a musical about street gangs, no less. We've added words like Sputnik and Frisbee to our vocabularies and removed (not a moment too soon) others like Edsel. It must indeed be true, as Jack Paar says, that time flies when you're having fun. Jack's having fun, taking over the *Tonight* show from my former *What's My Line* cohort, the multi-talented Steve Allen. In entertainment as well as world affairs, this year has been a veritable whirlwind.

Speaking of whirlwinds, Johnnie Ray continues to wow audiences worldwide, causing as big a stir over there as French import Brigette Bardot is causing over here. In June, it was England, then Rome again, now Germany. He did find time between trips to catch The King and I three nights in a row yet. I understand that he and Yul Brynner came up with hand signals so that the Cry Guy could let the king know from his seat whether or not the Yankees were winning. Only in show business!

 Johnnie

I come back from my '57 European tour, balls broke, but still free, white and thirty-one. Morrie has me on an itinerary so crazy even *Confidential Magazine* can't catch me. Still the mongers got me linked to sex-crazed sirens, swishy counts, every sheik and Sheba wanting their face on a scandal sheet: "Half-ass Celeb So-and-So, shown here with the weird kid, singer Johnnie Ray, the Prince of Wails."

The term, rock 'n' roll, is being tossed around, and I figure like most everything else here in Ikesville, it originated underground, probably at the Flame Showbar in Detroit. Detroit City. Wish I could say it like Jimmy Witherspoon, harsh and harmonic.

"Hardscrabble honky come to Detroit City," Spoon chided me back then, "sings the blues like Al Jolson crying for his mommy."

Me saying, "Who the fuck is Al Jolson?" Not for laughs but 'cause I really didn't know.

Last week some stiff-assed Brit stuck a mike in my face, told me I'm the father of the New Music. "Shucks," I say. He wants my opinion of Elvis. "Al Jolson, cryin for his momma's grits," I tell him.

Morrie calls while I'm unpacking. "Today's Times has your pic and says you broke the Palladium's numbers," he says in salutation. "By the way, you're booked Friday and Saturday in Chicago."

I'm lost in my own flat. Traffic noises drift up from 55th and Broadway. I start flipping stuff back into my bags. "You and Saul," I shout into the phone. "Dig up some tomato cans from our backyard. I need the bread."

"We got no backyard," Morrie reminds me, hanging up.

Sitting bedside, I worry. Blue devils ring in my hearing aid. I need a drink. I need Dorothy. I dial her townhouse, East Sixty-Eighth, posh end of Monopoly board.

Her butler takes the ring. "You wish Mr. Kollmar?"

"Come on, Vinson, get the lady," I say. "I'm falling apart over here."

After a silence, her heels on that cold marble, then her soft "hello." I can smell the lavender.

"I'm back," I announce. "Flying to Chicago tomorrow. Come with me."

"When is our flight?"

"That's my baby." The closet mirror sends me a look that must match my boyhood's smile, when life was full of freedom and those roving hills back home.

"One condition." Her harder voice from *What's My Line.*

"Ask."

"We catch Lenny Bruce."

"So you can write his obit?"

"That what you think of my column?"

"I remember how rough you were on me."

"That was before I fell in love with you."

I throw an honest-to-christ laugh at my reflection. "Well, all reet. Maybe I can warn the poor boy in time."

In Chicago, we imbibe a tad heavy after my Friday gig. By the time I'm done with the doubleheader Saturday, I'm spraying my throat with a vodka atomizer, popping aspirin for my tin ear. Strange, the noises you hear from your deaf side.

We catch a yellow for a small club called The Cloisters. I'm motating on fumes. Dorothy is sexy, dressed to the nines. She guides my hand under her skirt.

"Agitate me," she whispers. I sneak a feel. Her dark eyes watch mine. "Can't wait to see Lenny Bruce. He's post-existential."

"Post-existential," I repeat. Lenny would need a hand job himself over that.

Inside the club, we drink doubles served by a cocktail skirt, who bends over, hole in panties, runs in both net stockings, has no idea who we are in the darkness.

I wink at Dorothy. "Not my kind of town."

"*Sawr* a man dance with his wife here once," she sings. "And it wasn't that bastard Sinatra."

Can't get into that sore issue, so I excuse myself. She raises a hand.

"Lenny Bruce can be venomous. Protect me."

Backstage I find him in a suit looks metallic, no tie, polka-dot shirt with Billie Eckstine collar.

"Twerp," I say, remembering him when he was Leonard Schneider. "If you were my size, I'd trade you my Caddy for them rags."

He looks glad to see me, cups his balls. "If you were *this* size," he honks, "you got the suit and—as Mussolini once told his great Roman army—the boots off my feet."

I laugh. "We both know what happened to him."

"Shot. Burned. Hanged. Not necessarily in that order, and never excommunicated." On a harangue, he grabs my arm. "But he beget a son who I see—come to think—last week in L.A., playing piano with Baker and Mulligan."

"No."

"But yes. Chetty Baker looks at El Duce Junior in rehearsal and—you won't believe this, J.R.—he says, 'Drag about your dad, man.'" His head tremors. He walks about splay-footed, impersonating Jimmy Durante. "Shot. Burned. Hanged."

Two wrinkled suit types, shirt collars sticking up, try to pamper him. His evil eyes land on me, darkly alluring.

I remind him I knew him when. "Before you changed your name. Last guy I met named *Bruce* tried to kiss me."

Shaking his handlers, he busses my cheek. "Unfuck you, man. Last kiss you turned down was from Ethel Merman."

One suit keeps bugging him. "House is loaded with law," he says. "Best lay off the fag schtick."

"Fag's in," Lenny says. "But no dyke jokes, dig? Them dykes'll kick the shit out of you." He leans as if to kiss me again. "Thanks for coming, baby."

"I'm here with Dorothy Kilgallen."

"Prig with power."

I flinch. "Easy on her, Lenny. Keep her on your side."

"That ain't the way I work." His face is grave as the suits shove him toward the wings.

Rushing back to my table, I can't hide my six feet of ungrace. People spot me and buzz. I can tell some have picked out Dotty too.

"You were gone a long time." Her little triangular face is tight. "You tell him I'm here?"

"Yeah." I brush back my hair, give her my cornpone look. "He promised to tone it down."

Then Lenny finds the spot. Furious applause, the kind I know. He stands sideways to the house, turns his face full portrait like he's amused to catch three uniformed Chicago police leaning against the far wall.

Lenny shades his eyes. "I'm gonna get shot, burned, hanged. Give 'em the light."

Everyone follows the spot, sees a dick in plainclothes join the lineup of fuzz. Then their gaze returns to Lenny, who's baring his chops like a Bronx pimp.

"Granite." He pops the word into the mike. "A Mount Rushmore of cocksuckers."

Even I duck at that.

Dorothy's face is on fire. Under the table, her hand is warm on my thigh. I dress it left, and that's the side she's on.

I fake aghast.

"You like?"

"Speaking of cocksuckers." Lenny's voice and chuckles are gunshots now. "Let's have the light on the incomparable Johnnie Ray and his lady, the Voice of Broadway, Dorothy Kilgallen."

The joint splits its seams. Even the cops thaw and start clapping. I nod at Lenny, heedful there's a price for taking his thunder. Dotty's Lifesaver mouth flashes a grin at me, then at Lenny. The heart of the night is beating fast again.

Morning after, that's me forty stories above Chicago's Madison and Clark. Mystery people below scramble this Sunday toward the deep blue of Lake Michigan. In the early fall glare of the window, I go over in my mind last night's partying. Let's see. There was an after-hour loft southside, Lenny and his wife, Hot Honey Harlow, part doll, part gargoyle. And there were songs from me—*Cry, Walking My Baby, Sweet Lotus Blossom,* like Lady Day. Other shit was going on, too. Jesus.

A moan from the bed joins mine. Miss Kilgallen in the twisted sheets, Gina Lollobrigida tits exposed. Her face, what? Ribald, like she's played it to the edge down on the streets. "My fault," I utter, pressing fingers into my skull. My fault.

Her eyes open laced with panic.

She relaxes after scoping me. "Good morning." Her voice is smoky, gray, dry. She props herself up, stares at my nakedness for a long, long time. She messes with her tangled dark hair, and out of the fucking blue, man, she asks, "What's it like being with a man?"

I freeze, play it deaf and dumb without my wires.

Grimacing from what must be a hundred pains, mental and physical, she straightens a pillow behind her. Those breasts. I'm getting hard.

"What I mean, of course," she says, is what is it like for you? I know what it's like for me."

I stroke my cock.

Motioning me to come to her, she clears her throat with a raspy cough, notices I'm not moving. "You think the business you're in gives you license to behave bizarre as you wish?"

I stand sideways. "Look. The state of Florida." I squeeze my asshole muscle. "Rising." She don't laugh. I sit on the bed, hands pressing my lap.

"With those people last night, I saw something," she goes on. "A desperation you all seem to share."

"Yeah," I agree. "I saw some of that too. I saw Lenny pretty desperate to make a three-way with his wife and that cute ink blot from the Sunset Club." I don't add to this how interested Miss Kilgallen seemed in the plan. "I seen me some desperation in those talented musicians snorting horse through them pink cocktail straws." I don't embellish this with how Miss Kilgallen destroyed the career of tenor man Tiny Walsh for doing the same.

"Spare me." She cross-arms her chest, shudders.

I don't let her go. "Hey, I'm agreeing with you. Out amongst 'em without a gig, without a dime, without a hope—sometimes it can get a bit bizarre."

"You're saying it goes with the territory?"

"I'm saying last night you saw nothing compared to how it can really get."

She flings the sheet away, something she wouldn't do when we were new. "You articulate that loneliness in your singing."

Light strikes her flesh. I can't believe her marriage to someone else, three kids, her other life. "You sound like a journalist."

"You sound like you're evading my question."

I stand, stroke myself, inches from her face. She removes the pillow from behind her, holds it to her chest. I poke a finger into its softness. "Smother you?"

"No," she says. "Place it under my ass so you can fuck me with that monster."

"Lenny Bruce," I say. "His bit on pornology."

"Pornography."

"Yeah, that."

"You innocent," she says.

"You innocent too, girl."

Down there, her smile is colored soft. The smell of our sex, short hours before, raises from her. Our hangovers will hit really bad soon, so I don't wait any longer.

Dorothy's friend, Clara, Rollie's long-suffering better half, had come to Chicago with us and spent most her time visiting relatives. Lucky for us she shows up at the hotel with our return flight tickets. In the air, Dorothy and I drink tiny bottles of Smirnoff. She's bleary and nauseated.

"Maybe we should slow down," I tell her. "You have to make *What's My Line* tonight."

"That's why I have no intention of slowing down," she says.

Disboarding, we get looks from people, like they're hoping we'll lose control, make their sighting us bigger than life. Ikesville, man. Everybody golfers and deacons. Rollie is at LaGuardia to pick us up. I catch a glimpse of his barracuda grin, wave down a taxi for Dotty and me.

In the cab, Manhattan looms, sundown glinting off limestone and glass. Dorothy is antsy, hyperventilating, and don't ask me about hyperventilating.

"Wish I had a pill that could help," I say, "or a paper bag."

Rummaging through her purse, she finds a small vial, shakes out four capsules. "Doctor Feelgood," she murmurs.

I look at the cabbie's pencil neck. "How do we get them down?"

"*Voila.*" She comes up with a smuggled two-ounce Smirnoff. "The incredible shrinking Russian."

CBS Studios minutes away. Skyscraper air. Scents of dry-cleaned, cologned people rushing nowhere. I'm spinning, swirling down a drain. Trying to explain my randy ways to the lady this morning, shit. Cars are turning on their lights, a galaxy of revolving stars. Dorothy almost nods off next to me, her face serene, like she's satisfied life will go on for us, though I'm an old thirty-one and she's much older, trying to keep up in her high heels.

"I love you," I say to her.

"You love your music," she says, half gone.

Pencil-neck cabbie turns, throws his words back to us. "I got some dynamite boo," he offers, and I know nothing ever really ends.

 ## Dorothy

She'd held up the Kilgallen end of the panel on *What's My Line* that night after returning from Chicago like a Mick bantamweight. The following week's show didn't go as well, however.

She had closed the Stork Club with Ernest Hemingway the night before, and she would ride in Queen Elizabeth's procession from City Hall next week. No wonder she was so exhausted.

Marie, her makeup woman, didn't have her vodka ready when Dorothy returned to the dressing room after the show. She hadn't even set up the bar, standing grim-faced in front of the clock as if in court, waiting to be sentenced. Whatever her problem, it would have to wait. Dorothy couldn't deal with anything more challenging right now than the clinking of ice in a glass.

Her head had buzzed throughout the show, and she'd listened to herself speak as if through static on a radio. She'd blown two easy guesses, too, giving one to Arlene, the other to Bennett Cerf. What she needed to resurrect her self-esteem was Johnnie, but he was out of town again. She'd have to settle for a drink and after that, a quick visit to P.J.'s.

She wished she'd brought one of the remaining Smirnoff bottles from their Chicago trip, but at the last minute, she'd decided on the see-through Lucite bag and dismissed the idea, the first of many poor decisions she'd made tonight.

Taking a seat before the makeup mirror she smiled at Marie's stern reflection.

"I wasn't that bad, was I?"

"Wasn't your fault. Anyone can have an off night."

"Where's the bar? They cut the budget?"

Marie smoothed a drape over Dorothy's beaded gown. "Mr. T was back here looking for you tonight. Himself."

"Indeed." Dorothy gave herself a moment to regroup, watching her own image in the mirror as Marie removed the heavy stage makeup. She needed to cut her hair again, do something about the puffiness beneath her eyes. "Let's hope he didn't catch my humbling performance tonight."

"He said he'd be back after the show."

"Let's leave the rest of the war paint on then," she said. "And thanks for the warning, Marie. Arlene has a bad day or two, and no one utters a peep. Let me screw up once, and they're out to get me."

"It's because they're jealous of you." Marie handed her the box of tissues. "If you're going to keep the makeup tonight, I'll leave a little early. Is there anything else I can do before I go?"

Dorothy could hear the worry in her voice. It made her want to weep. Jesus, it would be nice to just put her head down and have a good cry. But she couldn't.

"Any good fan mail?"

"Peeked at a few," Marie said. "That club owner from Dallas sent flowers again. Over there."

Dorothy turned to look at the carnation melange. "What's his name, Rudy?"

"Ruby," she said. "Jack Ruby. Flowers should cheer you up."

"Did you read what Hemingway said about me?" she asked, addressing Marie's reflection again. "How much he loved my work on the Sam Sheppard case?"

"Miss Kilgallen—"

"A good girl, he called me, kissed my hand, too. We drank champagne all night, Marie, closed the Stork. Jack Kennedy was there, but that's, as we say in journalism, off the record."

"Miss Kilgallen, please."

Dorothy was rambling again, couldn't think straight, close to tears. "Sorry," she said. "I'm just tired."

"I know." The expression on Marie's face changed from concern to something else Dorothy didn't want to contemplate.

"I'm just excited about next week, the queen and all. Now, what were you asking me, dear?"

"I just wanted to know if I can do anything for you before I leave."

That look again. She couldn't stand that look. "Yes," she said. "I'll tell you what you can do. You can get the portable bar out of protective custody and pour me a goddamn vodka."

nine

 Johnnie

Using Lum and Abner for my writers again, I check into the hospital day before my birthday. I'm hoping to throw my own surprise party this time. A team of sawbones wait with what I hope is my new left ear. The place is a dump. I had Babe Pascoe smuggle me a taste. Nurses got uptight. Big black attendant scolds me while I'm walking toward this little toilet next to my room because my gown is on backwards, my Frank Sinatra swinging.

I give it a little finger flip. "Ever see an ofay dick like this?" Letting Amos and Andy hack a line for me.

Black nurse grins a mouthful of Hollywood teeth. "On my turf, that's nothin'. Black, tan or pink, it don't matter."

I laugh out loud. "There's a little pink in all of us."

Surgery is a shmeer. I wake up punchy and ask for Dorothy. Who? "Dorothy Kilgallen," I mumble. "This is my surprise for her."

"Earl Wilson's in the waiting room," a voice says.

"Who the fuck's Earl Wilson?"

"Hollywood reporter. You know that."

"There ain't but one reporter," I scream. "And that's Dotty."

The voice again. Shit, it's Morrie, and don't tell me I don't know the owl's hoot.

"Morrie?"

"Yeah, pal."

"Speak up." I free a trembling hand, touch a turban of bandages. I'm soaked in a rush of terrible pain, and worse than that, I'm flat-out scared. "Oh, God, Morrie. I can't hear."

Dorothy finds me later that day.

"You could have at least checked into Mt. Sinai instead of over in this borough."

Walls spin into focus. An axe splits my skull. "I wanted to keep it secret." I smell her lavender, thin whiff of vodka on her lips as she kisses me. "Jesus, Dotty. I'm still the weird kid. I'm hearing harmonics, dinosaurs crunching up trees from way back. Pre-historic, off-pitch music."

"You'll be making your own music again, Johnnie. I'm working on lining up a session with Billy Taylor for you. Jazz standards. If Morrie can't make the deal, goddammit, I will."

"Oh, man. Let's hope I can hear Billy's piano," I say.

Later they try to keep her in the hall while they tell me the surgery failed. She storms past the guards.

"What's going on?" I ask her. "Give it to me straight."

"They want to try it again," she says. Her voice hisses like the honeycomb radiator against the wall.

"Oh fuck."

The doctors chatter. I attempt to read their lips. The room is fogging up. They wait like a ghostly jury for my permission.

"Go ahead," I say, everything going black like if I don't hear, I can't see.

70

A week after my second operation, I'm onstage at Philadelphia's Latin Casino, winging it without a hearing aid. Earl Wilson writes that Broadway believes in miracles again.

Dorothy Kilgallen's column says my audience digs the drama. When I sent a grinning wink and snapped my fingers at the band, when I came to the lyrics about dark clouds passing in time, there wasn't a dry eye in the house, she said.

In truth, I did it all by rote. By instinct. By mirrors. Dog and pony show with a one-trick star.

Deaf as a post.

Cold day, light snow blowing with cinders. Winter birds scuffle in downtown doorways. Miss Cornshucks is at my side, lifting her yellow galoshes out of the slush. Not wanting to lay all my woe on Dorothy, I've asked the Shucker to be my scout. I'm determined to find a new ear.

"Slow down," she says, almost sliding off into the gutter.

"Bowl 'n' Bite." I throw her a hand. "Gutter ball."

"You racial."

"Ah, come on."

She throws my hand aside. Passersby gawk at her. Her dress is indescribable. Think bazooms. Think ass could bring down Jericho. "Where we goin'?"

"I need amplification."

"One thing you don't need, baby, more amps."

"In my ear," I say. "First they took what was left of my left, then stole half of my right."

Cornshucks cuffs my left ear with her mitten. "Let's get you the most powerful tin motherfucker they make."

I place her mitten on my other ear. "Only hope now is this side."

"What people going to think when you switch sides? They'll say you don't know your left from your right."

"What?" Clamor of traffic and street hubbub crest like the Lost Sea in my head.

She shoots me a sweet golden smile. "Let's head over to West 52nd. Know a place allows silly lookin' shits with freckles."

I work on a grin. "Now you're coming in loud and clear."

Striding the wet sidewalk, I scat a free-flowing chorus to *Whiskey and Gin.* She joins in. Damn, I forgot how pure she is. I go into a bit of Bing's *Goodnight Sweetheart.* She lifts her eyes, draws a square in the air with her index fingers. Then to my astonishment, she takes a jade from some fold in her garb, sets fire to it with a big Zippo.

"Jesus Christ, girl."

"No big thang." She burps after a drag. "Used to could do this along here, no hassle."

"Jesus."

"Don't be all hinkty now."

We walk a stretch between Fifth and Seventh. Brownstones are modified into street-level clubs. Under dark marquees, they sulk in the cruel daylight.

She stops, stamps her galoshes. "Sang here in the Club Onyx, first night Joe Helbock move it from over there."

I follow her point.

"Was a speakeasy that side of the street." Her gaze is dreamy. "First night booze was legal after Prohibition. First night they'd bust you for this." She holds up her joint.

"How old were you?"

"Was summer of 1934. Guess I was 'bout fifteen."

"Jesus." I reach for her.

"Goddammit," she growls. "Quit your crying." Her grip on my hand could be a small girl's. Looking off, she moans low in her throat. "Club Onyx. The Famous Door. The Hickory House. All mostly for whites, but my voice is around here."

We clutch in yesterday's echoes, both of us blubbering like a pair of lost kids.

Dorothy

Morrie called that morning as she was leaving to cover Queen Elizabeth's visit. Johnnie, she thought. Something must be wrong with Johnnie. One white glove on, the other still in her hand, she almost yanked the phone from Julian.

"Is he all right?" she demanded.

"Oh, he's just fine, thanks to you," Morrie said. "Couldn't you have picked out a bigger hearing aid? He'll have to push that one around in a wheel barrow."

She felt the tension leave her chest. Johnnie was fine. He and Miss Cornshucks had gotten drunk on West 52nd when they were supposed to be shopping, and she had no choice but to step in and help. Although in truth her selection was a bit cumbersome, it was supposed to be the best on the market.

"At least he'll be able to hear when he records '*Til Morning.* I should think you'd be pleased by that."

"Got it named already, do you? That's why I'm calling." Morrie's nasal voice took on a wounded quality. "We need to talk, you and me."

"I'm sure we will," she said. "I can't imagine how we can avoid it."

"Listen." His voice rose, then she could hear him force it down, trying to mimic her icy tone. "I'm just concerned about you butting in on this recording deal of his."

"Butt, my ass. I created the deal. If it were up to you, he'd be selling bowling balls. You should be glad I'm not taking a cut."

"Oh, you're taking one, all right, lady. You're taking a big cut, and we both know it."

She started to tremble, needed a drink to quiet her nerves, but it was too late for that now, thanks to this ungrateful asshole. Julian appeared in the doorway. If he'd heard her outburst, he gave no indication.

"The driver's waiting, ma'am."

She nodded, then spoke icily into the phone. "I want what's best for Johnnie, and you'd better just get used to it. I'm going to be around for a long time."

"We'll see about that."

"Yes," she said. "We will. Now, if you'll excuse me, I have a queen to meet." She handed the phone to Julian, without waiting to hear Morrie's next response. Still working her right hand into the glove, hurried out the door.

ten

Johnnie

I walk into Dick Clark's Saturday Night Show's debut wearing my new hearing aid. Pat Boone is here, doing the bump and grind with this plastic ring around his hips. Gives me his shit-eating grin.

"Hula Hoop," he says. I walk by, show him nothing but boredom. "Yoo-hoo," he hollers after me. "Earth to Johnnie."

Before showtime, Jerry Lee Lewis horses around on the piano, kicks the piano bench behind him. Bam! Into Dick Clark's shins. This action must remind Dick of me doing the same thing years back.

All in all, the show is a hit. I join Dorothy at Trader Vic's for a quick one. We end up breaking our old record for Scorpions downed in one sitting. Before we're too smashed, she tells me about my upcoming disc for Columbia.

"Billy Taylor has agreed to produce." Sounding like my new manager.

I smile at her enthusiasm, add some of my own. "I got the can't-hardly-waits."

"March 3 and March 6—two days in between so your voice is strong."

"Who negotiated that?"

"Not Morrie."

Little girl getting tough over there.

Billy Taylor is a genius at soft pedal, lulling the best out of everybody. He greets me at Columbia, those smiling eyes through windowpanes. "Hey Slim."

"Hey, professor."

"You sane and sober?"

"Certified."

"Solid," he says, "because we've got no two-and-a-half minute do-wa-ditties here."

Adrenalin splashes into my veins as he sets up. He runs Gershwin over the keys, cigarette in his playing hand. Soon he's got music from a hand-picked group, so lush I feel tears in the back of my throat.

In three hours, we lay out Gershwin's *They Can't Take That Away from Me*, Johnny Mercer's *Too Marvelous For Words*, Sammy Cahn's gems, *Teach Me Tonight* and *Day By Day*.

Digging deep, Billy lays color hues on these standards that dissolve the static in my head, leave it clear enough I'm proud of the job I do.

After work, we smoke and chat. The studio is dark and full of old voices, old refrains.

"You've a most distinctive voice, Johnnie." His back is against the wall, so he can view the entire room. "Your *Day By Day* will ring in my head forever."

I feel my face turn red. "Thanks for getting with Morrie. This session means a lot to me. Last week I thought my hearing had split for good."

"Morrie would have us doing Hi Ho Silver," Billy says. "It's Dorothy Kilgallen you should be thanking. Says she'll have you fronting Ellington before she's done."

"A reach for a hayseed like me."

"You are a reach, Johnnie Ray." He rises from his dark corner. "One hell of a reach." Extends his hand. "See you in a couple of days. We'll wrap this gig in gold."

I'm feeling pretty good right about now.

 # Dorothy

The Silver Wraith Rolls that Mr. Hearst provided her for the queen's visit was rumored to set him back more than $25,000. Dorothy perched stiff-backed in its massive rear seat and slid off her shoes, soothing her aching feet against the Persian lamb's wool. The sensuous gesture made her think again of Johnnie. He'd love this car with its gold fixtures and French walnut bar. Even more, he'd love watching her in this procession creeping past City Hall, just two cars behind Prince Philip's party and three behind Elizabeth.

She'd see him tonight, tell him all about it. She needed to keep his spirits up, get his mind off the failed surgeries and whatever propaganda Morrie was feeding him. At least Johnnie wasn't threatened by her involvement in his career. Quite the contrary, he loved it, and there was nothing Morrie Lane could do about that.

Cheering crowds lined the streets as the royal procession passed. Clever the way her driver had inched in right behind Governor Harriman's group in a position of prominence. Sheilah Graham and the other bitches would be beside themselves. Hearst would know she'd done him proud, and just maybe the publicity would keep Mr. T at bay about her streak of bad luck on the show. It was only television, after all.

The crowd pressed closer, reaching out in imploring gestures, cheering as if grateful to even witness such an event. Dorothy lifted her hand, palm facing her, in the slow circular wave of the Royal Family. At the moment, she felt like royalty. By god, in her own way, she was royalty.

She was supposed to meet with the decorator the following Thursday at the new apartment she'd found for Johnnie. Even the address was musical—163 East 63rd Street, and it was simply enormous, especially so without furniture. On a whim, she brought Clara along. Marilyn Monroe had once told Dorothy that blondes fade fast, and Clara was living proof. The bloom on her cheek came out of a compact now, and her once-spontaneous smile had taken on a forced quality. For some reason, these qualities endeared Clara even more to her. There but for fortune, and without Johnnie, she could be aging just as quickly before her time. Instead she felt like a girl as they strolled through the empty rooms.

"What do you think?" she asked walking along the row of windows opening onto 63rd.

"I think you're crazy, that's what. You're practically moving in with him." Clara's eyes widened at the delicious possibility of it.

"Not officially."

"What if Dick finds out?"

She shrugged inside her fur. "What's he going to do, kill me?"

"Don't even say that. He hasn't been very happy lately."

"He hasn't been happy for a long time. That doesn't mean that I can't be."

A soft knock at the door. Clara jumped as if caught doing something she shouldn't. "Who is it?"

"The decorator, I should hope." Dorothy threw open the door. "Max, it's about time."

He looked like an overweight undertaker, but Max was the best decorator in New York. Also the tardiest. Although you couldn't tell from the girth he carried and his boring, monochromatic suits, he was a master of color and design.

Behind him, two workmen balanced a large carton. Max sweated for both of them.

"The chandelier," he said, wiping his shiny face with a handkerchief. "I wanted you to see it inside, be sure it's what you have in mind."

"Put it there," she said, pointing to a spot on the ceiling above where the table would go. And to Clara, "It's absolutely massive, all cut crystal and burning candles."

"Well, not burning yet," Max said, as more cartons were dragged into the room. He spread the fabric samples out. Clara all but gasped at the salmon velvet.

"Your bedspread?" she asked, stroking it.

"Our sofa." The color was perfect for the room, perfect for Johnnie. "It arrives tomorrow. We'll put it here, the piano right there."

"What's Johnnie going to say about all this?" Clara asked, as the workmen secured the chandelier and a blaze of light reflected from its surfaces.

"He loves the idea of it, and he trusts my taste completely."

"He must. It's all very lovely."

"That far wall there. That's his gallery." She pointed out the large, black-framed photos of Johnnie and the queen, Johnnie and Lady Day, autographed photographs of Marilyn and Noel Coward.

"You couldn't find a more dramatic chandelier," Max said. "The dining table will go beneath it."

"Oak," Dorothy told Clara. "It's costing Johnnie a fortune. The chandelier's a gift from me."

"Do you want the bill sent to the same address?" Although he spoke in a fat man's gasp, Max still had that understated, casual tone, acquired over time, that people use to discuss large sums of money.

"That will be fine." Her secretary would just have to do some juggling this month, that's all.

"Of course," he ventured, as if sensing her hesitation, "we do have other styles, if you think this one's a little too large."

What he meant was too expensive, and he knew she knew it. She could always have Johnnie pay for it, but this was to be special.

"What do you think, Clara?" she asked.

She looked from Dorothy to the glittering pieces of glass above them. "The truth?"

"Of course. You don't like it, do you?"

"It's not that. It's just that it seems, well a bit ostentatious, perhaps." She crossed her arms across her chest, as if to ward off whatever blow came next.

"Oh, I think not," Max said, with more force than he'd used since he'd arrived. "If you consider the size of the room, the scale of the furnishings—"

"Ostentatious," Dorothy said. "You really think so?"

"A bit," Clara replied grudgingly.

"Would you have it in your home?"

She slowly shook her head. "No, I guess I wouldn't."

"Would Roland like it?"

"Heavens no."

"That settles it," she told Max. "I'll take it."

"I know you won't be sorry," Max said. "Marilyn Monroe and Arthur Miller bought a similar one."

"Indeed," she said, giving him her *What's My Line* smile. "I'll still take it."

Dick was waiting for her in the dining room when she got home. He held a drink in his right hand and stared at her with the squinting half-smile of someone who had spent too many hours in the dark.

"Where have you been off to?" he asked, circling her like a large animal checking for scent.

"Out with Clara."

"Spending a lot of time with her, aren't you, darling? That trip to Chicago? All of these afternoons."

Her worn-thin patience snapped. "I have no time for games today. Say your piece, if you must. Just be sure you can sit down here in front of the microphone tomorrow and resume our show with a semblance of sobriety."

"Say my piece?" He drank slowly, watching her face. "Okay, then. I came home only because I heard something this afternoon that I thought might interest you."

"Such as?"

"Tyrone Power."

"What about him?"

"He died today. I thought you'd want to know."

His statement knocked the air out of her as surely as a physical blow would have. She gripped the chair in front of her, trying to steady herself. She once dreamed of marrying Ty. How different would her life be if she had?

"How?" she managed to ask. "He's so young." Her age. He was her age.

"Overexertion, they said, doing a fencing scene for his new film. His heart went."

She shook her head, barely able to speak, remembering the idol she'd often praised in print. "He tried to teach me to drive," she said.

"I know."

"He was just a sweet man, not at all the Hollywood type." She felt the threat of tears again, not just for Ty but, damn, for what? Dick looked helpless, awkward now with the extra weight he'd put on, facial muscles working as if searching for something to say that mattered. "Thank you for letting me know," she told him.

He nodded, stone faced, took another drink. "Don't worry about this," he said, tilting the glass toward her. "I'll be fine in time for the show tomorrow."

She looked at his lips, still wet from the liquor, his hunched shoulders and swollen belly, and felt an inexplicable rush of tenderness. "Good," she said. "I appreciate that."

She waited until he left, then poured a drink of her own.

eleven

 Johnnie

Columbia is happy with the results of my new album. Dorothy is ecstatic. Morrie says the beatniks should like it. I don't ask him to explain that; the songs must not be corny enough for him. He's on his own road lately, thinks I'm Dorothy's puppet. As for me, I'm proud when people I respect tell me Taylor and I buried Sinatra's *Day By Day*.

Dorothy and I celebrated by opening my new apartment. We'd walked through it before, made love at twilight on a boat-long sofa of pink velvet. She had this two-ton decorator throw enough fuchsia and green around I'm singing *September Song* in July.

This hot Sunday a bunch of us are partying, waiting for Dorothy's show to air. When I saw her off earlier, she looked a bit bushed, and I'm apprehensive. *What's My Line* can be a stiff workout with those lights and close-ups. I drink cocktails double-fisted to relax.

Morrie's here trying to find his picture on my gallery wall. He shakes his head at my drink.

"Whitecoats break in, we're all in their butterfly nets," he says dramatically.

"Yeah, yeah," I say, rattling my ice. "That's their wagon down on 63rd."

He gazes with serious expectation out a floor-to-ceiling window. "Why you throw these big parties?"

"So friends can drop by bearing gifts," I answer, "except you, you cheap screw."

He looks crushed. "Gladys brung that clay thing."

I see his wife nibbling with others at the oak table. "An ashtray, Morrie," I remind him. "You brought me a fucking ashtray."

He cleans his glasses against his paunch, looks in my direction. "Whatever. It's a Picasso."

"Yeah, and Samantha over there is Rin Tin Tin." My Doberman wakes, rolls back in grassy shag.

Party time is building. Air conditioning is humming. Hi-fidelity is blasting. TV is warming up for the show. I pray for my lady, hope she has a winning night.

Christopher George struts into the den, throws his arms around me. Morrie turns all prim, shakes his wrist as George walks away.

"Another Hollywood pal?"

"Good friend is all." Knowing truth don't always prevail, I point out the actor's gorgeous wife.

"Maybe he throws from both sides of the mound," Morrie mumbles. "Amby-dextry, like you."

I do what I don't do often. I flare. "Maybe you pitch a bitch when your fucking opinion ain't needed."

Staggering from my rebuff, he blindsides Yul Brynner. Samantha bolts from a nightmare, bites his pant leg. His wife clutches him before he's an unintentional suicide out my glass. She gives me a depressed look. I take the opportunity to thank her for the Picasso piece.

She releases Morrie. "It's a fake," she whispers.

"Don't worry," Yul says. "Nothing is perfectly real."

About now, Carol Channing bellows by the TV, "*I've Got A Secret* is starting."

Fifteen people correct her. She eyeballs us like she's the Hirshfield drawing of herself on my gallery wall.

Amid famous performers and hard-ass show-biz types, I pray again for my lady. Jesus, nothing in the racket comes easy.

 # Dorothy

Marie wasn't in the dressing room when Dorothy returned after the show. Neither was the makeshift bar. In their place, stood Mr. T, a picture of solemnity in a dark suit, oiled-down hair and a scent to match. Her performance tonight, if not stellar, had been acceptable. At least she had been able to ace the last guest before Arlene could get another question out of her mouth.

"Good evening," she said. "Did you catch the show?"

"Never miss it. I just wanted to say hello. We so seldom get a chance to chat."

They stood facing each other across the room. Chatting was not something this man did well. His fair skin paled in the bright light of the room. With his arms stiff at his side, he looked mechanical.

"Forgive me, but I'm in a bit of a hurry tonight," she said.

"I know you're busy."

"Terribly busy. I'm covering Khrushchev's trip in September, you know." She gauged his reaction, unable to read beyond the expression of mild interest.

"Your schedule must be very demanding."

He made it sound like an accusation, damn him. "If you have a problem with my schedule, perhaps we should set up a meeting to discuss it," she said, as pleasantly as possible. She'd promise anything, say anything, just to get away from him right now.

"Oh, this isn't an official visit." He moved closer to the door, as if he too would like to get out of this stifling room. "I just wanted to be sure nothing was bothering you."

"Implying?" The question slipped out, icy and swift.

"Dorothy." He now stood only a few feet from her, so close she could see the beads of sweat on his poreless forehead and smell the unctuous odor of his aftershave. "You know I have only the highest regard for your work." The insincerity in his words irritated her more than his presence. She crossed her arms in front of her, trying to ignore her throbbing temples.

"My work," she said, "isn't pleasing you?"

"No. You've been off, Dorothy. You know you have."

"As we all are on occasion." She crossed her arms tighter to keep from trembling. "If Arlene has a bad night or bad couple of nights, no one says a word."

"That's not true. You know that I pride myself on my fairness. Both you and Arlene make your individual contributions to the show. You have different styles."

Now she had him on the defensive. She tried to sound hurt, injured. "Every time I open my mouth, everyone's hoping I'll make a mistake. I'm resented because of who I am, even because of my religion." Sweat glistened on his forehead now. Good. She hammered a little harder. "I'm the John Kennedy of broadcasting, discriminated against because I'm a Catholic."

"Oh, come on, Dorothy. You're the one who kissed Bishop Sheen's ring on national television. You flaunt your religion."

"Why shouldn't I?"

"It's not your Catholicism that concerns me," he said. "And you're right. We probably need to talk about this later. I just dropped by to see if there were anything I could do."

He reached for the door. In a moment, she'd be rid of him, rid of his sweet barbershop smell. "I appreciate your concern," she said. "But I do find it a trifle odd that you, this paragon of fairness, aren't equally concerned about others on the show."

His pasty face went pink as if she'd pinched it. "Others don't have problems with their speech, Dorothy."

That did it. How dare this sniveling little man in a cheap suit criticize her? "You're questioning my diction? You?"

"I'm questioning what it is that sometimes slurs your speech and makes it difficult to understand you, like tonight for instance." His face was now florid. "We can talk about it next week in my office. I'll have my secretary contact you to set up a time. Goodnight." He all but whispered the last word.

"Goodnight," she said, enunciating clearly, as he walked out.

She'd deal with his veiled accusations later, and if it came down to it, she'd walk off the damned television show. Her diction was flawless, she knew. He'd said it only because she'd bested him, as she always did, in their little battles of words.

Her makeup felt as if it were melting into her skin, and her parched throat ached for a cool drink. She'd deal with Mr. T later. Right now all she cared about was getting back to where she really belonged, back home with Johnnie.

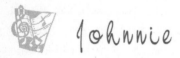 Johnnie

Dorothy's show was like watching the seventh game of last year's World Series. I kept pulling for the Yanks against the Braves, but each inning it got worse.

She arrives a bit late. We all rush to compliment her, tell her she was marvelous. I suddenly realize that much of her weekly job is bona-fide performing. I've considered it such a simple feat, not really art, but you boil it down and that half-hour viewed by millions is one intense gig.

"I need a drink," she says. Her mouth is tight, lips a line.

I guide her away from the fawning, see a few raised eyebrows from those who aren't actors. She is in the gown and make-up from the show. I dab at a moustache of sweat under her nose.

"Ran into trouble after the show," she says. "I'll tell you later."

I hand her a drink. "Big-time trouble?"

She turns her drink up and down. "Nothing I can't handle."

Grabbing Smirnoff's neck, I freshen our drinks. "That's my girl." I attempt to cheer her up. "What's that new phallic symbol next to the TV?"

This gets me a smile. "Remind you of anything?"

I make a deal out of looking around her at the sculpture. It's a polished oak pole, globe on top, full of crabapples. We hold onto one another, chuckling. Two lovers against the odds.

Things get sloppy later. Dorothy bristles at the crude remarks a flamboyant young woman makes about Mr. K's nightclub.

"And whom might you be?" Dotty demands.

Miss Razzmatazz turns red, says she's an associate of Max, our decorator. "I meant no malice."

Dorothy counter-punches. "Your claiming my husband's club is an homage to Art Wrecko merely points out your ignorance."

One thing about Kilgallen, she'll defend the son of a bitch.

Diehards stick around. Rafael is at my new white grand, playing softly. Dorothy drowns him with a platter by Dinah Washington and tells me again to get rid of him.

"His visa has lapsed," I tell her. "He's waiting to go back to Chile." I'm repeating his bullshit like it's gospel. "He's heir to a winery fortune."

Dorothy ain't buying. When he stops playing to look our way, she frenches me. I go along with it, and she breaks the kiss.

"Has he been staying over?"

Jesus. "Using the spare bedroom 'til he's leveled out."

"Take me in there."

"There's still a few guests."

"I don't care."

This kind of behavior I've grown to admire. It's like she makes a game out of being daring, wants to see how far she can push it. I like it, but it scares me.

"Jesus, I don't know."

"And when we get in there," she says, "leave the damn door ajar. And whatever you do, Johnnie, don't hold back."

We stagger into the spare bedroom. Rafael's cologne tints the air. I leave the door almost all the way open and move on Dorothy like a petting teenager.

"Come on," she says. "Get completely undressed." She's stripping fast, breathing hard. Past the door and the short hallway, noises of the others beat like music. I reach for the glowing bed lamp.

"No. Leave it on," she says.

The room is half lighted, half open. I feel that it's half closed up in another way, that there is barely a chance for escape.

twelve

 Dorothy

Christmas was her favorite time of year, especially this last Christmas of the 1950s. She arrived to meet Johnnie at the Waldorf Astoria that night feeling like a movie star. With its cut-glass chandeliers and Erte-inspired décor, the Waldorf made any occasion seem like a holiday. Tinsel and elaborate garlands added to its allure tonight, and the mood of celebration was contagious. In a week, it would be Christmas, and then her New Year's Eve party.

Dorothy walked briskly behind the maitre d', past the college boys in suits trying to impress their dates, through the seasoned New Yorkers, toward what Clara called Celebrity Central. Beyond the ghastly clock, an homage to Art Deco gone wrong, she waved at John and Jacqueline Kennedy taking a respite from the campaign trail, caught sight of Tennessee Williams and a friend deep in drink and conversation. Her territory, her beat, all hers.

Glances lingered, she knew, as she passed. She never would have dared to wear such a revealing dress before she'd known Johnnie. She'd softened the deep neckline with a double rope of pearls, a trick she had learned from her dear friend Sophia Loren, to whom some compared her. Not that they came out and said it. Silly, really. Sophia so earthy-ethnic, and she so Irish and, some might say, so elegant.

For a moment, as she tried to focus through the swarm of faces, her momentum shifted. She reached out, grasping only air. The maitre d' hadn't noticed. She took small, quick steps to keep up.

Faces blurred. That damned anemia again. When was the last time she ate? She did her best to maintain a smile, thinking of Queen Elizabeth. No matter how many hours she had been standing or waving, she always managed to make everyone feel acknowledged.

Then she saw him, dressed in a tux, glass held in mid-drink. He'd ordered for both of them, the darling, then drained most of the glass on her side of the round table. The maitre d' stood aside as she hurried to him. On his feet at once, he gave her a cool vodka kiss for the public, a warm touch of tongue for private. She pulled away feeling herself blush.

"Damn, you're gorgeous," he said. "Your hair! What'd you have done?"

"You like it." She'd taken a chance, had her stylist mimic Sophia's highly teased do. Her hair felt like a lacquer-coated hat sweeping straight up and over to the left side of her face.

"It's beautiful, you're beautiful. Sit down, sit down. Let me look at you."

"Must be the ring." She flashed the rose quartz he'd brought her from Brazil and settled next to him. "It complements the black dress, don't you think?"

"It matches your nipples." He glanced down at her cleavage, then back up, gazing into her eyes, all mischief and sex appeal.

"Come now. It's not that low."

"But my mind is."

She heard a noise, turned to see a patient waiter at the table trying his best to look unobtrusive. "Well, hello," she said, straightening the square neckline of her dress. And to Johnnie, "Care for some hors d'ouevres, darling?"

"Would I! But since we're in public, I'll settle for some food. Hell, I'll even go for a little grape tonight. You got to choose though."

They ordered and, when the waiter left, they huddled over the one remaining vodka, heads close. He smelled of leather and citrus, of man. The satin-trimmed tux smoothed out his angular body as if someone had gone over it with an iron.

From the side of their table, a voice shouted, "Smile."

Photographers. That was the one negative about the Waldorf. Johnnie turned like the pro he was, crossing his arms on the table, taking her left hand in his. She smiled into the lens, heard the click. Immortalized, she was, the two of them, together.

His job over, the photographer slid back into the crowd, looking for other subjects. Johnnie leaned forward, his expression serious. His scrutiny gave her pause. She needed conversation, laughter.

"You must have gotten here early," she said.

"Couldn't stand the thought that you might have to wait."

"I got tied up making party plans. Had a visit from Sophia. She's a beautiful thing."

"No more beautiful than what I have."

He gave her a lingering kiss. And why not? No photographer would dare snap them embracing.

The wine arrived along with the shrimp cocktails. Johnnie lifted his glass. "To the sexiest woman in New York, maybe the whole world."

She clinked her class to his. "And to the most handsome man who ever stepped out of a tux. The sooner, the better."

"Vixen," he said, moving closer.

"Hound."

"Crazy lady."

"Wild man."

It was the way they played in public, teasing each other with words and glances. He looked down at her cleavage.

"Careful or I'll kiss you right there."

She cut a fast glance to the bulge in his lap. "Then I'd just have to grab you there."

"Dare you."

"Remember the last time you did that here?

He grinned, brushed a strand of hair from his forehead. "Got a blow job, didn't I?"

"In the elevator, darling. I only wish someone had seen us."

"Dotty, please." Now he was the one to blush, narrowing his eyes the way others might clamp their hands over their ears.

His citrusy scent tickled her nostrils. She giggled, feeling breathless and silly, the way alcohol had once made her feel, when she was new to it. "That's what I'm going to do to you at the party. They say that what you do on near Year's Eve, you'll be doing all year long. I want to be on my knees in front of you—"

"Dorothy." He looked uncomfortable the way he sometimes did with her public displays, but she didn't care.

"I'll find a way to do it, too."

"Not unless you move the party to California."

"What?" Slowly his hesitant manner and serious demeanor made sense. But no. He wouldn't desert her New Year's Eve. He couldn't.

"Morrie insisted. I tried to tell you right off, but I didn't know how."

"That son of a bitch."

"Don't blame him. I'm a performer. This is what performers do. I'm lucky to have the gig."

"Lucky!" She took a swallow of cold wine. "Do you know how long I've been planning this party?"

"I'll call you the minute the show's over."

More wine arrived. A long swallow, she thought. Just cool off and get past the disappointment. Why did there always have to be so much disappointment?

"You look pale," Johnnie said. "Why don't we get something to eat?"

A minute ago she was the most beautiful woman in the world. Now he wanted to feed her before midnight, get rid of her. At that moment, an idea occurred to her.

"Is Rafael going to California with you?"

"Why would you ask that?" The hurt in his voice relieved her, but she couldn't be too careful.

"Well, he's living off you. He's practically your manservant."

"This is business," he said. "It's important to my career."

"And you'd perform on the moon if Morrie thought it was a good idea."

"He's my fucking manager. I don't need another one."

"The same manager who got you into that disastrous bowling alley business when he should have been worried about your recording career."

"That's none of your business."

"Your lack of gratitude astounds me." She felt her words slip together, bumping into each other. Too much booze on an empty stomach, too much sorrow. She straightened in her chair, made an effort to speak clearly. "You want to sing *Cry* for the rest of your life? Stick with Morrie. Spend your New Years Eves in dives all over the country. Turn your back on everyone who loves you."

"I'm not turning my back on you," he said, his voice drained now. "I'll never turn my back on you."

"You're doing just that, and you don't even know it," she said, unable to stop the tears. "The party's just a metaphor for what you're doing to me."

"Ah, c'mon, baby."

"Fuck you." The words stunned her like a slap across the face. Crude, unplanned, they couldn't have come from her, simply couldn't have.

"Dorothy." Shock etched his features. Miss Kilgallen didn't swear in public. Miss Kilgallen didn't shout. The next thing she knew, she was twisting the radiant quartz ring from her finger. Amazed, she watched herself bounce it hard across the floor of holiday merrymakers, doing her best to smash it and all it meant to her, to both of them.

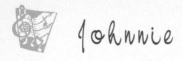 Johnnie

New Years Eve Day. Garden of Allah again. I toss my bags onto the bed. "Fucking L.A."

Morrie has followed me in. "Better than Frisco," he says. "There they got poetry readings, musicians playing jazz serums."

"Theorems."

"Thamo, thamo."

I pluck his cheek. "You're too much."

He collapses on the divan. Half the flight's supper is on his tie. "Got you ol' Errol Flynn's room again." Saying *Earl* for *Errol*.

I scope the place. By god, he's right.

He points above the bed. "Last tenant painted a face over the still life. Portrait in oil of Papa Hemingway." He says *earl* again, this time for oil.

"It's New Year's Eve." I sigh. "And I don't know where we're playing tonight."

"The old Earl Carrol Theatre." He finally gets it right.

"One out of three," I tell him. "Your Earls."

"Who?" He makes a claw, scratches his bald spot. "Anyways, the place is called the Moulin Rouge now. Frog décor top to bottom."

"I've seen the real thing in Paris."

"La de dah." He grunts, hoists his ass out of a cushion. "I'll be back for you in two hours."

"I'll be ready."

He starts to wave a fat hand, lets it drift, stands as if he's forgotten his way. Afternoon light glistens in his magnified eyes. "One thing I gotta give you, Johnnie," he says. "You're a pro."

Watching him fumble the door knob, I begin a thank you but figure no, it'll just confuse him.

Alone, I light a Lucky and unpack. I strip, stand for inspection in front of the bathroom mirror. "You lean motherfucker," I tell my image. "Still got your twenty-nine inch waist."

94

Under a blanket that smells of the beach, I stare at prism reflections on the ceiling. Must be coming from the pool. No starlets wearing bikinis out there today.

I struggle with dreams I don't want, remembering that nasty spat last week with Dorothy. We were dining at the Waldorf, or trying to, when she flung the ring I'd given her to the floor. A busboy retrieved it. Tablesiders applauded softly when, with aplomb, she put it on again with sheepish pride.

I'd said, "Found that quartz in Brazil, your color."

What had she said? That she wore it at risk, planned to flaunt it New Year's Eve? "And you won't attend my party because Morrie booked you in Tinseltown?"

More half-dreams, then the phone, sounding miles away. It's my sister.

"Elma," I shout into the mouthpiece.

"I'm in Hollywood," she says. Her voice is muted music. "With Ding Wakefield and his wife. We'll be in your audience tonight."

"Great." Tears sting my eyes. Cold fingers grab my larynx. "How's the folks?"

"Doing well," she says. "They loved the Christmas presents you sent. So did I, Johnnie."

"Nineteen sixty is our year," I say. "I'll make it home again."

After hanging up, I lay with a current charging me. Voices and sounds build from the Pacific. I bolt from bed, stand naked, fight my wanting to run to the sea, plunge into its foam. I know it would taste of my tears.

Morrie feels his way along Sunset Boulevard in our rental. Less time than smoking a cigarette, and we're at the theatre. Looks like the Ted Mack Hour out here, every amateur in town trying for the spotlight.

I bar the dressing room door. Inside, everything is laid out like I asked. There's even polish for my kangaroo shoes from

Australia. I try to make myself pretty. Adrenalin kicks in. I add two ounces vodka, pound the table with the pads of my fists, scale a voice exercise composed by Tarzan, run in place to an unknown hymn. "Jesus, Jesus, Jesus."

Only once do I allow myself to think about Dorothy's gala in New York. Then it's time. I burst through the door, stride past a gauntlet of faces ashine with hate, wonder and worship. In the on- deck circle, Babe Pascoe's drums rain on my tin. Morrie's face bobs up. It looks like a sore knee wearing goggles.

Cracking a smile. "Keep it mellow, kid."

"Fuck you," I give him. "Tonight I rip it up with my teeth."

Three hours no break, no book, no mercy. I open it wide, full throttle. Tease 'em. Kiss 'em. Stick my dick in 'em. I hit their jive, Jack. Drown my lonesomeness in their ocean.

Then, after the sad midnight song, I wish them Happy New Year. Exhausted musicians flash looks that say they'll remember. Everyone wants to touch me. My name rushes on thousands of breaths. I cry on my sis's shoulder. I toast the new year with Ding Wakefield and his wife. I wrestle Morrie around in a bear hug 'til he laughs out loud.

Finally, I trudge back to my dressing room, suffer a coughing fit.

Alone, man. So fucking alone.

But not for long.

It's two o'clock, L.A. Time. Dorothy's party in New York is wet ashes by now. I broke down, tried to call, but her butler was ice. Just as well.

An hour ago, Tempest Storm rescued me from my forlorn dressing room. "Get your skinny ass away from that mirror," she squealed. "We're going to a party."

The bash is in progress at Chip O'Hara's home, Laurel Canyon Drive. Chip was a PR man for me 'til he'd had his fill of New York winters. It ain't snowing here. In fact, about twenty of us are enjoying Chip's kidney-shaped heated pool. Phillip Matthews, another PR guy, is also there. He's tall, with dark hair going bald, too nice for a party like this. He comes over, limping slightly, greets me, holding a class of clear liquid.

"Potato?" I inquire.

"Club soda. I gave up the other stuff after the accident." I remember something about a car wreck, but don't warm to the idea of discussing the virtues of sobriety right now.

We party. That's me with Tempest on my left and Marcy, a young stripper friend of hers, on my right. Only thing we're wearing is the fog coming off the water. Holding hands, we drop off the edge of the pool. Tempest surfaces, throwing water from her long red hair. Her breasts come up like volcanic islands. Marcy's rise like strawberry sundaes.

Poolside, we snuggle under beach towels, Tempest and I laughing about old times in Detroit. Marcy shivers and stares at me with eyes so huge and clear I feel guilty about all the evil in the world.

"Remember the night I bailed you out of jail in Detroit?" Tempest asks me.

"Yeah," I say. "You bond me, we hit the night broke, go back to the jailhouse, ask if they'll keep us 'til morning."

This calls for more drinks. We watch the naked revelers. I can't help notice how Tempest and Marcy ogle the bare asses of the others. Two exotic dancers reversing their roles. My blood runs hot. Chip O'Hara is sharking some babe in the deep water. His on-and-off loverboy, an actor with violet eyes like Liz Taylor's, sits in a lounge chair not bothering to cover his erection. He keeps looking my way, not covering that either.

Tempest says that she and Marcy caught a couple of my songs at the theatre.

"You didn't go by the book," she says.

"Took my muzzle off."

Marcy squeezes my face, makes my lips pop out, kisses them. She's bottle blond. Looks like Marilyn Maxwell.

Tempest allows her towel to slide over her breasts. Her nipples stiffen in the cold. Boys and girls waiting for this gasp. "Don't lose your style, Johnnie. All we got is our style." Her breasts jut enormously as she hooks a silver necklace on. A pendant cascades into her cleavage.

"You're gorgeous," I tell her, meaning it.

"Remember," she says, poking a fingernail into my thigh. "You try to satisfy gray flannel, and you'll find black chinos are in."

"I promise to remember that," I say. Something tells me I will. It becomes a resolution.

The fog stream above the pool begins to clear. Couples have scurried inside. I wonder how many bedrooms this place has, or if anyone gives a shit.

Tempest and Marcy leave me alone with my vodka and a sore throat. I watch them go, Tempest's hair a wet mane down her back, reaching the sliding pillows of her ass. Jesus, Jesus, Jesus. I look for Violet Eyes. Guess Chip rounded him up, took him to the corral where it's warm.

Marcy returns from inside, house lights defining her curves, spiked heels clicking on the stone deck. She's wearing tasseled pasties and a jeweled G-string. Seems to be searching for sorrows of her own.

"Tempest was picked up by a friend," she says. "Another singer."

"Damn."

"Black singer."

"Double damn."

"You got no worries," she says, glancing down at me. She still looks too young, but wiser, a whole lot wiser.

thirteen

 # Dorothy

A couple of months into the new decade Dorothy realized that as she aged, she'd become more resigned in some areas, more resolved in others. She knew now that she would have to live with her health limitations. Once nagging anemia had grown so intense that she had to be hospitalized until her iron could be built up. At times her count was so low that her blood looked pink. Her doctors had told her to quit drinking, which is what they always said, regardless of the malady.

"You wouldn't expect them to say start drinking, now would you?" she told Dick.

"Well, it wouldn't hurt you to cut down," he said, "or at least eat."

As distasteful as he had become, she felt sorry for him. The club wasn't doing well, and he was convinced if he opened another, focused on food this time, he'd have the income and the recognition he craved. She hoped he were right. Even with almost seventy thousand from the radio show, they couldn't save a dime, let alone afford to repair the elevator or the leaky roof.

What had once been her dream home had become an albatross forcing her to remain in this life she no longer wanted and that Johnnie no longer wanted for her. Understanding as he was, he was as unhappy with their situation as she was. Only more money could free her, and Dick could provide that if his restaurant idea worked.

Although she'd acquiesced to her health limitations, she was more determined than ever to overcome the pitfalls in her career. That nasty mess about Nina Khrushchev's attire back in September hadn't helped. Five years before, readers would have loved her truthful take on Russia's first lady and her homemade slipcover dresses. Now the *Journal* had to hire four secretaries to answer the letters of outrage, and Bill Hearst himself admitted that they had overstepped the boundaries of tasteful reporting, an oxymoron if she ever heard one.

From the publisher who had encouraged her astringent style, it was the ultimate betrayal. She did what always worked for her when she found herself backed against the wall; she walked out. Monday came and went without the Voice of Broadway, while she refused then accepted her editors' phone calls and ultimately agreed to the conciliatory lunch at "21." Fortunately she just happened to have an extra column ready for Tuesday's edition.

She and Johnnie were finally back to entertaining friends after her Sunday night show. Even though they had mended their Waldorf confrontation with an evening of endless sex, she still felt remorseful about her childish outburst. She felt even worse when she found out that Johnnie rang in 1960 with his old stripper girlfriend, not that anything had happened. Johnnie had sworn on his life that all they did was drink. Still, while she was entertaining everyone from Noel Coward to Lucille Ball, he was drunk at a Hollywood party cavorting with a bunch of strippers. He said he'd tried to phone her, but he'd been different, more quiet and reflective, since his return.

This Sunday he seemed like the old carefree Johnnie, possibly because Cornshucks was back in town. Dorothy could hear him at the piano when she came into the apartment, which was as packed as a New York elevator. Morrie gave her a stiff nod, drink in hand.

"Kid's singing up a storm," he said, making myopic eye contact. "Gig in Hollywood got him going again, just not sure which direction."

Cornshucks slid in between them, a referee in a blond wig, black spike-heel boots and leather skirt to match. Holding a martini in each hand, she gave a deliberate bump of her hip in Morrie's direction as if knocking him out of the way. He actually seemed to bounce from them back into the crowd. Dorothy giggled and took the glass Cornshucks offered.

"You dressing like a black woman tonight." Cornshucks' enormous eyes squinted at the full-length ermine as if examining a diamond through a loupe.

"Want to wear it?" Dorothy asked.

Cornshucks drew a finger to her pursed crimson lips. "Now you know that little thing's gonna look like a bed jacket on my ass."

Dorothy set the martini on the entry table and slid out of the coat. "Shorter furs are in this year. Come on. You know you want to try it."

"Well, you sure I won't look like Miz Khrushchev now?" Cornshucks' smile flashed ivory and gold.

"How did you—"

"I do read the papers now and then." She reached out, stroked the fur. "I can't resist this stuff. I'd wear Sabrina over there if she'd let me."

"I wouldn't advise it," Dorothy said, eyeing the pensive Doberman staking out the dining room.

Cornshucks took the coat, stuffed herself inside it, smoothing it over her black leather skirt. The ermine was transformed from elegant wrap to second skin.

"No bed jacket was ever that provocative," Dorothy said. "Just look at yourself."

Cornshucks strutted before the full-length windows. "Not too bad if I do say so. When I'm a big old star, I'm gonna' have me one for every day of the week. Diamonds, too, like yours. No, better than yours, nothing personal."

Dorothy wondered if the woman had any idea how many nights of singing it would take to duplicate the jewels she wore on her fingers and earlobes tonight. No wonder she and Dick couldn't afford to repair the elevator. She felt a tightness in her throat, almost tears. Damn, she'd better get something to eat.

"You can wear it tonight, if you like," she said. "It's very becoming."

"You sure you don't mind? You won't get cold?"

"Actually, it's a bit warm in here with all the people," Dorothy said.

It gave her pleasure to watch Cornshucks preening in her wrap. She remembered how, when she was in school, girls would borrow each other's clothes, as if, through them, they could absorb the good qualities of the other. She had never felt close enough to another girl to do it. Now she felt connected to the solid decency of this woman who wanted nothing more complicated than stardom. She'd gone from being repelled by her, to trusting her, and she knew Cornshucks felt it too.

The piano music in the next room grew louder. Babe Pascoe joined them with fresh drinks and began chiding Dorothy for losing more weight.

"Just a pound or two," she told the drummer. "It was a hectic holiday."

"Look like she lost it and you found it," Cornshucks said with a light pat on his stomach. "You get rid of that before we hit the Flame. Want my drummer looking pretty for all the folks in Detroit."

"You don't have to worry about that," he said. "Ever think you'd be opening there, Shucks?"

She nodded, flashed him a dreamy smile. "Sure did. Just didn't think it'd take this long. Sometimes things just take longer than they ought, ain't that the truth."

And since it wasn't a question, Dorothy didn't answer. She did promise that she and Johnnie would try to attend Cornshucks' show at the Flame Showbar, and she accepted another martini, her third, she thought. She'd better keep track.

The piano music grew wilder, more distracting.

"What's he singing?" she asked Babe.

"Impressions." His usually expressionless face lit up. He's too much. Ever seen him do Billie Holiday?"

She nodded, remembering their first night at the Copa, as she followed Babe and Cornshucks toward the increasingly raucous crowd congregated around the piano. "Oh yes. I've seen him do Billie."

This was no *Sweet Lotus Blossom* with Basie backup taking place at the white baby grand. This was raw cabaret. Johnnie had loosened his tie, in the predictably irritating way he always did after his first song, and his once-crisp shirt lay resigned against his shoulders. He finished his song to applause and shouts, spotted her and blew her a kiss before launching into a full-scale impression of Lady Day.

His version of *Ain't Nobody's Business* would have brought down the house in any nightclub. Thank goodness it would never be witnessed by any audience but this one. Across the piano from her, Morrie glowered. For once, she agreed with him. Cornshucks and Babe snapped their fingers, and Rafael, wearing a television blue shirt, threw back his head in apparent ecstasy. Everyone else clapped and laughed uproariously, half-drunk, like rubes watching a freak show.

Dorothy stood motionless, her cheeks hot, as if watching someone else superimposed on her man. His movements were overdone, hilarious, if you weren't the woman who loved him. Of course men had performed the song before; she knew that. Jimmy Witherspoon had done it, Ray Charles. This was different. Johnnie sounded, acted like Lady Day. For that moment, he *was* Lady Day singing about her lover—her *man*. He didn't even change the word to *gal* the way Witherspoon and Charles did.

He finished to greater applause. A martini glass appeared in his hand, delivered, she noted, by Rafael, who lurked behind the piano bench. Oblivious to him, Johnnie crossed the space between them, took her into his arms and gave her a lingering kiss. Through his citrus aftershave, he smelled of sweat, an animal scent that she knew came from an excitement that had nothing to do with her.

"Thought you'd never get here," he said. "You were great tonight."

She knew this was the cue to say something about what she had just witnessed.

"I feel a little shaky," was all she could utter.

"Let me get you a drink," he said. "Here, baby. I'll be right back." He disappeared into the kitchen before she could stop him.

Cornshucks took her arm. "Come on, honey. You better sit down. Don't want you getting sick again."

"I'm fine," she said. "Really. It was just a dizzy spell." She sipped the martini to make her point.

"Hope you're happy." Morrie bobbed before her like an apparition. "You didn't like the Mitch Miller stuff? How you like this?"

Cornshucks stepped forward, glaring down at him. "Butt your ass out, you and your lousy timing."

"You're no better than she is," he retorted, florid face puffed around his glasses. "Damn broads don't care about his future. You forget I'm the son-of-a-bitch who made him a star."

"What is it about short dudes always make them such assholes?" Cornshucks asked. "Excepting Babe, that is, you all go around pissed off at the world, especially at any woman who got the gumption to say what she think."

"Well, you just go on saying it, honey," he shouted. "You, Kilgallen here, that stripper. What's happening tonight's just going to get worse and worse, 'cause the kid don't listen to me anymore."

Still carrying his glass, he stalked past them out the door, slamming it behind him.

"Guess he told us," Dorothy said, trying to regain her dignity.

"Asshole." Still wearing the ermine, Cornshucks put her arm around Dorothy, walked her toward the kitchen as the room swept past them. "Ever tell you 'bout the time back at the Flame, Laverne Baker and I tried to teach Johnnie how to bow like Al Jolson, and Johnnie ax who the fuck's Al Jolson?"

"You told me," she said, hating the weak, watery sound of her voice. "Al Jolson's one thing. Liberace's another."

"Cat packs a room," Cornshucks said, adding quickly, "Not to say Johnnie would ever want to be like him or anything."

"No, certainly not." Yet Dorothy felt herself shudder.

"Come on," Cornshucks said, as if talking to a child. "Johnnie's got a mess of Dago pizza pie in there. I'm going to get you some, and you're going to eat it, and everything's going to be fine."

"I know," she said. But she watched ahead as, from the kitchen, Johnnie came balancing a tray of pizza slices and two tumblers of ice filled with what must be vodka. He looked like himself again— all angles, a man moving to his own jazz beat.

"You make yourself eat now, even if you don't want to."

"Of course."

Dorothy heard the concern in Cornshucks' voice, saw it in the scrutiny of her black eyes. She had to get away from it, however well-meaning. What she needed, what she must have, was Johnnie, another martini, a bed, right now.

Johnnie

A rare afternoon. Dorothy and I on my bed in our robes look through glass at a lavender sky, darkness falling out there over those tiny Manhattan diamonds. We drink to ward off the post-coital evils. My shanks tremble as I stretch. Bet she's frazzled too. She was wild as me, maybe worse.

I been working on a theme since we lit our cigarettes.

"I'm gonna ride this year out my way."

"Retiring?" That wise-ass lifted brow, her voice uppidy.

"No. Just want to show them the real Johnnie Ray. Right now I'm in limbo, between rock and roll and jazz."

She sits up straight, hugs her knees. "You'll accomplish more in jazz. Think how close you are to recording with Ellington."

I hop from bed and pose in front of the window, motion to the sky like my mortality is flying by. "I can sing it all, Dorothy," I say. "When the smoke clears, it's still me."

"You quoting your top-heavy stripper girlfriend again?"

"Christ. She's an old pal, nothing more."

"One you've been telling others brought you ever-loving light."

"She got me thinking."

"I'll bet."

"But this is about what I think, not anybody else."

Her hands fly from her knees like moths in the dimness. "Oh, it's about you now. What happened to us, Johnnie?"

Stepping toward the bed, I soften my voice, like pouring syrup over a lyric. "I got to perform the way God made me."

"Spare me religion." Her eyes reflect the day's last light. "Is God's way that queer stuff you displayed at your grand piano the other night?"

"I was performing. God's way or queer, I was doing what I do best."

Silence. That word, *queer*, can do that. I stare at her—at her dark hair, petrified eyes, circle of blood-red mouth. A nipple peers blackly from a crack in her robe.

Her teeth glint. Still no sound.

"I'm going down, Dotty. I haven't been high on the charts for months."

"No." Her voice is a rough shout.

"But I can fill any small room. I can always be on top if I choose my spots."

"You better explain yourself."

"I'm a cabaret singer, Dorothy."

"No."

"I can control a room, make it mine, not the other way around."

"You'll do nothing but form a cult following the way you're going."

She rises, drops her robe. More ink blotches: The other nipple, dent of navel, glossy bush tucked between her thighs.

"Jesus." My voice is a moan. I want her again.

"I should shower," she says.

"Sit on the bed first."

"No. You're not here with me. You're with that god of yours."

"The one that ain't Catholic. That your problem?"

The bed sighs as it takes her fanny. "My problem is you."

"Not man enough for you?"

"You come here," she commands, displaying herself shockingly.

"I want to taste you," I say.

"Go down on me," she says, "and taste us both."

As I move for her, she says something I can't hear, something about finding a place for me. Something so full of hope it breaks my heart.

fourteen

 Johnnie

Springtime birdies are chirping on the sidewalk as we pull up in front of the Cathedral Studio on 30th, Babe driving, Morrie up front. I get out of the back, hold the door open for Dorothy and Clara.

Duke Ellington greets us graciously. His first lieutenant, Billy Strayhorn, scowls from a corner where he's marking up charts with colored pens. My throat clamps, my eyes water, my good ear buzzes, my hands shake. I stifle a cough.

"Ready?" Duke standing, those baggy eyes, complete picture of cool.

I smile. He inquires politely about my sister. Years ago when she'd met him, she'd shyly kept his hand for a moment, told him how, in Oregon outreaches, she and I had danced to *Take The A Train* on the car radio.

Soon I'm fiddling with the mike and music stand. I ask for a position closer to the percussion.

"So you can see Duke better?" Strayhorn asks. He seems truly concerned.

"So he can feel the drums," Babe Pascoe tells him before he surrenders me to Ellington's two drummers. This causes twenty-two or so musicians to give my hearing aid a second look.

The band flexes its muscles. Behind glass, my team gives me thumbs up. The red light goes on. Wham. That Ellington sound, man. I pretend like I've been shot, grin at the air splitting into fragments around me.

First out of the chute is *The Lonely Ones.* I got it down, come in just when I should. The tune free-flows. It leaves and comes around again. It leaps, finds its way down another time, then another. I raise my hands, take a step back like this is a hold-up. Everyone watches. Desperados waiting for me to empty my pockets. Duke hits a sustained chord.

"Gentlemen," I say. "At some point, even Errol Flynn has to climb off."

After that, everyone relaxes, and the session progresses smoothly. This band is so powerful I wait like a good boy for a chance to jump in. I'm soon drenched in sweat, weak, more from trying to contain myself than from exertion. Between takes, Strayhorn shows me where he's going on the charts.

"I'm confused," I say, "but enthused."

He's encouraging. Everybody tries to help. At times I'm amazed at how well I seem to fit, but my hearing won't let me be sure. Other times I find myself backing up like I'm about to fall into the drum kit.

When it's over, and we're driving back, I keep repeating in my mind my resolution, like it's my credo. I'm a well, I tell myself, a deep well. Only I know how deep and how to find the gusher, bring it up.

"Nobody can put a label on me," I say in the backseat.

Outside, it's almost another spring. Light pastels are breaking out on skeletal trees.

Morrie starts a wisecrack. Babe shuts him up. Dorothy pats my hand and looks straight ahead.

"*The Lonely Ones,*" she utters low, "will be a classic. People a hundred years from now will be listening to you with Duke Ellington."

"Babe," I say. "Don't let this limo lose its way to P.J.'s. My tonsils need some tonic."

Brave talk from the Weird Kid who's scared again.

 # Dorothy

The session with Ellington would prove to the musical world what she already knew about Johnnie Ray's talent. More important it would prove it to Johnnie as well. Morrie could label her concern interference or anything else he liked. Her rebuttal would be in the music, *The Lonely Ones.*

Babe Pascoe had somehow appointed himself their chauffeur, and they drifted from P.J. Clarke's to the Copa, toasting Johnnie's talent, her brilliance in recognizing it, their love, which could endure anything. A couple of times at the beginning of the evening, the drummer would clear his throat as if to censor their public displays of affection, but he soon either gave up or grew used to it. She, too full of the night and Johnnie's sweet voice, didn't care what anybody thought.

He sang the chorus of *To Know You Is To Love You,* one of the best songs from the session, lifting her hair, brushing her cheek with his lips.

Somewhere—was it the Copa or one of the clubs later?—Pascoe moaned and put up his hands.

"I give up. I can't drink with you pros."

"Don't go," she tried to say. It came out, "Don't grow," which threw all three of them into fits of hysteria.

"Good thing I ain't sensitive about my size," Pascoe replied. "One more round then, and I'm really going to split."

Was it then he'd left? Had that first attempt been one of many? She couldn't remember, didn't even know where she was. Warm, though. Johnnie's arm around her. But not right, tumbling, hurting her leg, unable, unwilling to move. Sleep. God, yes, just for a moment. Safe here for just a while on this hard hopeless sidewalk, reek of urine joining the wind from an alley.

Words filled that wind now, words from a nightmare.

"Dorothy, damn it. Johnnie. What the fuck?"

Fingers dug into the safety of her sleep. Obscenities. Didn't they know who she was? She forced her mind open. Saw the face that went with the voice.

"Babe. I thought you left." The cold closed in now, the darkness. The trembling started inside, moved to her hands. She turned to Johnnie, on his feet now, as she was, his eyes bleary and blank.

"We fell," he said, fear crossing his face as he studied her. "You remember, don't you Dotty? God, what time is it?"

"Time to get you out of here," Pascoe broke in. He all but dragged them into the backseat of his car. Dorothy felt her stomach roll as they took off.

Johnnie pulled her to him, and she curled against him, trying to get warm, rid herself of the trembling. Just get something to eat, tape her ankle, and she'd be fine.

Johnnie's scent was harsh and metallic against her nostrils.

"You need a shower," she said.

"Yeah. More than that. I'm really sick, honey."

He covered his mouth with both hands. In all the time they'd been together, she'd never seen him vomit, didn't know what to do to help him.

"Want Babe to stop the car?" she asked, trying to sober up. "Maybe we can find a service station, a rest room."

His answer was unintelligible, his voice muffled through his hands. Through the dull edge of intoxication, she felt the cutting fear. She lifted her head, trying to focus in the dark.

He removed his hands from his face, staring at them like a man in shock. "Oh, God." He held them before him, fingers in the shadows black with blood.

Blood, so much blood, poured from his nostrils, down his face, his shirt

"Babe," she shouted, although Pascoe was only in the front seat. "Take us to emergency. "Johnnie's hemorrhaging."

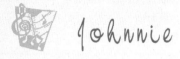 ## Johnnie

After the session with Ellington, I remember only pieces of the night—torn and fractured harmonies accompanied by visions that flash in my head like historical films of world disasters.

Babe Pascoe had tried that night to keep up with us, but our pace was too wild. We were losing control; I can see that now. Babe left around midnight to go home. He says at four in the morning, the killing hour, he got the call. A player he knew had found us, stumbled upon us. We'd passed out in some piss-frozen doorway on 52nd. Nightriders had picked us clean—coats, Dotty's pearls and purse, my wallet with a note to my sis from Ellington. Evidently the vultures were shooed away from our carcasses before they got Dotty's rings.

It must have been sheer hell for Babe. He'd thrown us in his Fairlane. I went into convulsions and started vomiting blood. By the time he got us to Sinai, Dorothy had come around but was hysterical. Babe lifted me on his shoulder, grabbed her hand. We spilled through the emergency doors, Babe says, blood-soaked head to foot.

The next two or three days you don't want to know. I must have had delirium tremens, the doctors tell me later. Shit, it was *Lost Weekend* all over again, the *Cry* Guy getting the Oscar this time instead of Ray Milland.

Must have tested my luck too far. They tell me my liver is turning to stone. Few more bouts with the booze, and I won't get off the canvas.

Then they give me the bad news.

X-rays proved my internal bleeding was more than just ruptured throat vessels. Seems I got a nice little case of tuberculosis.

They keep me down for days. At times I feel the straps and buckles. The nights are forever. Visions of a godforsaken world. Hallucinatory phantoms—Sinatra, Jimmy Witherspoon, Joe Williams, Billie Holiday, the Count—all their voices screaming like city sirens.

Duke chants a countdown for my burning. A metronome. One. Two. One two three four. Wham.

Around my fourth day in the wet sheets, real people gather above me.

Dorothy, looking strung-out, dashes my bedside water with vodka, and I see her eighty-sixed by the docs. Cornshucks, tears on her plum-colored cheeks, says in my good ear, "These doctors, they best not be fucking with you, J.R."

Do I see the beautiful Ava Gardner, or am I dreaming? Is that Yul with a gang from Broadway, smiling like cheerleaders, their team behind in the last quarter?

I beseech them all for just one more chance. One final gig. A *tour de force* finale in a cabaret room.

"I got to get up," I shout to the walls, the white nothingness of being alone.

When I wake, Morrie is sitting at my bedside, holding flowers I remember Carol Channing bringing by for me.

"For you," he says. "Wish it could be more."

"*De nada.*" My throat is so dry I scrape words out with my tongue.

"I come to get you out of here."

I raise a trembling hand, make a circle with thumb and finger.

"We got you some new dates," he says. "A great summer calendar. Engagements, kid, you won't believe."

fifteen

 Dorothy

Only she stayed. The others came and went. Morrie, after finding out his star would probably live, made a hasty departure clearly intent on using Johnnie's latest tragedy to propel him into a new recording deal.

"It's for the kid's good," he told Dorothy when she called him on it. "More than you're doing sitting here red-eyed day and night."

Only she stayed, even after they told her she couldn't go into the room if she wasn't a family member, even after she sneaked back, was caught with her glass of vodka at his bedside and ordered to leave by a nurse who looked as tough as her voice.

She wrote every weary word of her column from this institutional sofa that had become home. She washed up in the ladies room, took food and drink from Cornshucks and Babe Pascoe, the only ones who showed up regularly. Mostly she kept the vigil, praying, making deals with God. Let Johnnie live, and she'd leave Dick. Let Johnnie live, and she'd never fight with him again, never be jealous of Ava or Tempest or even poor, pathetic Rafael who burst into tears in the waiting room that morning.

That's what they called this place, the Waiting Room. She called it the Clock Room. The ubiquitous timepieces ticked from every wall, slowly counting out their reminders of mortality.

"Clocks," she said to Cornshucks. "I hate them."

"They okay. Only way you going to keep track."

They sat on the sofa drinking coffee they'd doctored with the vodka Cornshucks had smuggled in her zebra-print jacket. "But why in a hospital? Who needs to be reminded how long they've been sitting in this dreadful place."

Cornshucks shook her head. "I don't know, honey. Sure you can't get some food down?"

"Maybe later," she said. "You know, you'd better make it as a singer, because you'll never make it as a bartender."

"Just trying to keep you out of trouble with that old nurse."

In spite of the humor in her voice, Cornshucks looked exhausted, her dark eyes bright with too many hours of waiting and worry.

"I still can't believe it," Dorothy said. "There I was, covered with his blood, and they wouldn't even let me in his room."

"They got this thing about family, that's all. I could see them kicking me out, but you, you his woman, damn it."

"But not his wife." Tears filled her eyes, and Cornshucks looked away as if to let her have the pain to herself.

"Never know what will happen," she said, staring straight ahead.

Dorothy thought that once hospital officials were reminded of who she was, she'd be allowed in the room, family or no family. As it turned out, it was Johnnie and who he was that finally overrode the ruling. As his health improved, his famous friends continued to show up badgering the hospital staff until they, Dorothy included, were cautiously admitted one at a time.

Just last night, Dorothy thought he recognized her. This morning he'd been asleep, but his breathing had seemed less ragged than before. She wanted to wait until seven, which was when the nurses had told her he was most alert.

They'd decided that Cornshucks would go up first and return for her at once if he were conscious. She smoothed out the black-

and-white sheath dress. The hat she'd put on with it had taken up permanent residence on the stack of magazines beside the sofa.

"How do I look?" she asked.

"Beautiful."

She saw the lie in Cornshucks' eyes. "Bet I smell beautiful too."

"One thing about you, honey," Cornshucks said. "You could be up to your neck in shit, and you always look like a lady. Smell like one too."

Dorothy cringed at the analogy. She'd been too many hours in the place, drinking too much, eating too little, worrying— most of all worrying, scared to death.

"I want to look good for him."

"You will," Cornshucks said.

"Hi, girls." Dorothy jumped at the sound of the husky voice. Ava Gardner stood just a few feet from them, her hair wild, her body wrapped in a red, silky fabric. It was the way any woman would want to look moments after crawling out of bed, and it was not the look of a woman who slept alone.

"Hello," Dorothy said, straining her voice for a semblance of formality. "Have you met Ava, Cornshucks?"

"Oh, yes," Cornshucks breathed. And to Ava, "J.R. awake?"

"Not yet." Ava tossed her black, brambled hair. "And if he can't wake up for me, you better know he's sick."

"We know that all right," Cornshucks said. "He been here for days."

"I know." Ava's whiskey tone softened. "Been worried sick about the son of a bitch."

"He's going to be all right now," Dorothy said. "I'll tell him you were here."

Ava smiled and stretched to full height in the clingy dress. "He'll know," she said.

"Bitch," Cornshucks muttered after she'd left. "Who write her material now she's dumped Sinatra again?"

"Probably no one, and that's the problem." Dorothy's heart pounded as if she'd consumed a pot of coffee instead of a cup. "I guess she and Johnnie were really close at one time."

Cornshucks scowled. "Word is Sinatra beat her up first night she met J.R., so she use him to get even with Frankie."

"A woman using Johnnie? That'll be the day."

"So, maybe they use each other." She glanced up at the clock, and Dorothy followed her gaze. Almost seven. Cornshucks drained her coffee cup and stood. "J.R. never was gone on Ava like he's gone on you, not Ava or anybody else."

Dorothy sipped at her coffee-vodka and toyed with a magazine in the Clock Room as Cornshucks disappeared into the elevator. Jesus, she hoped it were true and not just one of Cornshucks' kindhearted attempts at consolation. He had to love her as much as she loved him. He just had to. And he had to get well so that they could have a real life together.

She'd just settled down with the magazine, when she heard, "Dotty," shouted from across the room. Cornshucks stood just outside the elevator, her face animated. "He's awake," she announced to her and everyone else within hearing. "J.R.'s awake."

Dorothy didn't care who heard or saw. She dashed across the room, gave Cornshucks a giddy hug. "Thank God," she said. "Thank God." He was conscious. He was alive, and everything would be okay now.

The bed, partially surrounded by a hospital-white curtain, was shaded, leaving his face in shadows. The room smelled of smoke. Ava, she thought, moving closer. She'd have the nerve to light a cigarette in a hospital room. Johnnie lay on his back, eyes closed.

"Darling. I'm here."

His eyes opened into a squint. "Dotty, man. I thought I saw you. Couldn't tell. They got me so doped up."

"I've been here the whole time, darling. I wouldn't leave you."

"I don't feel so bad." He reached out for her hand. "Considering."

"You don't look so bad, considering."

"Feel better if I had a drink," he said, the familiar grin lighting his face.

She patted her bag. "Got something right here."

"There's got to be a water glass or something," he said.

She looked around, spotted two glasses on the stainless-steel table. Next to them, a saucer held a crushed Kool cigarette, cerise lipstick coating the filter. *Bitch*. Cornshucks was right about that.

Dorothy poured the water from one of the glasses back into the pitcher and pulled the vodka from her bag. Her hands shook. A residue of fear persisted, making her wonder if she should be doing this.

"Did your doctor say it was all right to drink?"

"Who cares?" He'd propped himself up on his pillow, gown open at the neck. "I'm okay, and I ain't going to live like a monk."

She splashed vodka into the glasses. "Just wanted to be sure. I don't know if you were aware of my little tussle with your nurse the other night."

His drug-glazed eyes narrowed, and he managed a smile. "Saw you getting eighty-sixed. Thought I dreamed it. Dreamed a lot about you, baby."

She handed him the vodka and sat on the bed next to him. "I hope they were good dreams."

"They were dynamite." He glanced down at the swelling bulge beneath the blanket, drew her fingers down his thigh.

"Oh, Johnnie."

"Such sweet dreams. Must have had you a hundred different ways. Wish you could have been here for it."

"I'm here now."

"Oh, baby."

Her hand moved on its own now, fingers stroking him through the thin thermal blanket. Poor judgment, she knew. They'd have to stop. They would in a minute. But first, just a kiss. Damn, he tasted like always. Only a tiny bitter medication taste lingered beneath the vodka. "Oh, Johnnie, it's been so long."

He pulled her into another kiss, pressing his palms into her back as she covered the length of him.

"God, you feel good."

Barely able to breathe, she tried to speak against his flesh. "What if someone comes in?"

"Fuck 'em."

The way he said it aroused her more, pulled her out of the vodka fog. "Say it again."

"Fuck 'em." Louder this time. She reached down, pulling up her skirt.

"This damn garter belt."

"Take it off. Take everything off."

"Darling, we can't." But already her mind raced ahead of her body. Yes, she could take them all off—the garter belt, panties, her shoes. She slid her hand under the blanket, gripped him hard.

"You want that?"

"God, yes," she whispered. She sat on him now, fully clothed, kissed him again. "It would work like this, wouldn't it? You wouldn't even have to move."

"It'll work, all right. Can't promise I won't move though." He tried to take off the hospital gown, cried out.

"Don't," she said, slipping out of his arms. "You stay right where you are and let me take care of this."

"We're crazy, you know that?"

"I know." She left on only her dress, tossing everything else into the chair. "Now, come on, crazy man."

She climbed unto the bed, and on her knees, pulled the curtain the rest of the way around them. It made a safe circle enclosing the narrow bed.

Johnnie threw back the blanket and lay exposed and erect, his skin smooth and golden in the dusky light. He looked so vulnerable that she feared she would choke up. "Do you know how beautiful you are?" she asked. "Do you?"

"Tell me, baby. I'll believe it from you."

"You're beautiful, Johnnie Ray. And I love you."

"I love you, too, Miss Kilgallen."

He helped guide her onto him, her skirt straining as she skinned it up to her waist. She grabbed his bony hips, used them for handles. As she sank down onto him, he moaned softly. Dorothy began rocking against him, still holding his hipbones. Crazy or not, this was right. At that moment, straddling his naked body within the curtained cylinder of shadow, she couldn't believe she'd ever felt so much joy.

They didn't even hear the nurse walk in. Before she knew what was happening, Dorothy heard the curtains being yanked from around them and a firm hand grab her shoulder.

"Out," the nurse demanded.

Dorothy shrieked and tried to gather her clothes around her.

Johnnie pushed the nurse away. "Damn, give us a minute, will you?"

"I want her out of here right now," the woman said. Then glaring at Dorothy, "You're not allowed in this hospital again, not ever."

"Do you know who I am?" Dorothy said, trying to regain her composure.

"I know what you are. Now, out."

She should have been embarrassed, but the entire scene struck her as comical. Clinging to Johnnie, she burst out laughing. He joined her, and they held to each other convulsing with laughter as the nurse sputtered oaths and tried to pull them apart.

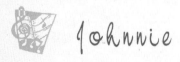

Out of the hospital, I stand on solid ground and set my jaw like my hardscrabble ancestors. I refuse to lose sight of my goals.

It ain't easy. Columbia rushes me through a record date with Mitch Miller. Even the Beard yawns his way from song to song. I try to give it some jizz.

"Can't make chicken 'ala King out of chicken shit," I say when we're done. My complaints rain on ears that are as tin as mine. Columbia stutters when I ask who is the market for this tripe.

Morrie says like he's found a cure-all. "Got you booked in Vegas."

"Big deal. Maybe I can take on Sinatra's Rat Pack all by my lonesome."

"Well, Tempest Storm is out there. Get her to nurse you, scramble your brains."

My manager trying to help. I find actual affection beaming behind his specs.

"Look," I say, grabbing onto his slumping shoulders. "I'll go to the desert, but I want some say in my destiny."

"Make enough money, and destiny will take care of itself."

"That's everyone's philosophy."

"What's wrong with that?"

"It doesn't work."

He shakes loose, bats his hands at invisible tormentors. "It don't work in the red either, kid."

So, I do five weeks at the Desert Inn, building my health and courage.

I call Dorothy, tell her this isn't bad. "The crowds seem to like me."

"You should be on bigger stages."

"This offers an intimacy. I feel I'm performing to people who've loved my work since I broke out."

"Ma and Pa Kettle."

"They pay for tickets with American currency, and I don't come cheap out here."

"Oh, well." She sounds tired. Her voice has a heavy-breathed echo. "Try to make it back by Thanksgiving."

After my getaway performance, I talk with Tempest Storm.

"Find the ones who love you, Johnnie," she says. "You'll fill any house if you don't try to be all things to all people."

"I'll just be me."

"You do and you'll beat the odds."

This in the desert night breeze, driving the Strip in her convertible, top down, streets soaked in neon, noises of desperation oozing out doors that never shut.

sixteen

Dorothy

Johnnie couldn't believe that she was serious about attending the Rat Pack party for John Kennedy.

"You didn't even vote in the fucking election," he said, when she told him about it.

"Don't you ever get tired of that adjective?" she asked.

"Thought you liked the word."

"Only in bed, darling."

"That so?"

He didn't add that it had been she who shouted it at the Waldorf the night he had told her he was going to be in California for New Year's Eve. That had been more than a year ago. They'd spent this New Year's together, if you didn't count Richard and a house full of people so drunk they wouldn't know who was kissing whom at midnight anyway.

She and Johnnie were more committed than ever. His capricious success and serious bout with his health had been unable to destroy their bond. He was the only man she wanted at her side for either inauguration party, and of course she would attend both. It was an honor, almost a duty.

In the end, she invited Clara to go with her so that she could take full advantage of the opportunities offered by the photographers and reporters instead of trying to avoid them as she would have to with Johnnie. It would be a night of glamour documented for the generations that would follow. History. The inauguration of President John F. Kennedy would be history.

Regardless of how much she loathed Sinatra, she wouldn't dare miss his gala if only for its news value. The hundred-dollar-a-plate event he and his Rat Pack gang were hosting the evening of the inaugural ceremony would help ease JFK's campaign debt. It would take its toll though by publicizing Kennedy's not so public friendship with the King Rat—a friendship whose days, if old Joe Kennedy got his way, were already numbered.

A blizzard ground Washington activities to a halt the week of the inauguration. Trolley cars were derailed, automobiles stalled. Various accidents claimed the lives of forty-seven people.

When she departed on January 18, the Journal-American photographed her boarding a train at Pennsylvania Station, which looked better in print than it would have in reality. She and Clara rode in the chauffeur-driven Silver Wraith Rolls.

They arrived at the Mayfair Hotel in time for her to change into her brocade gown and coat. Most of the other guests weren't that lucky. Bette Davis lost her luggage and performed in street clothes.

"Wear my coat," Dorothy insisted as they stood in the massive armory.

Bette smiled, shook her sleek head. "That's cute of you, but there's no use pretending I'm anything that I'm not."

Onstage, Ethel Merman belted out, *Everything's Coming Up Roses.*

"She's in street clothes, too," Bette pointed out.

"But she's a Republican," Dorothy said.

Rat Packer Sammy Davis, Jr. hadn't been able to make it, insulted, it was rumored, by Joe Kennedy's objection to Sammy's interracial marriage to Mae Britt. Dean Martin also bowed out, which didn't surprise her. If Bobby Kennedy as Attorney General did indeed target organized crime, Sinatra and the Rat Pack would be guilty by association. Martin had quietly begun divesting himself of his Las Vegas gambling interests. Showing up here would lose rather than gain him points with the new administration.

In spite of the absences resulting from the weather and other causes, traffic was as clogged indoors as it was out that night.

They sipped champagne in a long reception line, gossiping as if it were any other party. Yet the air was charged with anticipation—those high, apple-pie-in-the-sky hopes Sinatra was singing about.

"Feel it?" she said to Clara.

"Oh yes. I still can't believe I'm here."

Clara had let her hair grow, and she wore it pouffed, a baby-blond version of Jackie Kennedy's elegant do.

"This is a once-in-a-lifetime event." Her voice sounded shrill and school-teacherish.

Clara nodded toward the stage. "Are you worried about running into you-know-who?" she asked.

"Heavens, no." Dorothy took a steady sip of champagne. "He wouldn't dare pull anything at his own party."

"I don't know," Clara said, lowering her voice. "He's done some terrible things in the past."

Dorothy patted her arm. "Don't be silly, dear. He wants this to go smoothly so that he'll stay in JFK's good graces. He already has Jackie and the old man against him."

"But he's so vindictive."

"That's what Johnnie says, but you'll see, you both will. I'm the least of his worries tonight."

She prayed it were true, that Sinatra would have the sense to conduct himself in a respectable manner for once. He had, after all, sent a tombstone to her home. He had insulted her appearance in front of hundreds of people. He had also been close to her once, and this was a time of new beginnings. A time of high hopes.

Sinatra completed the song, and she and Clara joined in the applause.

"He is blessed with a wonderful voice." Clara spoke slowly, as if searching for the one kind remark she could make about Sinatra. "And he did help Kennedy get elected."

"Oh, he did that, all right," Dorothy said. "He and his friends."

Mobster friends she'd bet Joe Kennedy would write off now that he had what he wanted from them. She felt something close to pity for Sinatra, who so much craved acceptance yet whose only value was his cohorts' abilities to stuff ballot boxes.

By the time she encountered him, the champagne had spread its euphoric glow through her. Clara had stepped away to talk to someone, and she was momentarily alone when she spotted him coming in her direction.

He stood in his tux, smoking a cigarette, Peter Lawford at his side, as they moved through the crowd. Lawford once headed Sinatra's enemy list because of a rumored dalliance with Ava. After his brother-in-law began campaigning for the presidency, he had weaseled his way into Sinatra's good graces.

Lawford saw her first, and his face stiffened, mask-like, ready for the worst. His lips moved, saying something under his breath.

Sinatra stopped. Their eyes met across the room. For a second, neither of them moved. Dorothy tried to smile, but the muscles that controlled her lips refused to work.

Sinatra's icy stare hardened, then his features relaxed. He handed the cigarette to Lawford, strode across the room, arms out. "Dotty Kilgallen. How the hell are you?"

Odd that someone with such a pure voice when he sang could sound so harsh when he spoke. Still, she wanted to weep out of sheer relief. "Very well, thank you. Such a lovely event."

"Yeah. Hell of a note about the storm. Didn't keep anyone away though, did it?"

"Apparently not."

"We packed the place."

"Indeed you did."

"Well, enjoy the night."

"I intend to."

"And take care of yourself, Dotty."

"You, too."

Her smile came easily now as she stared into the blue indifference of his eyes. It was dialogue from a bad movie, but it didn't matter. At least he knew enough to behave for one night.

As he walked away, she let out a sigh. Peter Lawford approached, still carrying the cigarette. He looked uncertain of his job, as if trying to decide whether to smoke it or to continue following Sinatra.

"Good evening," he said, in the overdone British voice that always made her want to imitate it. "Enjoying the evening?"

"Quite."

"It's a marvelous night for everyone."

"That it is. Frank looks wonderful."

"Indeed he does," he said, his tone condescending. "Nice to see you two chatting."

"Equally nice to see *you* and Frank getting along so well, Peter."

He colored slightly, gestured with the cigarette. "That was different. Frank and I worked out our misunderstanding."

"Well, based on his behavior tonight," she said. "Perhaps we've worked out our misunderstanding as well."

Lawford watched a long ash fall to the floor. "Don't kid yourself."

"What do you mean?"

"Frank hasn't forgotten everything you wrote about him," he said. "There's only one reason he was civil to you tonight."

"What's that?"

"Ava."

"Ava?"

"That's right. She's the only one who can put a muzzle on Frankie."

She fought to control herself, to keep this scum from seeing the shock and humiliation she felt. "I guess it worked," she said.

127

"For one night," he said pleasantly. "That was the agreement. Funny thing. Frankie can't figure out why Ava gives a damn about how he treats you."

"Neither can I," she said with a shrug. "Nice seeing you, Peter."

"Same here." He glanced at the cigarette once more, frowned. Then he dropped it before her and crushed it into the floor with his shoe.

"Dorothy, what is it? Where have you been?"

Clara's voice cut through the thick air that enveloped her. She looked up through the darkness, couldn't see anything before her but an odd-shaped appendage the color of the moon. Dorothy squinted, tried to focus. Fingers. Oh, Jesus, it was a hand, hers. She couldn't even recognize her own hand.

"Dorothy, what's the matter? Are you ill?"

She tried to work her mouth, to speak. "Johnnie." The word came out thick. Her fault for drinking the Jack Daniels that nice musician offered her. It didn't mix with champagne. Now, she could barely speak or navigate. She knew she should be embarrassed, but she felt only anger.

How long had she stood like this, the receiver in her hand, tears running down her face as the hallway darkened around her? How long since she'd fed the telephone the coins that connected her to Johnnie? She could hear the buzz of his voice even now, trying to explain away her humiliation.

"You bastard. You saw Ava."

"I was trying to help. I knew Sinatra would listen to her."

"You fucked her, didn't you?"

"Of course not. I was trying to help you."

"And you fucked that stripper, too."

"What stripper? I didn't."

"New Year's Eve, 1959, when I wanted you at my party."

"Dorothy, you sound terrible. Is Clara there? Put her on the phone."

"Clara?"

"Yes, honey." Clara moved closer, a blond blur. Dorothy squinted to make out her features. "Tell Johnnie goodnight, and we'll get you out of here. We'll go out the back. No one will know."

Her head ached dangerously. She wanted to strike him, beat her fists against his chest, but he was in New York. "How could you do this to me?" she demanded. "How could you, Johnnie?"

"Baby, please." He sounded resigned. The excuses would continue, and they wouldn't matter. Nothing he could say would matter enough to erase what he had done by conspiring with Ava behind her back and making her look like a pathetic fool to Sinatra.

"Let's go now, dear." She felt a firm tug on her arm.

Clara's voice, Johnnie's voice. Concern from one; lies from the other. Nowhere to go, nowhere safe. And throughout her body, only rage, that aching need to smash and destroy.

"Leave me alone," she shouted in the mouthpiece. Then she yanked.

Nothing happened. She pulled harder—again and again—until she heard the snap and felt the receiver break free, until she held it like a club in her hand.

Johnnie

Another year. Do you hold over all your good intentions, resolutions from last year like it's one of those progressive jackpots in Las Vegas, the betting pool bigger every time there's no winner?

Don't ask me who finally cashes in.

Morrie goes easy on me over the holidays. I look like a relapse ready to happen. Dorothy calls, asks me to meet her at the Stork

Club for an early dinner. I jump into a cab, and like a yellow duck, it waddles in the circling snow, the car radio bopping to Charlie Parker's sax.

Inside, I check my coat, pass the captain's station, spot Dorothy among the Cub Room's banquettes. Instinctively, I glance at the dance floor, the empty orchestra stage.

"This place," I say, sliding next to Dorothy, "is dying." I meet the stiff-necked glances of a few bold refugees from the storm. "Tubesville."

"It's early," she says. Her expression is hard, frigid. I haven't seen her since before Sinatra's party for Kennedy.

I kiss her. She hurries it, says, "I thought we might talk."

Sherman Billingsly cruises by throwing kisses at his loyal patrons.

"So, let's talk. I got my ear on, can lend it to you if you want."

"Not funny," she snaps. "I'm still hoping you'll tell me why you felt it necessary to conspire with Ava Gardner while supposedly recovering in the hospital."

Oh, oh. "If Ava came to see me, I'm sure I was too foggy to conspire."

"You managed to clear up your head long enough to get me in trouble with the staff."

I cross my middle digit over my pointing finger. "That's you on top, me on the bottom, helpless in that hospital bed."

"Spare me." She drains a short drink in front of her.

"Jesus, can't you smile?" I return Billingsly's wave, give him both palms up, like where's the drinks?

Dorothy scowls. "Don't encourage that hoodlum."

"Thought you liked him."

"That old rum-runner? He's nothing but a lackey for Walter Winchell."

"Winchell's washed up. Talk nice about the dead."

"Quit changing the subject."

She is in a maroon suit, first time I've seen her in anything close to red. I move a table flower so I can follow the plunge of her collars. "You can't still be pissed at what happened at Sinatra's bash."

A waiter brings drinks, shows his dentures. "Compliments of Mr. Billingsly."

I toss a fin on his tray. "Tell the old bootlegger *gracias*." Then to Dorothy, "Where's the cocktail girls?"

Already, she's lifted her glass, glowering over its rim. "I was humiliated to find out how you plotted with your lover behind my back."

"I tried to help."

"Please."

"You were going into an enemy's camp, JFK or no JKF."

"So you and one of your lovers—"

I cut her off. "Christ, Dotty. We were briefly friends, nothing more."

"Ava is briefly friends with many men," she says. Her fine little teeth grind. In my hearing aid, it sounds like a two-man saw falling an Oregon redwood. "But she doesn't do for them what she did for you."

"Bend Frank a little?" I laugh like it's no fun to laugh anymore. "Shit, Ava does that just for kicks."

We drink, order another. I take in the room, see a few people waiting to be seated. They look cold, sad. So does the stork with top hat and cane, painted on the foyer wall.

"Come with me," I say. "We'll go see Babe and the Shucker over to Tabby's. They're working on her act."

"I must eat."

"Fine. We'll go after."

"Can't. I have a full day tomorrow, a full week. I have things to do, or have you forgotten?"

Right now I feel the funky reaches of the Flame Showbar. "Then I think I'll go to Detroit City with Babe and the Shucker."

She keeps her face down. We'd talked about going together. I know she's remembering, trying to decide how distant to be. "You sure you feel well enough for that?" she finally says.

"I feel okay. You could always come with me if you can break free from your schedule."

"Guess we have conflicting dates," she says, fingering her bare throat like she's lost a favorite charm.

seventeen

 Johnnie

It's a fucking blizzard outside, but Tabby's is glowing when I stroll in. Cornshucks is putting a cap on her first set with *People Get Ready*. She burns the song to embers. With the audience, I get on board that long train to Jordan.

At the end of the hymn, Babe Pascoe leaps from his drums to the mike, announces they need five, breaks from the stand holding the Shucker's arm. He catches my elbow, and the three of us wade through all the frenzy to a table in back. Pianoman and bass stop at the bar, mop their glistening brows. A girl with Orphan Annie hair rushes us drinks.

I raise mine in a toast. "Better warn Detroit you're coming with work like that."

Babe smacks a hand on a stack of his charts. "My Bible."

I grin at Cornshucks. "Didn't know you could read."

"I do it by Braille," she says. Her form is squeezed into a shimmering gold sheath. Her sweat smells like rich perfume and upturned earth. She shoots her drink in one easy motion. "Lord they," she says, big-eyeing the glass.

"Stinger," says Babe. "Brandy and crème de menthe."

Curious, I toss mine. It's hot when it hits bottom. I feel like I've discovered something that might save me.

"You goin' to Detroit with us?" Babe's shirt is wet against his muscles, his paunch. "We take off day after tomorrow in the Fairlane."

I fake amazement that he plans to go by auto. He can outdrive Jack Kerouac's buddy in that book *On the Road*.

"I'll fly," I say. "Meet you there."

"You got to go with us," Babe insists, folding his hand like a vise over my wrist. "We shoot up to Scranton, pick up my sister, head for Rochester, pick up Rosehelen's brother. Hell, we're at Niagara Falls for dinner."

"Rosehelen?"

Cornshucks stands, pulls at the bunches in her dress. "That's me."

"Niagara Falls," he repeats with furious joy. He's up now, giving the sign to the other two musicians at the bar. Cornshucks wobbles on her spikes. Tabby's window sign projects a garish display across her bumped-out ass.

Raising up, I call at their backs. Ginmill faces turn on me, like who's the clown with the Johnnie Ray hearing aid. I savor the warmth in my gut from the stinger. Been a while since I've felt this mellow.

"What's at Niagara Falls?"

Up ahead, Cornshucks' gold tooth shines. "Church," she testifies. "Babe and I are getting married."

Jesus, Jesus, Jesus. Cutting through the din, I sing, *"Let's Go Get That Church."*

And, by God, I hear someone say, "Look, there goes Johnnie Ray."

Dorothy

It was bad enough that Johnnie felt no remorse for conspiring with Ava. Worse, he had actually gone to Detroit after they had agreed he was still too weak to travel. At least Cornshucks and Babe would keep an eye on him. No one wanted a repeat of that terrible night at the hospital.

This morning she didn't feel the picture of health either. She stood at the mirror in her bedroom and forced her hands to steady as she checked her makeup. No one would mistake her for Sophia today with these puffy eyes and skin the color and texture of chalk. Thank God this was radio and not TV.

She couldn't screw up this morning, and she couldn't let Dick screw up either. They'd been more stale than usual, as much her fault as his. Any professional who read her column would know she didn't remember much of the inauguration. After that dreadful scene with Lawford and her telephone tirade, she had collapsed and had to be taken to her room. All she recalled of the night was the helpless feeling of being unable to move, call for help or even open her eyes.

No wonder her column lacked details. Even now, when she closed her eyes and tried to visualize the inauguration the next day, she saw only Robert Frost's hair, silver as the glare of the snow, as the bitter wind whipped the pages before him. Only later, in someone else's column, did she learn which poem he had read that day, "The Gift Outright." Only then did she piece together the historic scene she had witnessed and just as rapidly forgotten.

She needed a Valium. Dick wouldn't notice, and it might alleviate this terrible sense of dread she couldn't seem to shake. She swallowed the yellow tablet without water, as if the lack of ritual would make the act less important. It was just a pillsky, as Johnnie would say, and she needed it to face the microphone this morning.

They were waiting for her in the dining room. Richard stood before the microphone at the head of the table talking to the young blond technician.

"At least he's heard of Frost and Mailer," he said, gesturing with his empty glass. "But the very idea of a literate administration is a bit preposterous, don't you think?"

As he continued his banal assessment of Kennedy, his tone boomed with artificial energy. Still, he was trying. As Dorothy crossed the hall and joined him in the dining room, she saw why. Directly behind the engineer stood a large, crew-cut man in a dark suit.

"Hello, darling," Dick said, looking from her to the stranger. "We have a guest joining us this morning."

"So I see." She paused as he kissed her cheek.

"Mr. Marshall, my wife Dorothy."

The stranger stepped from behind the engineer, and she realized that he was just a kid in a good suit. Yet he moved with purpose as if he were in charge, and his handshake was firm. The hand itself, also large, was too moist for a man's hand, as if he'd just slathered it in lotion.

"Vince Marshall, Miss Kilgallen. I'm with the station."

"An engineer?" she asked, knowing better.

"No. With management."

His pale, almost colorless eyes contained only a touch of green, like the color of a good martini. This, combined with a fringe of dark lashes, made him look as if his features had been painted on, like the face of a puppet.

"They're promoting them young these days," she said.

"I've had the position for some time. This is just a policy change."

"What type of policy, Mr. Marshall? What exactly is your reason for being here?"

"Same as yours, in a way. Just want to be sure the show is a success."

"I'd hardly say we have the same function. I am the show, my husband and I, that is."

"Dorothy," Dick interrupted, his face already shiny with sweat.

"No, she's right," the kid said. "Without you, there is no show."

"And without you?" she asked, feeling the Valium smooth the demand into a polite inquiry.

"Without me, there is no you."

"I beg your pardon?" She glanced across the room, past his shoulder for support. The engineer bent over the controls, tending to invisible dials. Dick stared back at her, anger purpling his bloated face.

"That's one way of putting it," Marshall replied, his tone as calm as hers. "As I was telling your husband, I'm here to be sure you're both comfortable going on the air."

"Comfortable or capable? Dick, he's saying we're incapable."

"Perhaps that's too strong, but I don't know how else to put it. The station is concerned about your tardiness and, to be blunt, your condition on some of the shows."

"There is not a thing wrong with my condition. We've been absolutely capable of doing the show since 1945."

"That's probably true," he said. "I'm just here to be sure it is."

"And this comes from station management?"

"Top management, Miss Kilgallen."

"We'll see about that."

Julian arrived with a coffee server. She noted with relief that he'd known to omit the ice bucket this morning. In its place a silver bowl of fruit joined the microphones on the gleaming table. No champagne. No crystal carafe of vodka.

"Coffee, ma'am?" Julian asked already extending a cup.

"Please." She took it from him and sat beside Dick. He smelled like bitter lemon. "Ask our visitor if he'd like some coffee," she said, as if Marshall were not just a few feet from her.

"Mrs. Kollmar wonders if you'd care for some coffee," Julian asked, taking the cue.

The kid blinked then narrowed his colorless eyes as he figured out the snub. "Tell her thank you," he said through tight lips. "It could be a long morning."

"Since he probably skipped breakfast, perhaps he'd like some fruit," she said, gesturing toward the bowl in the middle of the table. She didn't care if he ate or not, but she liked the idea of addressing him through Julian. Before Julian could reach for the bowl, the kid replied, "No thanks. Coffee will be fine."

Marshall had been right. It was a long morning. He sat at the dining room table next to the engineer, taking every refill Julian offered. Thanks to the Valium she relaxed, and Dick continued his hearty display of enthusiasm throughout. As he did more and more frequently, he put most of the burden of the show on her.

"Tell me your favorite moment of the inauguration," he insisted, once the Juicy Gem commercial was out of the way.

"Robert Frost's poem," she said brightly, aware that Marshall was watching her.

"What did you like about it, darling?"

"The sincerity, I think. It didn't contain the imagery of, say, *Birches,* or *The Road Not Taken.* It was more intellectual than emotional, but exactly right for the occasion. Frost himself was majestic standing out there in the snow."

"I wish I could have seen him in person."

She looked up quickly to find only a bland smile from him. But he'd meant it as a dig, the bastard, right here in front of the station henchman.

"So do I, dear," she said.

"But one of us needed to stay home with the children."

"The Rat Pack Party was divine," she said, purposely changing the subject. "In spite of the blizzard, everyone came through. Bette Davis and Ethel Merman performed in street clothes."

"And what did you perform in, darling?"

Her head jerked involuntarily toward him. She caught the bland smile again. "Luckily, I had a brocade gown with a matching coat, which I offered to Bette Davis, but she is just so gracious. She could have worn a gunny sack and no one would have noticed. But enough about me, dear. Tell me what you did while I was gone."

Now, he was the one turning toward her. Let him discover how it felt to be put on the spot.

"Well, the other night, I raided the refrigerator. You weren't here, and the children were back at school."

"And what did you find?" she asked.

"Some wonderful chicken. It has an entirely different taste, you know, eaten ice cold while you're standing with the refrigerator door open."

Marshall didn't leave until the show was over.

"Show our visitor out," she told Julian.

"Sir," Julian said, leading the way to the door.

"Tell Miss Kilgallen I'll be back tomorrow," Marshall said, studying her with those disturbing eyes.

Dick already had the vodka bottle out.

"Pour me one," she told him. "Now, this is a cozy situation. How can we be expected to do a show with this spy breathing down our necks? And why the hell didn't you ask him to leave?"

"Wouldn't do any good." He tipped the carafe, let the vodka cascade into her glass. "They're out to get us. They think we can't do it anymore."

"And no wonder when you show up reeking and goad me right in front of him. And now he's coming back tomorrow, Dick."

He settled back at the table with a vodka bottle before him where the microphone had been. "You blame my goading for that?"

"Well, it didn't help to imply that I dumped you at home so that I could attend the inauguration alone."

"It was said in good fun, darling."

"It was not." Her voice was rising above the Valium. "You're constantly baiting me. It's not good radio, and incidentally it's not good for our marriage either."

"Don't you talk about what's good for our marriage." His voice boomed out, its sheer ferocity bringing tears to her eyes. His own eyes were no longer dull, their dangerous sparkle warning her not to challenge him. "Don't you dare have the gall to talk about our marriage."

She swallowed the vodka, watched the maniacal fire in his eyes until it burned down and she felt safer.

"I could say the same thing to you," she finally ventured. "You have been far from the ideal husband."

He glowered, his face so purple she feared for his health. She couldn't let him lose control now. "Let's just stick together," she said. "We have to if we're going to hang onto the show."

"Is that all you care about? Your children are being raised by strangers. Your husband's business is going down the tubes. And all you care about is the fucking radio show?"

"Dick! I will not have you address me that way in this house. And you'd better care about the radio show, too. If your club does indeed go down the tubes, it will be our only means of support."

He gripped the edge of the table. "I do care about the show, but I've had it up to here with you. I really have."

She started to retort that she'd had it with him, too, for God knows, she had. But something in his voice stopped her. The wrong word, and he could snap, maybe even hurt her. Jesus, had it gotten so pathetically bad, that she actually thought her husband might cause her harm?

"And speaking of reeking," he said. "Have you tried smelling yourself lately?"

"As you know, I haven't been well." She reached for the bowl of fruit, held up an apple, its waxy surface reflecting the gleam of the chandelier. "Please, Dick. Let's discuss this later. That man upset us both terribly today. I need to eat now. I feel absolutely faint."

To make her point, she bit into the apple. It filled her mouth with a juice so sweet she felt it could heal all of her ills, even the ache in her heart.

eighteen

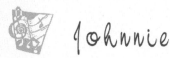 Johnnie

Sun-up Wednesday, Babe is waiting below my apartment scraping the blue Fairlane's windows as it pumps plumes of ghostly exhaust. He helps me fit my bag atop others in the trunk. Cornshucks pops out of the passenger side, an Eskimo in furry pelts. Jesus, she's shaken a bottle of cola and is spraying the windshield. The wipers cast Coke crystals, amber in the early light.

The car is warm. We move off, Babe cussing. Cornshucks gives his shoulder a teammate's pat, raises the spent bottle.

"Keeps the windshield from freezing up."

Babe's head rocks side to side. "Coke for douching, for windows. Shit, don't no one drink it anymore?"

"With rum," I say from the back seat. The city slides past us, monstrous vessels on a frozen sea. Babe and Cornshucks banter like mismatched lovers. Same as Dorothy and me, I reflect, thinking of my lady. Day's first sun pours onto my lap, warming my lazy hard-on.

We dash through the Holland Tunnel, Babe honking the horn for good luck. Effortlessly, he tools the Ford over the Jersey Turnpike. The weather looks like it's breaking. Cornshucks hums a bar. Babe grunts time, swats the wheel. Lyrics swarm in my head. Soon we got us a tune.

When we pause for breath, Babe indicates his stack of music on the seat beside me. "Score that mother on those sheets back there."

I write, get ideas for more. We commence singing again. Cornshucks' voice covers mine like molasses. It strikes me now why she's in such demand for back-up vocals. Babe winks in the rearview mirror.

When we turn the volume down, he tells me to sleep. "Sixty miles of snowdrift along here."

"Too charged," I say. "This country is like back home."

Undulating hills drift back to quaint farms. Stark orchards march in fields of white.

Cornshucks turns, catches me in a smile. "You a virgin to this kind of travel."

Her message is obvious. "Been mostly first-cabin for me," I admit.

"Drive these roads, Johnnie," she says, "you best learn how to twist the head off a yard bird, cook it roadside in rainwater."

"I'm no stranger to that," I say. "Momma fried chicken every Sunday."

"Hoo-wee," the Shucker yelps, and we join in song again.

We pick up Babe's sister at her brownstone apartment in Scranton. Her name is Lillian. She's a stringbean compared to Babe, looks much older than he and is kind of school-marmish. Her husband was killed over in Korea, and the woman seems angry, tormented. She sits primly next to me as we take off once more.

"Jesus, Lil, relax," Babe says. "It's been five years since I seen you."

Her eyes are riveted on the back of Cornshucks' wig.

"Her husband Jack was in the same outfit as me," Babe says softly as he drives. "We were all from Hell's Kitchen. Now most of us have moved on."

"Moved on," Lil says. "Yeah, Jack moved on, all right."

Babe sighs. Cornshucks tsks her teeth.

"I was 4-F," I say meekly. "My ear."

"What's wrong with your ear?" she asks. That gets a small laugh.

Next I know, we've stopped at a trucker's café. I must have slept for over an hour. Last sign I saw said Binghampton.

"Crosby and Lionel founded that town," Babe had quipped.

We eat burgers, drink thick shakes. I feel sixteen. Our booth has one of those jukebox selector things. I flip through it, see my two albatrosses, *Cry* and *Little White Cloud*. I put in a quarter, play Tony Bennett, Nat King Cole, Kay Starr. I notice Lillian holds her gaze mostly on Cornshucks.

"What do you think of Martin Luther King?" the widow asks.

Cornshucks slurps her shake through two straws, licks her lips, gives Lillian a full count of deadpan.

"Shit city," Babe sighs.

Lillian seems undaunted. "Reason I ask is the man preaches nonviolence, and just a year ago, a colored guy tried to rape me not a block from my home." She glares at Babe. "I wrote you about it."

"Said a black man propositioned you, Sis."

"Said he close to raped me is what I said."

The naugahide booth squeaks as Cornshucks shifts her weight. "I know the feeling," she says. To my surprise, she takes the widow's hand across the table. "Black and white sonsabitches have done the same to me." She nods in my direction. "Including that freckled fool sitting next to you."

This gets some smiles. I light a cigarette, blow smoke away from the table. I notice Cornshucks doesn't release Lillian's hand. The engagement ring on the Shucker's finger looks to be her only modest jewelry. Lillian's wedding band looks thin, worn.

Suddenly, I long for Dorothy. Nathaniel Cole spreads *Mona Lisa* throughout the café. We slowly crawl out of the booth. I spy Babe punching the numbers for my two songs.

"Still had some plays," he says. "Can you believe a place where they're still five for two bits?"

On the highway, the women snooze in back while I co-pilot with Babe. Snow swirls in the headlamps as the sky darkens. Babe refuses my offer to drive, finds some faint jazz on the radio.

"Listen," he says. "sounds like Symphony Sid, spinning records in his glass cage, Hi Hat Club late at night. Remember?"

I do. The year I met Dorothy, Symphony Sid's show would find us from Boston after our lovemaking. A trumpet's riff fills the car.

"Sounds like Diz," I say.

"Howard McGee," whispers Cornshucks into my hearing aid from the rear.

And of course she's right.

Then we hit the lights of Rochester, diamonds in the cold nightfall. We discover Cornshucks' brother in front of a flophouse downtown. He's in a suit short on leg and shoulder room for his young, athletic body.

Cornshucks embraces him, and the three of us take the back seat, Lillian joining her brother up front.

Off again, Babe informs us, "Hundred miles to Canada."

"They love you there, Johnnie," Babe says.

Lillian shoots him a sisterly look. "With this quintet, we'll need all the love we can get."

I settle back, listen to Cornshucks as she chats with her brother. His name, Carlton Banks, rings a bell with me.

"I play some guitar," he says when I pry. "But mainly I play ball. I'm waiting for the Yankees to start spring training in Florida."

Wondering what the Shucker is thinking, I peek at her face. She kisses the kid, holds him to her furs like a lioness would her cub.

"This boy's gonna be a New York Yankee."

"Major league does pay better than most club dates," I concede.

"Damn straight," Cornshucks says, rocking Carlton until he gasps.

Couple hours later Babe instinctively picks the right exits, ramps and tolls, and eventually we rumble onto Niagara Falls Boulevard.

Lillian mutters so we all hear, "Just another shitty street, ass end of New York."

Sadly, I think she's more right than wrong.

We cross a customs' bridge to the Ontario side of the Falls, find the motel Babe has reserved. It sports a neon rainbow on its sign just like, Cornshucks says, the one in the movie, *Niagara,* starring Marilyn Monroe.

Do I know Marilyn, the widow wants to know. I concede that we're old friends, and after a long look from the Shucker, I add, "Dorothy Kilgallen and I had dinner with Marilyn and her ex-husband right before they split up. He's a nice guy for a writer."

This gets me more questions like did I know Clark Gable and did Marilyn really cause his heart attack like they say by being late all the time when they were filming *The Misfits.* It occurs to me that the prim little widow is star struck, one of those people who keeps *Confidential* hidden under the *Saturday Evening Post.* What she hasn't figured out yet is that her new sister-in-law is the real thing.

The clerk doesn't hassle us but frowns when told it's Babe and Cornshucks getting married tomorrow. We peer through fogged windows at an odd little structure that, to our horror, is the wedding chapel.

"That the one in your brochure?" Babe asks. "It looks different."

I insist on paying for the rooms, take one for myself and don't worry how the others pair off.

After some rest and freshening up, we find a restaurant, eat like wolves while onlookers point at us with their forks.

Back at the motel, we join a gathering on a wooden deck, watch the American side of the Falls illuminate with colored lights. The steady sonata of the water petrifies us under a frozen circle of our breaths.

After a time, I find myself apart from the others with Cornshucks.

"Crazy, ain't we?" she asks. Her arms are folded like she's waiting for my reply.

"Lunatics."

"How you feeling?"

Jesus, this girl. Jumping into a mixed-blood marriage, and she's worried about me. "Stronger every day," I brag.

"Try hard, Johnnie. Stay off the booze and pills. You're too valuable."

"Worry 'bout yourself, dear."

Her chuckle joins the cadence of the falls. "What's to worry? Getting married tomorrow. Going to Detroit City, my career on the line. Carting a white widow lady for a sister-in-law, and the only brother I can locate out of six."

She looks off like she's piloting a ship, the Falls spectacular up ahead.

Carlton Hanks is silhouetted against the view. Her eyes glisten as she watches him.

"This his third, fourth shot at the Yankees," she says.

I put my arm around her.

"And he a clunker on guitar."

Her shoulder is a small boulder under my grasp.

"Look at him," she commands.

"Looks like he's waiting."

"He is, but he don't know for what."

"Maybe for Martin Luther King?"

"You better hope so," she says.

 # Dorothy

Two days passed before she heard from Johnnie, and the call only made her wish that she'd agreed to go with him. The happiness in his voice cut through the static that might or might not have been the sound of the Falls.

She didn't bother him with the dismal news on her front—the constant pressure of the kid from the radio station, Dick's continually dour state.

"Just come home to me," she said. "As fast as you can."

"I will, baby. You know, I look at the Shucker, what she's willing to risk, and I think maybe there's hope for everybody."

"I know."

"For you and me, I mean. Like maybe there's hope for us."

"I know there is, Johnnie. I feel it."

"We'll talk when I get home, okay?"

"Yes," she said. "We can talk after."

"After what?"

"You know."

"That's your problem, girl. All you think about is after. There ain't no before in your life where I'm concerned."

"And it's your fault, Johnnie Ray. You've turned me into a wild woman."

"You sure took to it. You better behave yourself while I'm gone."

"You, too."

"You know I will, baby. All I want is what's waiting for me at home."

"You sure about that? No old girlfriends from your Flame days?"

"No way."

"No Ava?"

"Baby, please." He sang a line from *Ain't Misbehavin.* "One thing's for sure, Miss Kilgallen. You don't have to worry about me. I got a woman waiting for me hotter than anything in Detroit City."

"That," she said, "just might be the truth."

"I know it is," he said. "Wish I were there right now. Know what I'd do?"

"What?" she whispered. "Tell me."

They spoke like that, in whispered eroticism, until he ran out of quarters and they reluctantly said goodbye.

After the phone call, Dorothy sat in her darkened room wrapped in the warmth of his words. Outside, a storm raged through the city, not an omen, she hoped, for Dick's grand opening that night.

Paris In The Sky was his last hope, their last hope if the radio show didn't improve. They'd lost their grip on the audience, and even at her best, when she'd had as much sleep as her body would accept, she sounded brittle. Dick came across worse. As much as she fought station management, she feared the day would come when they would cut back or maybe even cancel the show. She had to prepare.

She'd scheduled two buses to deliver their friends to New Jersey for the grand opening, and she had made up her mind to play the smiling hostess to the hilt. She rose slowly, still feeling close to Johnnie. Cornshucks' wedding gave her hope, as well, not just for Johnnie and her, but for Dick. He was still a young man, too young to give up. He deserved his dreams.

She dressed in a long white dress she'd worn when she had cocktails with Marilyn Monroe and Yves Montand. As she stood before the mirror, she heard Dick's knock at the door.

"Come in," she said. "Did you bring me a drink?"

"Right here." He came in, handed her the glass of champagne, sat on the bed, the bottle in one hand. "I know you don't keep clocks in here. Just wanted to be sure you know what time it is."

"I wouldn't be late for your grand opening," she said, lifting her glass. "To Paris In The Sky. Long may it wave."

"Longer than The Left Bank, I hope," he said.

"Don't give up on it yet."

"I have no choice." He shrugged acquiescence. "I'm fortunate this new opportunity presented itself. I have a good chance."

"Especially with your knowledge of music. Your taste is impeccable."

"Why thank you, dear." His voice deepened at the compliment. His features seemed more defined, sketched with the aristocratic boyishness that had once attracted women of all ages.

"I mean it. I think you're wise to manage the talent, not just employ it. Lee Evans is a great start."

"The RCA contract is almost in the bag for him," he said. "There's a chance of some TV, *The Gershwin Years,* they're calling it."

Dorothy sat next to him on the bed, holding her glass for a refill. "You know, she said. "Mike Wallace has been after me for an interview for ages."

He frowned. "Absolutely not. You don't need the publicity. He'll open all those old wounds, hound you about Sinatra."

"I like Wallace," she said. "I just had no reason to put myself through that before, but now I think I would."

"Why?"

"For Paris In The Sky. I'll agree to do the show if they'll include footage of the club, maybe have Evans appear on the show."

He peered at her steadily over the rim of his lifted glass. "You'd do that?"

"I will do it. Mike Wallace doesn't scare me."

"No." He smiled, showing teeth still shockingly white in spite of his constant smoking. "Wallace is the one who'd better watch out for you." He poured more bubbles into his glass, offered her the rest of the bottle. "I must say, darling. You're looking lovely tonight."

"Thank you, Dick."

"Your gown is very becoming."

"I've worn it only once, that night with Marilyn and Yves Montand."

"The actor with the long fingers and the French accent? Marilyn was foolish to walk away from her marriage because of him."

"You know how she is. She always falls for her leading men, and he's very charming. She's just a little girl looking for someone to take care of her."

"She had someone to take care of her, and look what she did to him." He patted her leg, rose from the bed. "Not smart to leave what you have just because something else looks better. She'll be sorry."

She returned his gaze steadily. "Maybe she'll find happiness," she said. "I hope so. Now let's go open ourselves a nightclub. Paris When It Sizzles."

"Paris In The Sky," he corrected, swinging the empty bottle. "Let's go."

Although the love she once felt for him had long departed, she felt a mutual bond connecting them. For this evening at least, they'd be a team. They'd open a nightclub. She'd do the Mike Wallace show, too. She'd help Dick reach his dream regardless of how she felt about him as a husband.

He bobbed ahead of her down the hall, humming like a man whose luck had changed. And all because of a woman named Cornshucks he'd probably never meet.

nineteen

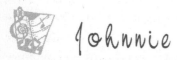 Johnnie

The wedding day breaks yellow with sun. We tunnel-trip the Falls in rented rain gear, laughing at our own childish wonder. Just before noon, we dress sharp as we can, gather in the small chapel.

Looking splendid, Cornshucks has poured herself into a pink hourglass suit, stands in six-inch heels, glances from under a floppy white hat with veil. She smiles, holding flowers I've ordered. Babe is elegant in a tux I got for him over in Italy last year.

An assortment of curious witnesses stand about like flood victims. Carlton strums the Wedding March on a rented guitar. The rites are performed by a wild-eyed preacher, half-drunk in preparation for his own Armageddon.

Cheers rise when Babe hugs his bride. Carlton plays *At Last*, Cornshucks' favorite, one she always said I should record. I wail it above the Falls, thinking Etta James couldn't do it better. Jesus, I mean I throw it up there so it's all alone for the Shucker, high and mighty for her to share with Babe.

We toast with paper cups of champagne. Cornshucks and I ham it up a bit for the assemblage. Preacherman almost kisses me when I hand him three twenties.

Finally Babe lays down the word. "Let's blow," he says. "Five-hour drive to Detroit City. We got a gig tomorrow night."

"Meet in one hour," Cornshucks shouts.

"Should take off sooner," Babe warns, looking at his Timex.

"Any sooner and you in trouble, Drummer Man."

Like I say, nothing really ever changes.

 # Dorothy

That Saturday Clara insisted they attend the cocktail party Joe DiMaggio was holding for Marilyn's new film, *The Misfits*. Since she'd inadvertently stood up Clara on at least two other occasions recently, Dorothy agreed, although she would have preferred going alone.

It had been a dreadful week. Marshall, the kid executive from the radio station, had her under constant scrutiny, and this morning had actually acted as if he were trying to smell her breath. She retaliated by lighting a cigarette and directing Julian to inquire if their visitor would like one as well.

They arrived after nine and were greeted at the door by Joe himself, a picture of restrained sensuality in a light suit only he could wear. If anyone could turn Marilyn around, it was he.

She was having a difficult time, more lost than ever since Clark Gable's death in November. The heart attack had struck the day after they finished filming, and Marilyn clearly blamed herself. So fragile had she been the last time they met, that Dorothy couldn't bring herself to print the rumors about her behavior on the set or about the pills that were reportedly flown in from her Beverly Hills doctors. It was unsubstantiated gossip, after all.

Dorothy wanted to attend to show her support for Marilyn but also because her reporter brain smelled a possible reconciliation between Marilyn and Joe. He certainly acted in charge as he saw to their wraps and ushered them through the hundred or more guests moving like slow traffic through the rooms of the penthouse.

"Marilyn will be so happy you're here," he said, squeezing Dorothy's arm.

"How *is* she doing," she asked, hitting the *is* to convey to him that she knew more than she was reporting.

"Better," he said, his tone careful as if he were choosing his words. "She considers you a friend, you know. There are no other reporters here."

"I appreciate that," she murmured.

"Have some champagne, and I'll get her." He indicated a waiter with a napkin-wrapped magnum.

"Sounds good," she said.

The champagne went down in a rush of icy bubbles.

"Lovely," she said to Clara.

"Expensive," Clara said.

Clara had lightened her hair again, and with it, taken on an air of aloofness, as if a change in hair color required a personality adjustment as well. She stood in an extended fifth-position ballet pose, as if someone had arranged her feet that way. Dorothy liked the old Clara better, the one with bangs and dark roots.

"Well, I think Marilyn's taste is impeccable."

"I hear she had taste for little else on the set," Clara said.

"Perhaps you should write your own column, dear." She lowered her voice to a whisper. "The poor girl's had her share of problems lately."

At that moment, Marilyn arrived, softly easing up to them. From head to toe, she was beige, blond, bone, ivory. The monochromatic tiered dress that enclosed her was made up of varying shades of off-white, and her short curls complemented the rest of the attire like a whimsical hat she'd placed on slightly crooked. The only color she wore was a slash of scarlet on her lips.

Everything about her was slightly yet charmingly askew, from the hairdo to the tilted champagne glass to the way she cocked her head to study them.

"Dorothy. Thank you for coming."

They embraced briefly. In spite of her curves, Marilyn felt brittle, like a stick figure any pressure could splinter apart.

Dorothy gently let her go, introduced her to Clara, an act of courtesy she'd performed countless times.

"We've met," Marilyn said, as if she really remembered.

"I've been thinking about you," Dorothy said. "I was so sorry to hear about you and Arthur."

She shrugged, took another sip. "Me, too. He is a wonderful man and a great writer."

She said it in a sing-song, memorized tone, and Dorothy knew that she would ultimately see it in print.

"I can't wait to see the film," Clara put in. "Hard to believe it's Clark's last."

Marilyn's glass froze midway to her lips. Her eyes grew larger.

"Clark was a dear man," Dorothy said quickly.

"I kept him waiting," Marilyn said, in a dry husk of a voice. "Kept him waiting for hours and hours on that picture."

"He wasn't well, dear," Dorothy said. "It would have happened regardless of what picture he was working on."

"You think so?" She looked up wistfully from her glass. One tawny curl fell over her arched brow. This was her appeal, the combination of sexuality and vulnerability, and even when she tried, there was nothing planned about it.

"Yes," Dorothy said. "For that reason, I've refrained from printing anything about the problems with the film in my column."

"Oh, I know. Thanks a lot for that. It's been hard enough, losing my marriage, losing Clark." Her voice trailed off. "Here I am getting divorced and releasing a picture, both in the same month. Johnnie will get a kick out of that."

"He's in Detroit," Dorothy said. "He sends his love."

A tender smile wiped the sadness from her face. "He's such a dearheart. Why aren't you with him?"

"I have too much business here right now. I've even consented to an interview with Mike Wallace."

"Mike Wallace," Clara butted in. "You can't be serious."

"I think he's nice," Marilyn said.

"Mike Wallace?" Dorothy asked.

"Him, too, but most of all Johnnie. He doesn't have any meanness in him at all. You two are the sweetest couple. I wish—"

Dorothy leaned closer, trying to hear the last words she spoke, but Marilyn only smiled apologetically holding her empty, lopsided glass between them.

Joe soon joined them, leading her away into the crowd.

"What do you think will ever happen to her?" Clara's voice was hushed.

"I don't know," Dorothy said. "Joe's a strong man. Maybe he can do something."

"Yes, maybe he can," Clara said, as if repeating a prayer she neither understood nor believed.

After Marilyn's departure, there seemed little reason to remain at the party. They finished their champagne and left. Insisting that it was too early to go home, Clara suggested they stop at the Drake. Dorothy acquiesced but dreaded it, half-expecting a lecture. She'd caught the disapproving frown on Clara's face when she'd mentioned the Wallace interview and didn't feel like defending herself tonight.

The Drake's dim, opulent interior soothed her. The booths on the other side of the room looked like shadowy caves, giving the place a clandestine ambiance all good drinking bars had. And like it or not, this was going to be a drinking bar tonight. The champagne, like Marilyn, had provided momentary enjoyment but little solace. If anything, Dorothy felt more depressed than she had earlier after her confrontation with Marshall. She ordered her martini extra dry and straight up. It slid down like liquid ice.

"You can't be serious about Mike Wallace," Clara said without preamble.

She lit a cigarette she didn't really want. "I'm not worried," she said. "What can he do to me?"

"Don't you know?"

"You mean the Sinatra stuff? I'm a big girl. Nothing he has said will bother me."

Clara sat stiff as a doll. "Oh really?"

"And if you're thinking of the Rat Pack party, it wasn't Sinatra who upset me. It was Lawford and what he said about Ava and Johnnie."

"I'm well aware of that," Clara said, lifting her drink.

"Besides, I wasn't at all well."

"Your anemia."

"Yes. And Dick needs my help right now, Clara. This interview will draw attention to Paris In The Sky."

Leaning across the table, drink in hand, Clara looked like an Erte painting, an Art Deco lady, all arc and hue. "If you cared about Dick, you wouldn't consider doing the show."

"How can you say that? He needs the business."

"But you don't need the publicity." She patted her blond, helmet of hair. "I don't think you realize how much he depends on you. You're his life, his strength."

"Dick and I both do fine independently," she said, looking down into her drink. "And when the chips are down, we stick together as we vowed to all those years back."

"I know it's none of my business," Clara began, then sighed before Dorothy could agree. "He just doesn't need to hear rumors when he has such pressing business concerns."

Dorothy felt a gnawing dread. Perhaps just vodka on an empty stomach. Perhaps Clara's inability to say what she meant for fear of offending. She crushed out her unfinished cigarette, watching it break into a messy pile in the glass ashtray.

"Rumors are my job, dear, or haven't you noticed? And if I listened to everything that was whispered about Dick—"

"You're stronger than he is," Clara said. "You can take it."

"And he can't?"

Before she could answer, an elderly couple approached the table and asked for her autograph, a gesture that Dorothy found especially touching at the moment. She signed her name on a cocktail napkin, and they thanked her repeatedly before disappearing into the shadows.

"You see," she said to Clara. "I am a public figure, and I have to live with what people say about me, good and bad."

"You don't have to let Mike Wallace have a field day with your life."

"Dick wants me to go. He knows I'm just doing it to help him."

"That may be what Dick wanted at first," Clara said. "It isn't what he wants now."

"And how do you know what my husband wants?"

She looked down into her drink once more. "I'm not supposed to tell you."

Dorothy sighed, lit another cigarette. So that's what this whole meeting had been about. "Go ahead," she said. "What did Dick say to you?"

"Not to me, to Roland. They met last night. Dick was beside himself. He's heard terrible rumors about you and Johnnie. He's furious."

She thought back. Yes, perhaps he had been chilly for the past few days. They hadn't really had a conversation since she agreed to do the Wallace interview.

"If those rumors were going to bother him, he would have divorced me years ago," she said.

"He tried to ignore them, especially with the other things he's heard about Johnnie."

"That he's gay? Come on, Clara. You've seen us together."

"I didn't say I believed it," she said, her voice a pious whine. "At first, you were more careful. If you went out of town with him, you used me as your beard. Now it's as if you don't care what Dick hears. You flaunt Johnnie, and you think no one's going to say anything."

"There is a certain courtesy in our profession," Dorothy said. "You don't see the media rushing to report on Jack Kennedy's private life."

"People still talk." Clara's face had gone pale as her lipstick. "Roland will kill me if he finds out I told you this. Dick said he heard that a nurse walked in on you and Johnnie when he was in the hospital. He couldn't believe the story, and frankly neither could I. It was tawdry, Dorothy, and it's not the kind of thing you want repeated about you."

Being a journalist had taught her that there was a time to talk, a time to listen, and a time to leave. She wouldn't have any trouble hailing a cab at this hour. Dorothy swallowed the last of the vodka.

"I don't care what you believe," she said, gathering her bag and her wrap. "I'm going to do the Mike Wallace interview and get Dick what he really needs, which in case you haven't noticed, is a source of income. The next time we meet perhaps we can discuss something more interesting than my sex life." Exhausted and annoyed, she started to slide out of the booth.

"Wait." Clara grabbed her arm. "It's not your sex life I'm worried about. It's your husband. I tell you, Dorothy, there's something wrong with him. Roland and I both think he's ready to blow."

"I appreciate your concern," she said, disengaging herself. "I really do." And she left before she could hear another dreadful word.

She knew that sooner or later she'd have to reevaluate her friendship with Clara and Roland, who had grown closer to Dick than to her. She didn't need friends to judge her and try to make her feel guilty. She could still see Clara's caustic glare when she described her behavior at Mt. Sinai. Hypocrite. She'd probably trade a lifetime of Roland for a moment like the one she and Johnnie shared in that hospital bed.

Clara was probably also miffed that she'd forgotten a few of their dinner parties. True, her social calendar was a bit less organized now, but she did her best to keep up, and Clara's weren't the only events she forgot. She shouldn't take it so personally. Perhaps it was time to start easing Roland and her out of their lives.

Dorothy gauged Dick's behavior for the next couple of days. Yes, he was definitely upset about something, probably the salacious hospital story. She almost wished he'd come out and ask her instead of drinking, brooding and berating Julian for imaginary infractions. Surely she could convince him that the stories weren't true. He'd be the first to agree that she wasn't capable of such wanton behavior.

"Do you still want me to do the Wallace interview?" she asked that Wednesday as they waited for Marshall to arrive. She had a dreadful hangover and had nearly vomited when she tried to gargle away her sour breath that morning. Dick didn't look much better, his eyes all but hidden behind puffy flesh.

"Why wouldn't I?" he said. "I thought you wanted to help me."

"I do, darling. I just wanted to be sure you wouldn't be bothered by anything Wallace said."

He took a swallow of coffee. His cup shook as he replaced it in the saucer. "He's not going to say anything worse than I've already heard, you can be sure of that. I just hope you generate some customers."

So much for Clara's concern. Dick, as always, cared about Dick. He might have been shocked by the hospital story, but he'd probably dismissed it and was counting on her support with his new business venture.

"I'm sure I will," she said. "I'll certainly give it my best effort."

"Good. I'm depending on you."

His eyes darted from her to the coffee to Julian, trying to feign nonchalance. She couldn't take it, the drumming fingers, the clatter of china when he tried to lift or replace the cup, the sour, hopeless smell of him. Finally she rose from the table, lit a cigarette and demanded of no one, "Damn. Where is he anyway?"

At that moment, the doorbell chimed.

"Right there," Dick said in a chiding voice. But his eyes remained dark and distanced, as if he couldn't trust himself to look at her too closely.

twenty

 Johnnie

I wake up to a hard, shiny Friday, stare at the ceiling. The bed's held me since Babe dropped me off sometime yesterday. Takes me a moment, but I remember this is the Statler Hilton, so I call room service for bacon and eggs.

A sudden languorous desire nudges me. I want to hear Dorothy's voice, more sex talk, like my call to her from Canada. Kollmar answers, and I follow the old rule for when a man answers—I hang up on the son of a bitch.

I call Morrie Lane. Of course he ain't around. I convey my message carefully to his secretary.

Her voice is new. "Didn't catch your name."

I spell it out for her.

"Oh, Mr. Ray," she says, like I've run amok. "Give me your number and I'll have him call you."

"I'm in Detroit," I say. "Now repeat my message."

"You want him to dig up a couple of his tomato cans."

"Good, very good. What's your name?"

"Heather."

"That's beautiful. Your voice is beautiful, too."

"Thanks. Your voice sounds—" She hesitates. "Like it does on your records."

"That bad?" I stretch my legs out on the bed, count my toes, play with myself as I bid goodbye to Heather.

Rested and squeaky clean, I bundle up, walk the streets near the hotel. A flower shop lures me in. The florist is as lavender as the flowers I choose for Dorothy in New York. He's confident his Manhattan contact can match my choice, make a delivery this evening.

"No problem." He blushes like he's committed a lewd crime. "Anything else I can help you with?"

"A white orchid corsage," I say, "delivered to The Flame Showbar by seven o'clock."

I scrawl mushy cards that bring tears to my eyes, pay the guy and breathe in the shop's fragrant smells. Outside the windows, the bright sky has dulled, and thin snow falls.

"These winters must be tough on business," I say.

"Not too bad," he says. "We hope to add a bit of color to the blandness."

"That's noble," I say.

I walk a block or two in the light flakes, watch harried people running away from another week of labor. With time to kill, I duck into a blue-collar pub, walk across peanut shells to the bar.

The bartender is a mean bastard who smirks when I ask the brands of his drafts.

"Greisedick's our top seller."

I grin at two old wry soldiers down the bar. "No Slippery Richards for me."

"How's Michelob, two bits a glass?"

"That during Happy Hour?"

"Son, that's for fuckin' ever."

"Dad," I say, winking at the pair of ancient warriors, "pour me two dimes' and a nickel's worth."

I'm uncommonly limber leaping from the taxi, corner of Garfield and Canfield. "There it is," I say to the driver. "Place looks evil as ever."

Cabby checks my tip, smiles. "It's been here all the time, just waiting for you, Mr. Ray."

It looks like it. I blink at the pink neon bubbles rising into the cold night, the crimson tongue of electric flame. People devoted to the ceremony of nighttime strut and preen with decorous bravado under a brilliant marquee that displays Cornshucks' opening.

The Flame Showbar. A place jammed with promises, all of them lightweight, flirtatious. All of them worthless lies that roar in your ears the morning after.

But I stride in like an ex-champion. The attention I expect don't bowl me over, just occasional nods, hip gestures from figures more anonymous than familiar.

A bartender looks sixteen, asks what's my poison. I boldly hiss, "Stinger," instead of staying with beer. Word travels the bar that Johnnie Ray is here. Old sports gather around. Young strangers stretch their necks. Red lips smile, and you can smell the blood in the air. I play it with my best boyish look, letting a hank of my pompadour drop over my right eye.

Some man holds my hand a count too long. I allow my innocent demeanor to stiffen. "Don't be keeping that hand from its drink."

The man is my height, heavier but carries himself like a dancer. He hasn't shed his topcoat. His face under a short-brimmed fedora is finely sculpted and as white as his silk scarf. His age is hidden in the perfection of his features. Maybe he's forty.

He drops my hand and steps back. My vision narrows so I see him like at the end of a tunnel or a path lined with trees. Funny, but I see him this way, his hand still poised like he expects me to reach for it, join him in some kind of match.

"What's your game?" I ask.

His lips part as if to answer, but he is bumped away by my fans. He retreats like a boxer, tipping a hand to his brow. For a moment, I'm trapped in the wake of his energy. I feel cold. It's as if the space around me is frosted with danger.

Thin martini music is winding down. Mean rhythm and blues honkers stomp in anticipation to play for Miss Cornshucks. I join them near the bandstand, slapping their hands, watching them seize the stage like victors.

Then I see the Shucker.

She's wearing the corsage I sent her in a nest of multi-colored hair, some of it actually hers. Standing with her brand new husband, she grasps his hand in both of hers. A fire burns in her eyes brighter than the neon outside. She's damp, soaked in her own vapor. Her darkness shows through her white gown.

I kiss her cheek. "You're too much."

"Bought this dress today," she says. "Think it's too see-throughish?"

Shyly I turn away from her bosom, its twin halos of rich sienna spreading like stain. "Nah."

"In the store, it showed nothing."

"Your undies are too sheer," Babe says, wearing his sad, worldly smile.

She thanks me for the orchid, moves off for a last-minute chat with the piano man.

I grab Babe's arm. "This gang ready for her?"

"Shit no. She balked during rehearsal."

"Don't sound like her."

We watch her near the stage, a picture of pugnacious non-chalance. Babe swears under his breath.

"Her kid brother boosted her money last night, split the scene."

"Carlton?" I swallow a knot. I can feel Mr. White Scarf's intense gaze on me from across the tables. His lips are parted as if mouthing a silent message.

"Yeah," Babe says. "Carlton."

"That motherfucker."

"That's what my sis said."

"Don't let it drag you down."

"What the fuck?" He shrugs his thick shoulders, runs a hand through his matinee black hair, turns for his stool on stage behind his drums. "I seen you go on with worse troubles."

From a table reserved for the Flame's elite, I view the stage, Babe's beat jolting Cornshucks alive, rest of the band coming in. Before I brace myself, the Shucker reaches those sacred, stained-glass notes black women hoard deep where nobody else can find them. She opens now with *Why Don't You Do Right?*, miming terrible anger at Babe.

Babe cowers, drums a pratfall.

Hands on hips, she lets him have it. No frills, just honest-to-God song. How I admire her! I promise myself to take heed, search for more honesty in my own voice.

Faces around me glow. She spreads light—indigo as she flattens notes, brassy as she raises them to glory.

Across from me, Quincy Jones beams up at her. Next to him, his first mate, Joe Reisman, shakes his head like he's lost for words.

I'm so thrilled I re-order drinks. A sleek black woman I remember from the old days stops behind my chair. Cool, dry fingers gingerly cover my eyes. "Guess who?"

I pull her hand to my mouth, kiss her soft palm. "Only one lady with your charms, Annette," I say.

Cornshucks, in mid-note, watches from above. The ways I can get fucked up tonight blur in front of me like a flicked deck of cards. I feel the points of Annette's nipples brush my neck and scalp. I close my eyes, listen to the band.

Her breath is hot in my naked ear. "You're looking fine, J.R."

"Fine as wine," I say, trying for suave. On stage, Babe's signaling a break.

Annette says something, sounds like a warning about evils imminent, as Yul Brynner might orate. It's half lost to my deaf side, in the applause for Miss Cornshucks.

She steals away. Jesus, her ass, that haughty carriage, spark memories. In the far quadrant of my gaze, Mr. White Scarf stands as if he's spying on Annette and me.

Quincy Jones is watching also, waving a no-no finger. Does he mean Annette, or is his hand above my drink?

I put a name to him. "Mr. Impeccably Cool."

"Horseshit," he says. "Just concerned."

"That's Morrie Lane's job."

"He still pull your strings?"

"When I let him."

Quincy draws a horizontal line with that fucking finger. "Decide which side of the fence you're on, Johnnie. Then hold to it."

I sulk. Goddamn, am I always the bad boy, the Weird Kid, can't find his way? I know Quincy and Joe Reisman have been planning to produce an album for me. Have been since Reisman wrote my last Tahoe charts.

"I'm motivated." I put on my most convincing smile. "Fuck Morrie Lane's road back to the Top Forty."

"You mean that?" Quincy's handsome face assesses mine. "Meet with Joe and me, Brass Rail, after hours."

"Solid."

Babe and Cornshucks join the table, soak up our congratulations, accolades for their first set. The Shucker drains a club soda, drags on my cigarette, scowls at my stinger.

"Only my second," I lie.

"My ass." Furrows crease her wet brow. "I promised Dorothy I'd watch over you."

Nothing to say to that. I light another smoke. "Your show is the most."

Her tough attitude melts. "Sing one with me, baby."

I play shy. "Nah."

"Join me in *People Get Ready*," she pleads. "For old times' sake." She switches her glance to Annette, who hasn't exactly disappeared. "Join me, cousin," she repeats. "That the only old time you gonna' be getting."

Closing time. I'm shit-faced. Babe and Cornshucks left after their last set looking like wrestlers who won a tag-team match. I sang with Cornshucks, I remember that. The joint came apart, and I played it cool, letting her have the spotlight. Babe's hot on us recording together. Christ, that's all Morrie needs to hear.

Anyway, I'm under the Flame's marquee with other gritty characters, hanging onto the night by my fingernails. I sort of swoon, pass out on my feet. I snap out of it, realizing I promised to meet Jones and Reisman after hours at the Brass Rail.

Shit, I ain't gonna make it. Best I wave down a taxi, get my skinny ass back to the Statler-Hilton.

Another lapse. Man, those stingers. I look about, find nobody. I'm abandoned. No snow is falling. Marquee lights dim as I inspect the ruin of the world against the vacant sky. My face is stiff, hands numb. Musical aftershocks rock in my tin ear. This is a drunk makes you fear tomorrow. I think I see a taxi down Garfield, wave like some forgotten survivor.

"Gotcha." Strong hands under my arms keep me upright. "You're in good hands."

Standing straight, I fear my bladder will burst. "Got to piss," I announce to this overlord behind me.

"The alley."

I look for stars to guide me. All is beyond stars, more than night.

Footsteps join mine, those strong hands again, balancing me.

"Here." The voice is soft.

I open the wings of my coat, press on them with my elbows, assume a wide stance. I unzip, pull my dick out.

"Might be drunk," I say, "but know better'n to piss on my shoes."

Urine splatters. Steam rises from brick. Another stream suddenly jets alongside mine. I chuckle at a goofy thought—two buddies after a high school beer bust.

Just dribbles now, and I shudder in the cold.

"Shake it more than once," my pissing partner says, "and you're playing with it." His words are so close they percolate against my cheek.

I rock back on my heels, throw out a hand, touch icy brick.

"I'm wasted."

"Let me help you."

His hand on my cock, squeezing.

"No."

"Steady," he whispers.

"You're hurting me."

"Bullshit. You're getting hard as a nigger."

His grip tightens. Thin light, maybe moonlight, shows me his white scarf.

His other hand catches my fingers. He jerks them onto his cock.

"Now you got a nigger in your hand."

"No." I tremble. My knees go weak. My teeth chatter as I mouth street babble I hope will slow him. "No. Please, the pain, man."

His hands tighten more. "Stroke that motherfucker, Johnnie."

My feet slip from under me. He holds me suspended.

"Chicken by its neck."

I scream in pain. "Oh, God. I'm begging now, man, please."

He releases my cock, grabs a fistfull of my hair, forces me onto my knees.

"Fucking faggot. Go down on me."

Our shadows are illuminated against the wall. Light. A light strikes us from down the alley.

"Help." I've found my breath, yell into the beam of light.

I'm shoved over on my ass. Above me, the white scarf hangs down, touches my face. I see him now. He's removed his hat, and his dome of short, blond hair glows in a flash as the light moves. He is zipped up, composed, standing in great calm.

He's mob. Or law. Or something born more dangerous than both.

Another voice approaches with the light. "You in trouble, Zellnik?"

"Nothing I can't handle."

The light blinds me. "Help me."

"Who we got?" The other man is a monster in his winter uniform.

"Johnnie Ray, the singer."

"Hell you say."

"Cry for him, Johnnie."

"What's with the motherfucker, Zellnik?"

"Fucking queer tried to grab my shlong while I was taking a leak."

"He tried that?"

"Not for long."

"What now, Zell? It's three in the fucking morning."

"I don't give a fuck what time it is." The man's voice is so quiet it's no more than sound waves slipping against my hearing aid. "Read the nigger-lover his fucking rights."

"Shit."

"Do it. Then cuff him, take him to your car."

"Shit."

"I said do it." The voice takes on a quality of force. I feel the danger. "This whole move on the motherfucker isn't about you or me."

"No?"

The voice waits like I'm being studied. I go into a position fetal, pathetic, my hands protective on my shrunken penis.

"No." The voice has found its secret level again. "It's about something higher up, something more complicated."

Dorothy

The Voice of Broadway.

Wedding news from Niagara Falls. Talented R&B singer on the rise, Rosehelen Hanks, who performs as Little Miss Cornshucks, wed Johnnie Ray's drummer Babe Pascoe last Saturday. Best man was the Cry Guy himself, who will be on hand when Miss Cornshucks opens next week at Mr. Ray's musical alma mater, the Flame Showbar in Detroit. Congratulations to this dynamic duet.

The Black Room held enough of the day's light to allow her to read. Newspaper on her lap, she leaned back on the sofa and sipped cold vodka. Reading her own words filled her with an optimistic pleasure. As Johnnie had said, if Cornshucks and Babe could defy the obstacles to their happiness by getting married, there was hope for all of them. Johnnie had been right to go with them, and she was happy he had. Somehow he and she would overcome their own obstacles. She would do the Wallace show, help Dick succeed. Then maybe she and Johnnie could find some happiness together.

Her biggest problem was sitting back and not taking action, waiting for her life to improve. Yet every success in her life resulted from taking charge. She needed to do the same with her personal life, and from now on, she would.

She stood and stared out the window at the silver reflections cast through the drizzle. She needed a little rainy day music, something Johnnie would croon to her if he were here.

"Ma'am?"

She whirled from the window. Julian stood in the doorway, his wooden form poised as if he were sitting for a portrait. Although he would be the last person to judge, she didn't want him to know how often she came here to drink and brood after the radio show.

"I was just taking a rest," she said. "That officious boy from the station is driving me crazy."

"Miss Cornshucks is on the phone for you, ma'am."

"That's wonderful. She probably read what I wrote in the column about her wedding. Thank you, Julian."

She dashed past him on the way to take the call, thinking that he seemed more reserved than usual. Their station visitor was probably getting to him as well.

"Cornshucks," she said when she picked up the phone. "How does it feel to be a Mrs.?"

"We got trouble." Cornshucks voice scraped out the words. "He wanted that I call you right away."

As she stood clutching the phone in her wet fingers, she saw that Julian had followed her in. He waited at the door, holding the vodka bottle, his expression bereft. Dorothy began to tremble.

"Tell me," she said, motioning to him with her empty glass. "What's happened?

twenty-one

Dorothy

The charge was accosting and soliciting. The words played over again in her mind as she drove to Johnnie's apartment. Dick had tried to stop her when she briefly explained where she was going and why.

"But the club," he'd said. "What will people say?"

Lost in a blur of pain and fear, she barely heard. Johnnie needed her. She could see the headlines now. *Johnnie Ray Accused on Morals Charge. Vice Squad Police Nab Singer.* She couldn't get to Detroit in time for the summary arraignment that morning, but she'd be waiting when he returned to the apartment.

The place looked like a sanctuary of crystal, velvet, leather. Sabrina greeted her then settled next to the elegant salmon-colored sofa where they'd entertained their friends, shared private conversations, made love. Dorothy pressed her fingers into her aching forehead. Damn, how could this have happened?

Sabrina stirred even before Dorothy heard the rattle of the door. "Johnnie?"

The door opened. He stepped inside, depositing his suitcase on the floor, quieting Sabrina, staring at Dorothy across the room. He looked freshly shaven and pale in a navy suit, the tie still knotted tightly.

"God, I hoped you'd be here," he said, reaching out to her.

"Oh, Johnnie." She ran across the room to his outstretched arms. "It's going to be all right. We'll fight the bastards."

He held her away from him. Tears covered his cheeks. "You know what could happen, don't you? If I'm found guilty, they'll yank my cabaret card. I'll never work in New York again. I'll be branded."

"No, you won't," she said. "I have contacts. I'll call the presiding judge myself. By God, I'll be your character witness."

"You mean it, don't you?"

"Of course. We've got to fight, Johnnie."

He wiped the tears from his face. "You're something else, little girl," he said. "You come in here loaded for bear, ready to risk everything to save me. Most women I've known would be demanding to know what happened. You don't even ask me if I'm guilty or not."

"I don't have to," she said, feeling the certainty that had flooded through her when Cornshucks had told her the charges. "I know you didn't do it."

He put his arm around her, drew her next to him on the sofa. "That cop set me up," he said. "Waited 'til after closing. Got me in the alley. First I thought it was because of the black thing."

"Prejudice," she said.

"Yeah, they think I'm too close to the blacks. Mob and the law both. Someone's put my name on an enemies list."

"You think they'd set you up?"

"In a heartbeat." He paused. "I need a drink, baby."

"Me, too." She located the vodka bottle and poured their drinks tall with lots of ice. Vodka, ice. That's what would get them through these first dreadful hours.

He took a mouthful, swallowed, then put his glass on the table. "That's my first since all this started. Kind of lost my thirst."

"Had you been drinking?" she asked. "When it happened, I mean?"

He nodded. "Way too much. Cornshucks was a sensation. She couldn't possibly keep her eye on me. I got blasted, and this man just came up out of nowhere, followed me when I went to take a leak, began violating me." He cringed drawing up the memory. "Real rough stuff. Lucky for me, a uniform came along wanting to know what was up. Son of a bitch in overcoat and scarf told him, 'This isn't about you or me. It's about something higher up, something more complicated.'"

"That proves you were set up, Johnnie."

"Cold motherfucker will tell his own version in court."

"Let him. The truth will come out."

"Not the whole truth." He reached for the tumbler again, rattled the ice. "Know who's out to get me?"

She shook her head. "You have no real enemies."

"I have one. Who owns Detroit? Who has mob connections there? Who said I'd better never set foot in the town again?"

"Sinatra." Her skin crawled. "But why?" She paused. "Not Ava?"

"He's obsessed with her," he said, "just like you wrote in that article about him. When she asked him to go easy on you at the inauguration, he agreed, but it pissed him off. He's been after me a long time, babe."

She swallowed more vodka, felt its heat spread through her as her anger grew. "So it's back to Sinatra again."

"I can't prove it, but it's what I think."

"We'll win, Johnnie. We're going to beat this thing."

He smiled slowly. "You really think we've got a chance?"

"We do because you're innocent."

"Innocent people don't always win."

"This one will," she said, "because I'm your secret weapon."

That got another smile out of him, but he still wasn't the old Johnnie. What had happened had robbed him of his spirit, left him guarded and doubting.

"You do believe me, don't you?" she asked.

"I believe you'll do everything you can to help me," he said.

"We'll dance on Sinatra's grave, just watch."

"I kind of doubt that one," he said. "The bastard made his point. I'm never going back to Detroit City again."

"Of course you will," she said, "once this has blown over. You love the place."

"No." He moved closer now, and she could see the flat conviction in his eyes, something too powerful to put a name to. "I'll never go back to Detroit City, not as long as I live."

She wasted no time making good on her promise to Johnnie. The chance that Sinatra may be behind it just pushed her harder. Friends and colleagues dealt with Johnnie's arrest the way they dealt with any unpleasant subject; they simply ignored it. Johnnie's associates reacted differently. Marilyn Monroe phoned late one night after the news was out.

"Tell Johnnie I don't believe a word of it," she said in a soft whisper. "I know what it's like when everyone's out to get you."

New Yorkers like Clara and Roland voiced support but kept their distance, not just at social events but at Dick's club as well. While Dick struggled to attract a tony clientele to Paris In The Sky, she worked putting pressure on the presiding judge, calling in favors owed her by power-wielding officials.

"You've got to stop this," Dick said one night shortly before Johnnie's trial in March. "Everyone's talking about it."

"They've talked before."

They had met in the dining room after dressing for different destinations that night—his the club, hers drinks with Johnnie's attorney. She knew he'd expected her to go with him.

"How can I hope to attract the right crowd, when my wife's out defending some queer on a morals charge?"

"That's enough." She poured a quick drink from the bar, didn't offer him any. "Watch your name-calling. People have said as much about you behind your back."

He stood in the doorway, unmoving. "You'd do it, wouldn't you? You'd destroy my business, our family, me. You'd destroy it all for him, wouldn't you?"

His theatrics were the last thing she needed tonight. She tossed back the last of the drink, waited for it to kick in and lift her past this ugly scene. "Leave the family out of it, Dick."

"That's what you've done. You've left the family out, all right, paid to send your kids away so you have more time for God knows what with him."

"You haven't been the ideal parent yourself." She glanced at the gruesome bell jar and its clock within. "I'm late," she said, brushing past him. "Don't like to keep attorneys waiting."

He grabbed her arm, hard. "You'd better not be his character witness," he said, squeezing harder.

She tried to pull away, couldn't. His muddy eyes looked unfocused, mad. "Let me go," she said.

Slowly he released her. "I mean it," he said as she hurried for the door. "No wife of mine is going to stand up for that bastard."

As it turned out, she didn't have to be Johnnie's character witness, but she would have done it in spite of Dick's threats, if the attorney thought it would help. Yes, Dick was right. She'd risk anything to save Johnnie.

Icy winds cut through Detroit the day of the trial. At least last night's rain had ceased, but the steps to the courthouse were wet and slippery. The jammed courtroom made her claustrophobic. She sat in front and surreptitiously eased her hand in her purse, feeling around until she found the tissue-wrapped Valium tablet. She swallowed it without water, then folded her trembling hands in her lap as the trial got underway.

Already the effects of her influence were visible. The jury was made up entirely of middle-aged women, motherly types who would think of Johnnie as a son.

Johnnie looked the part, dressed in a suit, watching with a serious expression as his attorney argued passionately for at least an hour and a half. It was a simple case of enticement, he said, a long-time vendetta this person and others had against Mr. Ray. Dorothy felt tears in her eyes, looked around the courtroom and realized that she was not alone.

Then it was Johnnie's turn. Jesus, please let him be all right.

His hair lay sleek against his head, and he looked like a little boy who'd just gotten ready for church. At Cornshucks' insistence, he hadn't joined in the drinking the night before, which probably contributed to the clear blue of his eyes. No one could convict this man, no one.

He answered the questions politely.

"How did you meet Lieutenant Zellnik?"

"He asked for my autograph."

"Inside the bar?"

Johnnie nodded politely. "It was inside. I gave it to him, and he invited me for a nightcap."

Court was adjourned, and Dorothy began to relax.

When court reconvened, the prosecution began vigorously. As Johnnie's attorney had predicted, the prosecutor brought up Johnnie's prior conviction in 1951. Dorothy listened intently as he answered. They'd discussed it before when they had first fallen in love. If only he could tell the story now as he had told it to her.

"I was unknown back then. Penniless," he said. "My appointed attorney said the only thing I could do was plead guilty, so I did."

The judge's instructions to the jury were careful. "Remember," he cautioned, "police officers must not assist or encourage acts against the law."

He was doing his best to help, to give her the favor she'd requested within the boundaries of his job. She looked up, found Johnnie's gaze, smiled her encouragement. Then she looked down into her lap and did something she hadn't done for too long. She prayed. Dear God, let the verdict be fast. Let it be right. Let Johnnie go free.

 ## Johnnie

From the prisoner's box, I get a glimpse of Dotty's dark blue eyes. She looks hard Irish, raises her clinched fist in encouragement, then drops her eyes as if she's counting off her Hail Marys.

I had a bad moment this morning outside the jammed courthouse. I felt my body go into this kind of spasm that sends my legs into a Saint Vitus. I've had the sensation before on stage. Maybe Elvis stole it, maybe he's got the malady. Who knows? I'm clutching my knees, waiting for the jury to come back with a verdict, hoping I can control myself. The jury is all women, which is like a set up for me. Shit, they been giving me magnanimous twinkle winks since the trial's get go.

They file in. I figure it's been about an hour since they retired. My attorneys have told me anything under six hours is okay in a case like this against Detroit's finest.

The judge asks the foreman to read the verdict. A juror I've named Granny for Dotty's amusement adjusts her specs.

"Not guilty."

My legs go. Christ, I'm herking and jerking so bad I fake a full-out faint so I can hit the floor, stretch my scarecrow legs.

"He's fainted," screams someone. I think it's Granny.

It is. She's helping my attorneys plant me back in my chair. She fans my Norman Rockwell portrait with her purse.

"Praise the Lord," I say.

Then I see Dorothy, and I feel like a club fighter who's come off the canvas to win one more time.

There's a fear that is like a mate to this feeling of victory. A fear that my luck could be running out.

The crowd rushing the granite stairs reminds me of swarming locusts. I'm being congratulated, slapped on the back, when I catch the terrible dead-on stare of Lieutenant Zellnik. A well-wisher tilts me so I'm lined up right in front of the dick.

He's hatless but is wearing the white scarf. His hair could be brass in the war-torn light of the afternoon.

"We'll see you again in this town, Johnnie," he says.

I let a moment pass. "The fuck you will."

twenty-two

Dorothy

The Voice of Broadway.

In all the hubbub over Peter O'Toole as Lawrence of Arabia, don't miss *To Kill a Mockingbird,* based on Harper Lee's poignant novel. I hear Gregory Peck is a sure Oscar nominee in this one.

Congratulations on the year's perfect box-office couple, Doris Day and Rock Hudson, for their hilarious performance in *Lover Come Back.*

Congratulations are also due Walter Cronkite, who's succeeding Douglas Edwards as anchorman of the CBS Evening News. Look out, Huntley-Brinkley.

Marilyn Monroe looks the picture of health once more and lovelier than ever. Could that glow be the new, top-secret man in her life, even more powerful than Joltin' Joe?

Dorothy finally appeared on *The Mike Wallace Interview,* although she didn't think any interview she did could help Dick or Paris in the Sky.

As she expected, Wallace asked about her feud with Sinatra and his public attacks on her.

After a pause, she spoke the answer she'd planned. "Some men turn into little boys when they don't get their way," she said, "and little boys can get vicious when their egos are damaged."

The story spread at once. Frank Sinatra had been turned down by Dorothy Kilgallen and still hadn't gotten over it. That's what they'd say any time he attempted to degrade her or insult her appearance on stage.

Dick couldn't understand why she'd want to start a new round with Sinatra, but Johnnie cheered her victory.

"Mark Twain said not to fight with someone who has more ink than you," she said. "Today it's more TV time."

It was a hot August of muggy days and oppressive nights. She and Johnnie had plans to attend a book-launching party for Helen Gurley Brown later that Saturday. Early that evening she dined with Phil Matthews, a public relations man Bennett Cerf had recommended. Phil had been part of Johnnie's party crowd in California until he'd almost lost his leg in an automobile accident.

At the Stork Club, they chatted about John Glenn's orbit and made small talk as she summoned her nerve. Tall and a bit stooped, Phil was Johnnie's age but he looked older. If she were guessing his line, she'd take in the narrow forehead, thinning hair and quiet demeanor and say a studio musician, a college professor, anything but a PR man. That sense of decency he conveyed was the secret of his success in an avaricious business.

She suspected that he had a quiet, unspoken interest in Johnnie, but he was too much of a gentleman to step out of line, especially since he didn't have the excuse of alcohol.

"Do you miss drinking?" she asked as they looked over the menus, he with a glass of club soda, she with her vodka tonic.

He looked down at his right leg, which rested stiffly in the chair.

"Not the way I miss this."

"One would hardly notice," she said.

"Thanks, but you're being polite. Besides, I notice. It hurts me all the time."

"Poor boy. You're just lucky to be alive." She looked at her own empty glass, decided to forego another out of respect for him.

"I want to talk to you about Johnnie."

"No one can make him quit drinking until he decides to," Phil said.

"Quit drinking?" she asked, annoyed. "I'm talking about his career. He's finally wise to that opportunist Morrie. You've got to help him."

"The business is bubblegum right now," he said. "Do you see Johnnie singing *Surfin' Safari* or *Palisades Park?*"

"Of course not. But look at Ray Charles. Look at Miss Cornshucks."

"Rosehelen," he corrected with a smile.

"That's right. On the Top Forty, no less. There's a place for Johnnie."

"I agree," he said.

"We just have to get him to break it off with Morrie once and for all."

"Morrie's the same as the booze," Phil said. "Johnnie has to make the decision himself."

After dinner, she drank a grasshopper while Phil toyed with a cup of coffee. With all that green, minty ice, it was practically dessert, not the same as ordering a real drink.

"It's really very refreshing," she said.

He smiled but said nothing.

Finally, she pressed her knuckles into the table, looked directly at him. "Phil," she said. "If I can convince Johnnie to get rid of Morrie once and for all, will you be his manager?"

His scrutiny was as intense as hers. "You'd want that?"

"Yes," she said. "I know it's the last chance for Johnnie. Would you do it?"

He reached out, took her hand, and held it in both of his. "You're quite a lady," he said. "You know that?"

A dozen responses spun through her mind, a hundred second thoughts. But she'd already made up her mind. "Does that mean you'll do it?"

"It means I'll think about it," he said.

She awoke that morning to the sound of hammering far away. Workmen so early? Oh, God, her head.

She must be late for the radio show again. No, they'd decided to record it. Today was Sunday morning. After she'd left Phil last night, she and Johnnie had drunk away the evening at a party for Helen Gurley Brown's new book, *Sex and the Single Girl*. She could write a year of columns just from the guest list, everyone from politicians to film stars to one or two mistresses of powerful married men.

How did they ever drink so much? Jesus, how did she end up strolling in the hot summer night, flirting with a blond Texan who'd arrived with friends of the Vice President? What was his name? August, he'd said.

"Just plain August."

"I like games," she had said, "but I can easily find out who you are."

"I'd be encouraged if you try."

She had glanced then at an attractive brunette standing alone across the room. "Why would you want me to know your true identity?"

"It would make us even if I tried to find out more about you."

She knew she was blushing. "I'd guess your line is something in the government, something covert, an agency identified by three initials."

He grinned. "Such agencies require vows of silence."

"That leaves you speechless then."

"Not so speechless I won't call you sometime," he drawled. "If you don't mind."

He was off before she could respond, moving gracefully to the dark-haired woman, who seemed to be waiting for him.

Dorothy, in that instant, identified the woman in her mind. She'd seen her before—once in a clandestine huddle with John F. Kennedy—another time on the arm of a man rumored to be a major player in the Mafia.

"Mrs. Kollmar?" The pounding grew louder. No, not workmen. It was right outside, on her bedroom door. "Mrs. Kollmar. Can you hear me, ma'am? Mrs. Kollmar."

"Mrs. Kollmar?" The pounding again.

"Coming, Julian." She had little voice. Must have given most of it away in meaningless conversations last night. "Coming." She threw the door open, then stopped when she saw the look on Julian's face.

"What is it?" she demanded.

"Your editor's on the phone ma'am. I told him you we're sleeping, but he said to wake you up. Marilyn Monroe—They're saying she killed herself last night. He wants you to write the story."

"Oh, Jesus." Dorothy reached out for his hand. "Tell him I'll call right back," she said. Tears gathered in her eyes.

Marilyn gone? Suicide? How goddamned unfair.

"Somebody should have taken care of the poor girl," she told Johnnie as they held each other at his apartment that night. "She shouldn't have been alone. And of course the caller on the phone had to be Bobby Kennedy. Perhaps he had called, realized what was happening and reacted the Kennedy way, dodged any involvement."

"You're not going to print that, are you?" Johnnie asked.

"I don't print my suspicions," she told him.

In a way, she did, though. She just omitted Bobby's name. She owed some mention of the truth to her readers, and she definitely owed it to Marilyn.

Marilyn's strange death couldn't be, she wrote, but of course it was the way it would have to have been. The pills, the nude body, and all alone.

How could someone she knew in that superficial way celebrities know each other matter this much to her? She knew only that Marilyn's death took something from her own life, that she was less for it.

 Johnnie

Reaction to my arrest is mixed. Some think I'm poison, but shit, that bunch always did. Most aren't rattled. A few see it for the setup it was. Now I know who's in my corner and who's not.

Phillip is for sure.

Dorothy proved she's a champ.

Morrie's hiding.

Saul, bless him, has kept me in cash.

Babe and Cornshucks—what can I say? They've taken flack for standing by me. Jesus, how'll I ever repay them?

And Marilyn, she took my side as long as she was around. The newspapers have tried to beat me up on this bad as they did her, dead and alive. I'm on page one when I'm busted. I prove entrapment. I'm acquitted. They bury me on the back page.

Scandal sheets are deaf to my claims of a frame-up. Don't want any part of my story about the Mob and Sinatra.

It's more than a month since my trial when Morrie pops up to my pad. He walks in without knocking. Raphael is prancing around bareass. Morrie doesn't see him at first, then catches him in his specs.

"Jesus, God a'mighty."

I cinch my terrycloth robe, go to the bar, fire up a menthol with my Zippo. "Over here, Morrie," I say. "Follow the flame."

Raphael is loaded, jumping around all campy. He grabs two magazines, interprets a fan dance. Samantha chases him off stage. Raphael falls at the doorway to his room. Samantha almost bites his nuts off before he slams the door.

Morrie raises his hands. "I can't take this."

"Quit breaking and entering," I say, "you won't have to."

"Visiting my client is a crime?"

"It's a crime holding my money for weeks."

"You want money, Johnnie, you got to work for it."

I make a short movie out of pouring vodka out of a cut-glass decanter. He stands next to my phallic totem sculpture. Fat. Sassy. Like he figures it's honorable work, his skimming from me.

"Watcha want, Morrie?"

His scrunched-up face is flushed with authority. "First, lay off all this police vendetta shit."

"You weren't there," I shout. "That sadist came close to killing me."

"And lay off the Mob."

Something Dorothy has told me comes to mind. "They're homophobic."

"Homo what?"

"They hate blacks too."

"Shit, what else is new?" Morrie does a little whirl, collapses on the sofa. We're both quiet, except for our panting. He squints, closes his eyes. "Columbia is dropping us."

"Nothing lost there." I chug my drink.

"Only the Beard. All your hits he played a part in."

"Fuck 'em. Get another label."

"Already have. Decca gave us an option I want you to okay."

I try to act chesty, get dizzy, hang onto my bar. My fingers leave a wet trail across the glass top. Morrie's mouth is working on words, sending a message I'm not receiving. I point to my naked ears.

"I said you look yellow, Johnnie. Your gut is all pooched out."

"Get me some work, see I get paid for it, and I'll unpooch it," I say, praying to God he'll leave. I'm about ready to fall apart, and I don't need any witnesses.

Morrie struggles out of the titty-pink sofa. "We record next month for the new label."

"Peachy."

"I thought you wanted work."

"I do."

"Can you make an engagement after the recording date?"

"You book it, I'll be there." I'd pour more courage at the bar, but I'm afraid I can't handle it without breaking glass.

"We got five nights, Angelo's in Omaha."

"Nebraska?"

"Last I looked at a map."

"Jesus." I heard him right.

"It's a hotspot."

"What's the deal?"

"One dollar cover."

Heard that right too.

Praying hard that my legs don't go, I clench my teeth, suck in my stomach. Off stage, Raphael must be retching, or Samantha is howling.

"Like I say, man," I reply, "I'll be there."

PART THREE

Tell the Lady Goodbye

twenty-three

 Johnnie

Springtime sixty-three, and I'm a pariah in the business. I chide Morrie on the phone, "If we can't score on the charts now, cousin, we never will."

He gives me eighteen reasons I won't catch the top rung, starting of course with my morals charge.

I give him eighteen reasons I oughta: Bobby Vinton, Walter Brennan, Richard Chamberlain are the first three.

"Christ, even Dr. Kildaire beats me to the top forty.

I haven't done dick on wax. Decca has buried my singles before they're released. No gigs on the horizon to brag about.

I'm crying in my beer with Dorothy in the deep shade of Tabby's back booth.

"Why don't you call Phil Matthews?" she suggests. "PR is his thing, and he's always offered his expertise."

"You think?" I'm trying to let her out of this, thinking wow. She knows Phillip is gay.

"Trade him for any one of your hangers-on, and you'll be ahead."

"He is smart." I feel the idea strike me in a lot of ways. I cast a look into the deep part of Dotty's eyes. I want to inform her my hanger-ons have jumped ship or have sunk lower than I. I place my hand atop hers, hope her eyes will brighten, but they do not.

"Hold the fort." I lurch off to relieve myself. Short trip since I've placed us practically in the pisser. My bladder. Man, I'll be in rubber diapers soon. Last night Raphael put a waterproof mattress cover on my bed.

Returning, I study the back of Dorothy's head, her dark hair, slim, white neck above her gauzy summer dress. So young-appearing from this angle, so tender. I touch her bare shoulder before I slide in across from her—to bring her back, from where I don't know. It's like she's from too fine a species, out of place with me.

Hoping to lift her mood, I suggest a quiz game she's invented.

"Give me a song fragment. Remember your rule. No fewer than two words, no more than four."

"What shall we bet?" She's leaning forward in her seat, rubbing her palms together.

"A blow job."

Her lips twist into that pixie smile. "No clear winner in that wager."

"Okay. Winner buys another round before we split."

"You operator." A vertical wrinkle divides her forehead as she concentrates. "Okay, here goes. *Whose broad.*"

"Whose broad?"

"Did I stutter?"

"That's from a song?"

"One down, nine to go."

"*South Pacific?*"

She mimics John Daly turning over a prop card. "Not even close."

"*Nothing Like A Dame?*"

"You're so chauvinistic. You'll never get it. Give up?"

"Yeah."

She hums a key, sings in perfect pitch. "Whose broad stripes and bright stars…"

"Jesus, the anthem."

"Yep."

And there it is, that smug bit of lonely loveliness that killed me when she took off that blindfold after another game a hundred years ago.

I use my beer napkin to blot my eyes. She fishes in her purse, hands me a tissue that smells of lavender. Past her, the waning light strokes listless figures at the bar.

"I've got tickets for tonight," she says.

"I don't know."

"*Swan Lake*'s opening. Nureyev and Fonteyn."

I picture us being ushered into choice seats, the covert glances sighted over blue noses.

"They'll be laying in wait out there, baby."

"I'll be ready. I bought a new gown. Gossamer. You'd think Gatsby picked it out for me."

"New guy in your life?"

"Great Gatsby."

"Oh, that Gatsby." I'm grinning with her now. "I'll wear white head to toe, a picture of chastity."

"I'll hire a limo, ask friends to join us, hit a supper club after."

"Deeper into enemy territory."

"We'll go to one where I'm on the license."

"Jesus, Dotty."

"To The Left Bank," she says. "Dick will be across the river in Jersey at Paris In The Sky."

"I don't know," I say, but I'm starting to like the idea.

Our party dances into The Left Bank, each of us doing a version of Rudolph's or Margot's ballet movements. My legs react to an unknown puppeteer, and my bladder threatens to burst. I enjoyed the ballet but, God, it seemed to go on forever. The theatre was hot, and there was no booze in the limo because Dorothy had put Rolly in charge of transportation.

I'm betwixt the bar and the restroom when I see Kollmar holding court with a sparse bar crowd.

I pull Dorothy aside. "Thought the bastard was across the river."

She stops cold. Her eyes blink like she's seeing something in her husband's image that she's forgotten.

Kollmar raises his drink to her. Two women drift away from him like weary sirens. He shrugs his wide shoulders. His eyes are black holes in the surreal light. I feel like a matador with bad kidneys.

"Excuse me, Dotty," I murmur. "Got to run to the men's."

She relaxes her grip on my arm. "Don't be gone long, Johnnie."

I piss in Kollmar's cheap ass trough-style urinal. Rolly comes in while I'm washing my hands.

"Grand ballet, wasn't it, John?" Sees the urinal. "Holy Christ."

Rollie. Only guy I know calls me John, but strangely the fucker can grow on you. Before I answer him, he breaks into a laugh.

"I mean *Swan Lake*," he says, shaking himself, "not the ballet that could happen in the lounge."

I find Dorothy alone at the rearmost table. Clara is waiting at the door.

"The others have elected to go to your apartment," Dorothy says.

Clara intercepts Rollie, and they leave, waving. In the dimness, I count a dozen patrons finishing dinner or just listening to the piano near the bar. Kollmar is behind the counter now, kidding the bartender in front of the two women, a few diehards and a cocktail waitress.

Dorothy takes my hand and places it on her gauzy bodice. Her nipple is like hard rubber between my fingers. I start to remove my hand when a waiter walks by, try again when the cocktail girl brings drinks.

"No," Dorothy says. "Don't remove your hand."

The girl is cool. "Two vodka martinis with olives *and* onions, Miss Kilgallen."

When the girl has gone and we've dipped into our drinks, Dorothy places her fingers on my hand again. "You feel cold, Mr. Ray."

"Too cold."

"Let me take it," she says, moving my hand under the table, "to someplace warm and wet."

At least one table hears this. I know others can tell what we're doing. Dorothy is oblivious as she leans across to kiss me.

Breaking the kiss, I ask, "Why?"

"It's time," she says.

We're breathing open-mouthed, and my legs are weak and shaky when we take a minute to finish our drinks. Dorothy clucks her tongue when I break loose to visit the john again.

 ## Dorothy

They hung onto each other as they stumbled into the elevator. Against his ear, Dorothy sang a line from *Walk Like A Man.*

"Four Seasons," Johnnie said, naming the group, as if he were on a television game show. "Now they got guys that sing like girls, and no one thinks anything of it."

As the elevator door slid closed, Dorothy pressed herself against him. "I took off my panties at the club," she said.

She could feel him swell in response.

"Damn. In the ladies room?"

"At the table. I just slid out of them while you were talking to Roland. Want to see?"

She picked them from her purse, dangled them in front of Johnnie. As the door opened, the stolid frame of Julian greeted them from the other side.

"Hi there, Vinson" Johnnie said, hastening past him.

"Have a nice evening, Mr. Ray, ma'am," Julian said.

"Wait for me," she said, catching up with Johnnie. "He's blind to what we're doing." She handed him her panties. "For you, darling."

He took them like a bouquet, sniffed. "Ah, my favorite flavor."

"That made you smile," she said. "Why so nervous back at the club?"

"Just didn't like the look on your old man's face."

The Black Room was truly black tonight. She lit candles. He poured drinks, slid next to her on the leather sofa, pulled a brown plaid throw over their laps.

"I didn't think Dick would be there," she said. "But he doesn't give me an itinerary when he leaves the house in the morning. Besides, I don't care anymore."

"You mean that?" he moved close to her, sliding his hand up her skirt, past the tops of her stockings, to her inner thigh and beyond.

"Oh, God, Johnnie. Do that again."

"Here?" He stroked her softly. She could smell her own moist scent filling their small world of leather and wool. She arched her back, sliding down beneath him.

"Keep that up and I'll explode right now."

"Good. I want you to."

"We have to wait," she said, pushing his hand away. "I have a surprise for you."

"What kind of surprise?" He moved beside her, sticking his tongue out, tracing her lips with it.

"I bought one of those new Polaroid cameras. Thought we might take some photos."

"You did not."

"Did too. I hid it in the closet. Come on. Let me pose on the drum table for you."

"Right here?"

"Why not?"

"Where will you hide the pictures? What if someone finds them?"

"I don't care." Her body moved on its own now, making small strokes against him. "Kiss me," she said.

He slid his hands inside her skirt as they kissed, making slow teasing circles with his hands on her bare buttocks.

"Beautiful ass," he said against her lips.

"Tell me you want it."

"I want your ass, baby. I love your ass." She could almost reach orgasm like this, his fingers stroking her buttocks, his tongue in her mouth.

"Johnnie, please. Now."

"Oh, Dotty." His hair had fallen over her face. Through it, she could see jagged candlelight, strange shadows. They lay body against body now, her buttocks almost entirely off the sofa. She wrapped her right leg around his hip, felt the pressure of his erection as they kissed repeatedly.

She heard the door click open, saw the splash of light from the hall.

"Get the fuck away from my wife."

His voice, Dick's. Jesus. Dorothy grabbed for her skirt as Johnnie tried to cover her with the throw. "No, Dick, no. Oh, God, no."

"I said get the fuck away from her, you two-dollar has-been."

Dick towered over them. Flickering shadows from the candles made him look like a distorted caricature of himself. She pulled her legs under her and drew back against the sofa.

"Look, man," Johnnie began, straightening his shirt.

"I'll kill you if I ever see you with my wife again."

Dorothy gasped and tried to find her voice. Dick waved his fist drunkenly, and she didn't doubt for a moment that he could kill her and Johnnie right now.

Johnnie held tightly whatever composure he could muster. Robot-like, he reached for his drink. "That's up to her," he said.

"It's up to me." Dick grabbed the glass from him, threw it hard against the wall.

It smashed into pieces before the fireplace. Dorothy screamed. "Dick, please."

"Shut up, bitch." He spun toward Johnnie. "I want you out of here, you fucking queer, out of her life."

Johnnie slung his jacket over his shoulder and looked at Dorothy. She had waited for years for the time to be right. This was it.

She rose from the couch and went to him. She trembled so hard that she could barely speak. "I want to go with you," she said, her voice a thin whisper. Tears filled his eyes, and she knew he heard, bad ear and all. Dick heard it as well. He seemed frozen in his rage. "Please take me with you, Johnnie" she said. "I don't want to be in this house anymore."

"Your children," he murmured.

"They'll understand."

"You'll lose the column, the TV show, everything you've worked for."

"I don't care." Her throat tightened. She felt the desperation in her voice. "Johnnie, please."

He looked at Dick, who appeared stunned by her words. They both turned to Johnnie.

"I'm sorry, Dotty," he said. "I gotta get out of here. Shit, there's no other way."

"No."

He waved a hand in the charged air. "You'll lose it all if I don't. I can't let it happen this way."

She began to sob, but he turned from her, stumbled through the door and into the hall. She wanted to run after him, but it would do no good. Nothing would do any good any more. Nothing.

"Oh, God. Oh, Johnnie." Through her tears, she saw the glistening shards where his glass had broken against the fireplace. She crossed the room, knelt before the fireplace and picked up a large piece.

"Like Humpty Dumpty," she said, looking at the hopeless, ragged piece. Blood oozed out of her fingers, the palm of her hand. "I didn't even feel it," she said. "I didn't feel a thing."

"Dorothy." Dick came across the room, wounded, bent. He handed her the wool throw, wrapped it in a clumsy, oversize bandage around her hand. "Come on," he said, reaching out for her. "Let's get you downstairs."

twenty-four

 Johnnie

Back at my apartment, Raphael is bartending for a full house. Clara and Rollie are long gone, but a cast of characters that look like they're from *Guys 'N' Dolls* is milling about. I instruct Rafael to shoo them out.

They're slow to depart. Some clown I don't recognize answers a ringing phone, hands it to me, mouths Dorothy's name. I shake my head, walk off toward my bedroom.

Raphael follows me in, hands me a tall drink.

"You look shook," he says, watching my eyes. "Dorothy's called a bunch of times."

"I am shook," I say. "Give me something with this." I hold up my glass.

He leaves, comes back with a pillsky. I wash it down, hope for sweet dreams I know won't come.

"The motherfucker kills me if I stay in her life, Rafe."

"That won't stop you." He looks like an oldtime Apache dancer sitting sadly on my bed in tight T- shirt and a beret.

"I stay, she loses everything."

He says nothing to that.

"Her column, radio, TV, everything she's worked for all her life." I shake my head in despair. "Her children."

"What'll I do if she keeps calling?"

"Tell her I love her, but it's over."

Raphael runs a hand along my arm. "Your beautiful white suit," he says. "It's a mess. Get out of it. I'll draw a hot tub."

"You understand. I don't trust myself to tell her myself."

"I understand," he says. "We all understand."

"Did she say much to you on the phone?"

"Not much, Johnnie. I'm not one of her favorites."

"Not much?"

His head is down, and I can't make out his answer. "Rafe, look at me. Not much?"

"That she'd kill herself," he says, lifting his chin. She said she'd kill herself if you didn't return her calls."

Next day I refuse her calls. Says something about me. Says I'm scared shitless of Kollmar is what it does. That man put the fear of God in me. I saw something in his eyes, man. Same as I saw in that dick's eyes the night in the alley outside the Flame Showbar.

I receive a letter from Dorothy. It's handwritten on stationery that carries her scent. Jesus, her words beg in a way I know is killing her. Sunday comes, and I tune in *What's My Line?*, shaking all over so bad Raphael helps me park in front of the RCA.

"She ain't on the panel."

I moan.

"Hold on," Raphael says. "They might tell us why."

The phone rings. I jump up, stand petrified. Raphael answers it, hands it to me.

"Mr. Ray, this is Julian."

"Who? Please speak up. My hearing—"

"Julian, the Kollmars' man. One you call Skinhead Vinson."

Oh, my God. "Yes?"

"I'm not supposed to do this, call you, I mean."

"Yes."

"But Miss Killgallen, they taken her to Mt. Sinai just this afternoon."

Oh, mother. "Did she—?"

"She didn't try to hurt herself, but she seemed about to. I went on and called her doctor."

"Bless you, Julian."

"Well, I'll go on now."

"Where's Kollmar?"

"The mister was sleeping, but he's awake now, gone after the ambulance."

"Julian, can you call me when he comes back and goes to sleep?"

"Mr. Ray, she's in a guarded room."

"I'll get in somehow."

"Just answer her call, Mr. Ray, if she calls you. Just answer her damn call, man."

She's in the hospital for more than a month. I pull every string I know and, careful of Kollmar, I get to sit bedside with her on three occasions.

"I prayed you'd come tonight," she says my third time up.

The room is dark save a soft night light. Dorothy is sitting up, her face in a blue halo, ghostly. She talks, her voice rising with an inner timbre that I thought was gone.

"I'm getting out of here day after tomorrow."

I pull my chair closer, kiss her cheek. Rain strikes the dark windows in gusts.

"Maybe the sun will come out in New York in a few days."

"Maybe we'll be together in Washington, D.C.," she says. "Nice, quiet hotel suite."

"You're going back to work?"

"Nothing I can't handle. I'll do it all on the phone. We can picnic three days in satin sheets."

"Silk."

"Okay, champ. Silk."

And here it is again. Perpetuity—ain't that what it's called?

 # Dorothy

She returned home on a Monday night, still weak but determined to do the radio show. They told their friends her anemia had taken a turn for the worse. Maybe that's what had happened—after Johnnie left her, after she refused to eat, after she went on a steady diet of vodka and pillskies. At least she knew that Johnnie really loved her. Their relationship would have to change, but they could still see each other.

Dick, who had been using guests on their radio show since she had been hospitalized, had sounded thick-tongued and uninspired.

She woke up shaky and cold that morning. She could never get warm these days. Her faded pink chenille bathrobe had seen better days, but it was at least cozy. No one downstairs would care. She'd worn it before to broadcast the show. She and Marshall the station spy had long established a relationship built on friendly sparring, and she knew he wouldn't mind what she wore as long as she showed up.

He and the engineer had already settled at the dining room table when she appeared.

"Look who's here." Marshall's colorless eyes widened with surprise, then he quickly glanced away.

"Do I look that disreputable?"

"Not at all, but I'm saving up to buy you a new robe."

"Think you can afford it?"

"At least a down payment," he said. "Glad you could join us today."

"Me, too."

Julian entered the room with a carafe of coffee. A smile broke through his solemn expression when he saw her. "Good morning, ma'am. Welcome back."

"Thank you, Julian. Would you ask Mr. Marshall if he'd care for some coffee."

It had become a joke now. Julian took the cue, repeated his lines.

"Thank Mrs. Kollmar for me," Marshall said, "but I prefer my coffee on a silver tray."

"Julian?" Dorothy nodded.

"Yes, ma'am." He returned in moments with the coffee on a small tray.

"Very nice," Marshall said to Julian. "Please thank Mrs. Kollmar for me."

"I'll take mine any way I can get it," said the engineer. "We need to get going."

As Julian poured her cup, Dorothy squinted at the bell jar. Where was Richard? She glanced at Marshall, and they both turned toward Julian.

"I'll knock on his door again, ma'am," he said.

"Break it down if you have to," she said. "The show's starting in minutes."

She was already poised at the table over the microphone when Dick stumbled down the stairs in a bulky jacket that failed to cover his girth.

"Sorry," he said. "Thought we were pre-recording today."

"Sit," Dorothy hissed. Already she felt weak. She needed someone to lead the show, and it wasn't going to be Dick.

His metallic smell nearly gagged her. God, what had happened to him in the short time she'd been gone? He paused far too long between speeches, giving the show a drunken, drawn-out pace. Out of nowhere, he began speaking of endangered species, penguins.

Dorothy stared at Marshall, whose face had gone white. "Who needs them?" she said.

Again, a long, weighty pause. Then, "We need each other."

Marshall pounded the table, made cut marks with his hand. "Out," he whispered, stabbing a finger at Dick.

"Oh," Dorothy said, trying to carry it alone. "That reminds me of a marvelous party I attended last week. I've been meaning to tell you about it, dear." She stumbled over the words, as Dick made his noisy departure.

She did her best during the rest of the time, but the copy on the commercial she read was too long and the type too small. She looked up only once to see Marshall, his head in his hands.

"I'm sorry," she told him when it was finally over. "Maybe I came back too soon."

"At least you tried." He waved away Julian, who returned with the coffee carafe. "Where's Kollmar?"

"He left, sir," Julian said.

"Okay. We'll pre-record tomorrow," he said.

Once the news would have thrilled her, but now it seemed ominous. "But you hate pre-recorded shows," she said.

"Yes, I do." He rose. "I have to think about our sponsors. "They're paying good money for this."

"But the station's still making money on us," she put in quickly. "Don't forget that."

He nodded. "I'm not forgetting anything, Miss Kilgallen, but we can't keep taking these kind of risks."

She took his arm. "I'll talk to Dick, I promise. It's just that I've been ill, and he's had too much to manage properly." She couldn't even convince herself. The look in Marshall's eyes softened. What was he feeling? Remorse? Pity? Jesus, not pity.

"I have to talk to some people," he said. "Then I'll get back with you."

No arguments of hers, no promises, would change what happened now. "Fine," she said, stepping back from him. "Thanks for your help."

"Thank you. Better get yourself a warmer robe. You look like you're going to blow away."

She forced a smile to her lips. "I'll be fine."

The New York Times ran the announcement. The *Dorothy and Dick* program would cease broadcasting until further notice.

Dick blamed her, but she felt almost relieved. Now she had a chance to reclaim her journalism career. She'd covered real news once, not just movie-star gossip and radio babble. *Dorothy and Dick* might be finished, but she wasn't. Somewhere out there was a story of the magnitude of Lindbergh, Sheppard and the stories of her past. Without the weight of *Dorothy and Dick*, she'd have the energy to pursue it.

twenty-five

 ## Dorothy

That Thursday she decided to risk Dick's venom and meet Johnnie for lunch at P.J. Clarke's. The loss of the radio show had reduced Dick to a barely coherent drunk, who depended on her even for pocket change. The explosive night that nearly destroyed Johnnie and her was his last burst of strength. She no longer feared that he could do violence to her or Johnnie.

They were still together, although she had been changed by that night in the Black Room. She had begged Johnnie to take her with him, and he'd refused. Although she still loved him, she knew they'd never be together. Her true love now was her career. She had to reclaim the journalistic respect she'd lost over the years and prove herself a professional once more.

It hadn't been a good morning. Upon wakening, she'd immediately thrown up the drinks she'd consumed the night before.

Just a week before Thanksgiving, and the holiday spirit already sparkled from the city. She liked the festivity of it, and wrapped herself in a maroon coat that smelled of wool and the perfume of a happier time. She hadn't seen Johnnie for several weeks, and when she met him in front of P.J. Clarke's, his appearance stunned her. Scarecrow-thin, he had the distended belly of malnutrition, and his once-golden skin had yellowed.

"You look gorgeous," he said, before she could speak. As a stiff wind struck them, he brushed the hair from his forehead. "That coat's your color. Matches your you-know-whats."

"Thought you said the ring did," she said, lifting the rose quartz he'd given her.

"That too. Depends on how hot you are. How hot are you, Miss Kilgallen?"

He never changed. She took his arm. Once they were sitting with their drinks, she would find a tactful way to question him about his health, encourage him to see a doctor.

Blowin' In The Wind blared from the jukebox, the voices of Peter, Paul and Mary in a consummate blend of purity and conviction.

Johnnie made a face. "That folkie stuff is everywhere now. Grow my hair long, give me a guitar and call me Dylan."

"It's just college kid stuff," she said. "But as I said in print, if I had a hammer, I'd take it to that song and a few more just like it."

"At least Sinatra's having as hard a time making the charts as I am." He pulled out a patio chair, looked into the tavern. "What's going on in there anyway?"

P.J.'s, which usually milled with bodies in motion, sat still, the people within frozen.

"Some game on the television?" she suggested. She slid into the chair beneath the Michelob sign. "It's a little chilly, but let's sit out here anyway for old times' sake. Be an angel and get me something to drink."

"Dom Perignon," he said.

"You don't even like champagne."

"But you dig it, and we're celebrating your return to journalism." His features blurred momentarily then came into clear focus. The sparkle had left his eyes. He looked even more gaunt than he had that time at Mt. Sinai.

"Why don't we try a mimosa?" she said. It's early. We could use the orange juice."

"Be back in a flash." He kissed her quickly. "A mimosa for the lady and a boilermaker for the tramp."

He didn't return from inside, and she grew irritated. Women still approached him the minute he was out of her sight. The men she could handle; the women were a different story. He knew how jealous she could get. She tried to send him a mental message. *Don't make me have to go in there and get you.*

She pulled back her chair anyway and stood. At that moment, he appeared at the door.

"It's about time," she said. Then she noticed that he carried no drinks, that his face was drained pale.

The music had stopped, replaced by the muffled buzz of a television. "What is it?" she asked moving closer to him.

"The President," he said. "He's been shot."

Dorothy never had a chance to talk to Johnnie about his health. Instead she witnessed, along with the rest of the nation, the whole surrealistic drama, replay after replay, narrated in Walter Cronkite's hushed tone, as if repeating it all would make sense of the senseless.

Dorothy and Johnnie sat on his velvet sofa, which they'd barely left since the assassination. Her children were flying home, and she'd have to leave soon. In the meantime, this was no time to worry about appearances. John Kennedy was dead, murdered. It was time to weep and to sit speechless beside someone she loved.

That night, as her driver headed toward home, she asked him to go around the East Side. On Fifth Avenue, Shelley Winters, exiting a restaurant with a group of friends, waved at her to stop. They embraced, shed more tears. "Pray with me at St. Patrick's," Shelley said.

"Of course," Dorothy said, hugging her again.

Afterwards, she stopped at the Stork Club, where Winchell and others sat, then Jim Downey's, and finally back to P.J. Clarke's for one last stop. A sign reading "No Music," now covered the jukebox. The unbelievable circle was complete.

The weekend was a collage of images: The black convertible. The pink suit. The blood. Then, the ghastly image of Lee Harvey Oswald cringing and clutching his abdomen as a man in a drab suit and fedora—a man with a pistol—was wrestled to the floor.

"Jack Ruby." She repeated the newscaster's identification of the man who had just shot Oswald on live TV. She looked at Johnnie. "I think I know that man."

 ## Johnnie

Last few days I'm wounded from all the unreal shit on TV. I'm a casualty when I begin a string of appearances in Ontario. My total collapse happens on stage in Windsor. This is the big fall, and it happens a stone throw across a narrow strip of water from Detroit City, so close to the town that turned on me.

I go down hard. Bam! A pile of tired, brittle bones.

This time it's over. Before, I was too invincible to die. Not this time. This is the instant that slams you into that dark space, all the way to a dimension in which you see the start of your life, then the finish. It's like the whole movie has played, has spooled out, and it can't be spliced, altered one frame.

It's over. It's so fucking over.

Death is a dream. I hear pure music. Sights are brilliant, cinematic marvels. There is perfection. It becomes a fight for death rather than life.

"No."

It's my own voice.

"No."

Another dream. I'm supine. I'm being rocked, gently like I'm strapped to a raft. No, it's not a sea under me. It's a road, and I'm aboard a vehicle. A solemn male voice speaks of an equinox. I beg someone, anyone, to prop my head to a rectangle of frosted light. Someone shades my eyes with dark glasses, and I'm lifted carefully.

Ghostly landscape rolls by. I know it in reverse from the trip to Niagara with Babe and Cornshucks.

It spreads now in muted springtime, a hallucinatory marvel under a black sun.

"This is a point in time," I say.

I don't know if anyone hears.

I'm sure of no time and place, but I fight like a mother-fucker. I see vague figures I know are doctors. They ignore the chart they post on the end of my bed.

"Too far gone."

I fight.

"Slow down, give it up."

I fight.

Heads shake gravely, side to side. Dead-still eyes observe. Hard-line mouths utter epitaphs.

I fight harder.

Once, keeping my eyes closed so not to lose a dream, I say to no one, "Black sun."

"He talking some old stanky blues," a man says.

Must be the big son of a bitch, all starchy white uniform over flesh the color of eggplant.

"You'll have to speak up, nurse," I say without raising an eyelid.

Another voice lands heavily. "You know who you are?"

"I'm Johnnie Ray."

"You know where you are?"

I don't answer. Somehow I'm sure it's not a doctor, not the starched nurse.

"You're in Montfiore."

"What?"

"Hospital in the Bronx."

I refuse to open my eyes. I look instead at my dream. "I was in Canada."

"You died there. More ways than one."

"When?"

"Weeks ago. You lost a Christmas, a new year, a birthday."

I give him no reaction, study my dream—ancient wonders, skies so old and blue, songs I wrote when I was a boy.

"Open your fucking eyes," the voice demands.

"Don't need to. See it all anyway."

"Shmucko."

"Where's Dorothy?"

"Away for a while."

"Can't hear you."

Rapid chuckle. "You know who this is?"

Suddenly I do, can't believe it. "Yeah."

"Really?"

"You're Lenny Bruce."

"Heh, heh, heh. You may now remove your blindfold."

I walk into the sun. It's cold, but March offers soft promises. Behind me, Phillip Matthews guides me with a hand on my back. Ahead, Dorothy leads with birdlike steps. Her form looks flexed as if she's frozen from her vigil. She and Phillip must have worn out their rosary beads.

At Phillip's Oldsmobile, Dorothy turns to face me. "I've asked Phil to stick close by you."

211

"Let's go home. We'll talk about it."

Emotions war in her eyes. Her brave little chin trills like a trumpet man's. I scan from her to Phillip. He seems to be hunched, weeping or ready to.

"Dorothy wants me to move in, help you for a while," he mumbles.

He helps fold me into the passenger seat, shuts the door, canters stiffly around the front of the car. I wait for him to get in, start the engine. I lower my window, watch it pass in front of my lady's face. Painful melancholia grabs my heart, then all time—past, present, future—seems to flee. I'm lost in an emptiness.

I squeeze Dotty's hand through the window, let it go, and the sedan carries me away.

twenty-six

 ## Dorothy

Dorothy spent the early part of 1964 helping with Robert Kennedy's campaign for the Senate. In February, she traveled to Dallas. Although she had not been assigned to cover Jack Ruby's trial officially, she knew there was a story there and planned on filing her own exclusive report.

She had lunch that Thursday with Ruby's two attorneys, Melvin Belli and Joe Tonahill. Joe showed her a ten-page letter he had written to J. Edgar Hoover, to each member of the Warren Commission and to Robert Kennedy. The letter requested all of the reports and minutes and evidence in the possession of the Warren Commission. Hoover refused to cooperate. The assistant attorney general's staff turned over material gleaned from more than fifteen hundred Warren Commission witnesses. Information concerning Oswald's assassination of the President would not be available, Tonahill was told, because it did not appear to be relevant.

"How could information about Oswald not be relevant?" she asked. "Why hasn't anyone written about this?"

Tonahill shook his head. "You tell me."

She filed her first assassination exclusive February 21.

The day her story appeared, Joe Tonahill summoned her to the defense table during the noon recess. Jack Ruby sat next to him, burly but exhausted looking, dark hair slicked straight back.

Tonahill was a huge man, pure Texas, and not much for small talk. "Mr. Ruby wants to talk to you," he said.

"Good," she replied. "I'd like to talk to him, too."

He made the introductions, then settled on the other side of the table.

Ruby continually rubbed his hands together, as if trying to wipe away his fear. One index finger ended abruptly, bitten off in a fight, she had heard.

"I'd like to compliment you on your composure," she said, trying to relax him. "I always appreciated your letters regarding *What's My Line.*"

"You're the best one on that show." He gave her the nervous smile of someone who was used to having his every move watched. "Here I am, should be in the hospital. Never happen though. Imagine, Crissake, I set half these cowboys up in my clubs. Now they're trying to lynch me. This is a felony on my record. Did you know that's a first?"

"What do you mean"

"Not one mark on my record like this," he said. "Once the trial's over, I might talk to you about it. You'd be amazed."

"What are your feelings about the trial?" she asked. "Are you anticipating questions about your sexuality?"

"Sure. I don't put moves on the girls at The Carousel. Because I'm their boss don't mean I'm not a gentleman. Single you get painted a funny way."

Tonahill moved in his chair. The recess was almost over.

"I would like to talk to you when this is behind you," she told Ruby.

He nodded, narrowed his eyes as if the light pained him. "You should be talking here with someone wearing medals the things I been through."

214

That night she answered her motel room's phone.

"It's August." The voice carried an inflection like others she'd heard today.

"Like the month," Dorothy said, as if completing his message. "This your home territory?"

"I'm calling from New Orleans," he said.

She stole a glance at her drink, looking lonely on top of the hotel's circular table. Should she admit she remembered him from Helen Gurley Brown's party? He was intriguing.

"August." She purposely sighed into the phone. "It's a bit late, and I've had quite a day."

"Do you ever get in the mood for Shrimp Creole, some great jazz?"

"Really." She sighed again. Then she ventured, "The woman you were with the night I met you—"

"I wasn't with her." He sounded as if he were smiling. "I was her escort."

"And she yours, I'm sure."

"Dorothy," he said, in three firm syllables. "If you're the reporter I think you are, you'll let your appetite pique for some Creole or Cajun food."

She carried the phone to the table and took a swallow of her drink. Then she opened her narrow notebook.

"What do you have in mind, August?" she said.

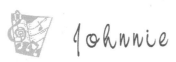

Johnnie

I sit on a park bench realizing it's been a month since I saw Dorothy off to Dallas. I'm wondering if things will be the same between us when I spot her coming across the green. She strides awkwardly, self conscious in slacks, frumpy sweater.

I stand to greet her. She removes enormous sunglasses to kiss me on the lips. When we sit down, she winds a wool scarf around my neck.

"I'm not an invalid," I say. I run a glance over her. "Some kind of disguise."

"Yes."

"Who you hiding from?"

"Start with Dick's cronies." Her eyes are round as if alarmed. "Go from there to just about anyone you wish to pick."

"Come on," I encourage her. "They can't kill us."

She takes a swipe at her windblown hair. "The hell they can't."

Something tells me Marilyn and Kennedy are names caught in her throat. Maybe others are there too.

As if to help solve the question, an elderly man stops at the bench. He's stooped and regards me out of the tops of his eyes.

"You're what's wrong with this fucking country," he says. Nodding agreement to himself, he trucks away.

Watching his thin legs, slack ass in the worn pants, I start to laugh. Dorothy looks about to cry, rummages through her purse.

"Nothing for the pigeons," she says.

We sit in silence. A breeze comes up, carrying small leaves, a hot dog wrapper.

"I testified yesterday for Lenny Bruce," she says, biting the inside of her cheek.

"Can you imagine him, coming into my hospital room? Asking me to get you to help him?"

"I told the court he's a very moral man."

"You believe it?"

"I believe he didn't violate the New York Statute on Obscenity." She pulls at an eyelash, breathes deeply. "I was asked about *motherfucker, shit, asshole* and plain old *fuck*."

"What happened to *cocksucker?*"

"I must have looked too innocent."

216

I think of that night in Chicago after Lenny's show. "You are."

"Told them I'd heard the words before."

"Yeah?"

"From James Baldwin, Tennessee Williams."

"Couple of cocksuckers right there."

A smile, thank God, tugs at her round mouth. She's quiet again for a long time.

I light two cigarettes, hand her one. She inhales and stares ahead at two Frisbee players. She smiles at a woman walking a baby stroller. I can tell by the way the woman stops, returns her smile, that she'll carry her recognition of Dorothy Kilgallen with her. "Guess who I see sitting in Central Park with some skinny dope fiend?" she'll tell a neighbor.

"You got claimed," I say.

"Wear pants and still can't hide." She rubs her cigarette ash out on the cement path, shakes the tobacco and filter fibe into the wind, rolls up the remaining paper, flings it.

"First woman I ever see field strip her smoke."

"First woman to do a lot of things."

I can see she's serious, yet not taking an ego trip. "Yep."

"Johnnie," she says, turning to study me. "I've got an exclusive interview with Jack Ruby. I leave again for Dallas tomorrow."

I feel like I'm aboard a glacier or riding those freezing Niagara Falls. Shadows from that alley behind the Flame Showbar fall darkly over me.

"Is it cleared?"

She looks at me, puzzled.

"I mean with the FBI, the CIA, the government, Jesus Christ, fucking Hoover, Johnson, whoever. Is it okay?"

I reach for her, hold her in my thin arms. I'm shaking and trying to ask her questions. My battery pack falls apart. I start cursing.

The old, stooped man has come back. He stands near a tree like he's spying.

After a moment, I let her go, square my shoulders. "I got a gig myself coming up."

She pulls away. "Too soon."

"At the Latin Quarter."

I can tell she's worried about how I'll stand up under the pressure. At the same time, she's thrilled. "Headlining? How long?"

The old man under the tree is grabbing his crotch like he's trying to clamp off a piss.

"*Mano en mano* with Johnny Puleo."

"The same Johnny Puleo that has the Harmonicats?" Her eyes go dim.

"Hand in hand. That's me doing the polka."

"Morrie's choice?"

"The only choice."

Mustering all the brightness she can find, she rises. "You'll kill 'em."

"Yeah, yeah."

"Must go. How did you get here?"

"Phillip."

"Come with me." She waves an arm into the wind. "I'm that-away."

"Gotta be here when he comes back." I study my watch. "About twenty minutes."

And there it is—that small, sad resigned smile. I wonder about the hand I'm playing. She's still willing to give up everything.

Or almost everything.

"This Jack Ruby thing," I say. "Be careful."

"After that, I'm going to New Orleans. Johnnie, I think I'm onto something."

"Jesus, is there an end to it? Is it worth disturbing the water that's finally coming to a rest?"

"It's what I do."

We kiss goodbye.

Watching her move swiftly across the green, I catch sight of the old man. He's doubled over, shifting his weight from foot to foot.

Approaching him slowly, I give him my Johnny Appleseed grin. "Restrooms aren't far away, Sarge. Can I help you locate one?"

"I'll wet myself, Junior, if you can't."

His thin fingers in mine, I assist him along a path, then break away. "Bear right at that fork in the road, and you can't miss it."

I don't go any farther. Holding a man's hand near public facilities, no matter he be young, old or in-between, isn't something I should be doing.

The sun hides, then jumps out from among the treetops. Pigeons run behind me like I might find something for them in my empty pockets. I see Phillip standing up near the bench. Two boys, two girls, college types, pass by. One is singing a Beatles song. The others strum imaginary guitars.

"I want to hold your hand," screams the singer.

When I reach Phillip, he's wearing a rare smile. "Kids," he says.

"Same kids that buy records," I say. I smile too, but it don't come easy.

twenty-seven

Dorothy

The case occupied her life as Johnnie once had. She finally made arrangements through the judge for a private interview with Ruby. Again Tonahill was the go-between.

"Well," he said. "Guess you know you're the first newspaper person to see him alone."

He led her to a small office behind the judge's bench. The four sheriff's guards agreed to remain outside the room. At the noon recess, Ruby joined them. He already looked older, more helpless, like a man moving toward his inevitable end.

"Good to see you again," she said, as Tonahill departed and they took their seats at the dingy metal table. "I want to talk to you about what happened. I want to tell your story."

"Better think twice about that," he said. "They're going to kill me is what's going to happen."

"Even if you're found guilty, you can appeal."

"They'll see I don't go down in history burnt by Texas. It's bigger than me and Dallas, so big I die and no one shows up dirty for it."

"No one can get to you in here, can they?"

"My brain is turning to cancer, so you tell me."

His eyes wandered around the room, the only room, the attorneys had assured her, that wasn't bugged.

"Who wants to kill you?"

"Who don't want me to talk? Go figure. You talking to me is cancer. But you're a reporter. You gotta chance the truth. What's going to happen to my family? Are they going to go after them after they eat my brain? Do you know the network, these people? The cancer cell labs?"

He was too rattled to make sense. An exclusive interview, and she couldn't get a comment worthy of print.

"Listen," she said. "I know that the whole truth has not been told. I've said so in print, and I'm going to say so in my book. The eyewitness who described Oswald to the police was too far away to see him. Who was behind it, Jack? The FBI? The Mob?"

"They're the same, in the same network. Why do you think Hoover won't cooperate? This so-called Warren Report won't listen. They'll march these witnesses out so they can go down like ducks in a shooting gallery."

"Why did you shoot Oswald? Tell me the truth."

He looked down at his empty, open hands on the table. "I used to love this country, no questions," he said. "Would you want Jackie Kennedy to have to go through a trial? Her little boy holding her hand—did you see that? So now they put cancer cells in my food, straight to my brain, so no one will believe me. Eight to five, you'll never print this. You're scared likewise. Blue ribbons we ain't going to get. I thought, Christ sake, they'll put my statue up in D-Town."

"D-Town? You mean Dallas?"

He shook his head. "Dago Town, Chicago—two, three blocks from the action. A little kid, and I run numbers for Al Capone."

"A Jewish boy in the Italian section."

"That surprise you?" He gave her a bitter look and chuckled. "You'd be amazed the things."

"What things?"

"The things you do to be made. What it means to have Mo's approval, his personal handshake."

A knock on the door was followed by Tonahill's lumbering return to the room. "It's time," he said.

Ruby leaned forward, his eyes tortured, pleading for help.

"But we've had only ten minutes," Dorothy said.

"Eight, to be exact. Keep in touch, Miss Kilgallen."

She caught Ruby in a last glance. His hands covered his face. "In my head, behind my eyes, I see the killing of my brain," he mumbled. "Can you imagine that? It's like Hitler if you want to know."

Later, she spoke with one of Belli's attorney's, a strictly business woman close to her age. "Who is 'Mo' to Jack Ruby?" she asked.

"Sam Giancana."

She'd heard the name, knew he was high in the Mob hierarchy. Was he the man she'd seen with Judith Exner, the brunette who'd been with August that night, the woman who was also rumored to have been Jack Kennedy's lover?

Links. It was all about links.

She pressed the attorney. "Ruby told me I'd be amazed at things a man would do to be made. What could he mean, and don't tell me it's the same as getting laid."

"Being a made man, taking someone out."

"Whack him?"

"Whack, clip, hit."

"Would Ruby do that for money?"

The woman gathered her folders, glanced at her watch.

"I'm trying to find out why Ruby wouldn't do it. Sorry, I've got to meet with our client."

"I don't think he'd do it for money," Dorothy said. "But he'd do it for fame, self respect in his old neighborhood."

The woman smiled, shook her head. "Not bad, Miss Kilgallen," she said. "Not bad at all."

With or without Jack Ruby, this was her story, hers alone. Crazy or not, Ruby feared for his life. This only supported the reports she'd already heard about witnesses being threatened by the Dallas Police or the FBI.

Through another source, she gained possession of the police log covering the department's radio communications after the assassination. The police chief, riding in the first car of the motorcade, directed officers to get a man on top of the overpass. Yet, the day after the assassination, he told reporters that the shots had come from the Texas School Depository and that he radioed officers to surround that building.

The description the Dallas police radioed of Oswald was provided by a steam fitter. He was more than one hundred feet away from the sixth-floor window where the kill shots were said to have been fired.

Late one night after she had returned from Dallas, she solicited Dick's help in an experiment.

"What do I have to do?" he asked. He'd already had too much to drink, but that didn't matter. She would be the clearheaded one.

She handed him a broom. "Go up to the fifth floor and lean out of one of the corner windows with this. Just don't fall—and don't shoot."

"Don't tempt me," he said, waving the broom, and she felt a chill, remembering the night she'd feared he would do just that.

She left the house, on East Sixty-eight Street, pacing approximately one hundred feet. If anyone were watching, they'd think she and Dick had devised a new parlor game. She looked up, squinted. No way could she discern Dick's features from this distance and this angle. Someone had lied.

The Warren Commission Report was due to be released in late September. Dorothy called in more favors and obtained one hundred and two pages of it, much dealing with Jack Ruby's testimony. Of course she wouldn't reveal her source, Jerry Sartor, a former journalist and colleague, who had acted as a liaison between the Commission and the FBI.

Convincing her publisher wasn't easy. This would be the first glimpse the public had of The Warren Report, probably the most anticipated document of the decade if not the century. Although it wasn't verbalized, she felt her publisher's reluctance to anger the administration. It was breaking news, she argued. She hadn't broken the law to obtain it. The newspaper couldn't afford to turn it down.

The ultimate decision was in her favor. The excerpt, with sidebars of questions and speculations, would run in three parts, starting August 18.

"The administration won't be happy," Johnnie told her on the phone when she shared her good news with him. "Guess you won't be going to any parties at the White House."

"Lyndon's a bore," she said. "Who wants to go to his parties? It's J. Edgar Hoover who scares me."

The report also stated that the steam fitter witness was in an excellent position to observe the window from which Kennedy was purportedly assassinated. Dorothy remembered trying to make out Richard's features from the street, and shook her head. The report was not telling the whole truth.

Three days after her first excerpt appeared in print, Julian told her that two federal agents were waiting downstairs. She wasn't surprised.

After the introductions were made, she said, "Do come in and have some tea."

One talked. One took notes. Neither drank tea. The talker, sharp featured and well-dressed, had smooth, freshly shaved skin and stark, prematurely white hair. His overweight partner, eyes enlarged by rimless lenses, was around the same age but looked years older.

"Miss Kilgallen," the talker said. "How did this material come into your possession?"

"Well, it wasn't John Daly," she said.

"I take it that's a joke?"

"An attempt at levity. John's the MC on *What's My Line.* He's married to the daughter of Chief Justice Warren."

"I know that," the agent said. "Look, Miss Kilgallen—"

"Mrs. Kollmar to you."

"Is that what Johnnie Ray calls you?"

"What my friends call me is none of your business."

"Everything about you is part of our business now, Miss Kilgallen, even your disrespect for President Johnson."

"You think I disrespect LBJ?"

"Perhaps you do. Perhaps you even find him boring. You don't like his parties. We're interested in all of it."

Jesus. They'd listened to her calls. The house had to be bugged. "I don't have anything else to say to you right now. You are aware that I'm writing a book."

"*Murder One,*" the talker said in a bored voice. "Already four years late at Random House."

"But, as my editor Bennett Cerf says, worth the wait," she countered. "Be careful what you say. You may see yourself in print."

The note-taker looked up at this. The talker glanced at him, then back at her.

"There's no need to threaten," he said. We simply want to know where you got the copy of the Warren Report excerpt. Are you going to tell us or not?"

Still shaken from the realization that her home phones were bugged, she replied, "You want me to name my source?"

"That's right."

"Sir," she said rising. "I'd rather die."

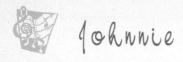 ## Johnnie

"It all started at the end of last year when you walked into the Latin Quarter," Phillip Matthews says.

He's rubbing my back with Tiger Balm.

"This your last can of the stuff?"

I'm in love with the powers of this Oriental salve.

"Yes. Brought it back from Hong Kong PR-ing that film with Bill Holden."

He grunts as he digs into my shoulders.

"But we're talking about you."

"Hong Kong, where you bought all them stylish rags?"

He spanks my bare ass. "Remember the Latin Quarter?"

"Couple months after my final rites."

"Reviews agreed you stripped down to your soul."

"Yeah, right there in front of the Harmonicats."

"That's when I realized I'd never give up on you. That and later when you showed such fortitude in Vegas."

"Came into the Tropicana to jeers, performed to cheers, left 'em in tears."

"Dorothy wrote that."

"Yes. She was there nearly every night."

His smile is contrite. "Oh, don't I know."

My bedroom is moody, blue afternoon shadows, Samantha thumping as she scratches her ear. No Raphael. He wasn't fibbing about his family's estate, even offered to stay, divvy up his inheritance.

"*Sayonara,*" Phillip had said.

Of course this was Phillip's way of taming the apartment's wildness. In a way it worked, but I still am on the sauce. I try not to flaunt it in front of Phillip.

"Got to keep my liver marinated," I quip when he shakes his finger at me.

On the edge of my bed, I reach for a towel from him, watch him turn to leave the room. His limp is bad today.

"Hop over here, Phillip," I say. "Let me work on that leg."

"Some other time," he says. "Things to do."

"Like what?"

"Like lining up a flight to L.A." He wipes his hands on a towel stuck in his belt, appraises me with a level gaze as I pull on a pair of jockey shorts. "I want to have a meeting before your West Coast dates."

"These dates. They amount to anything?"

"Truthfully, no. That's why the meeting. Morrie, Saul Rosen, you and me.

"Morrie ain't going to like what we have to say."

"You ain't going to like what Saul has to say."

I can tell, as Phillip lumbers down the hall, this is one trip west that won't be like old times.

Dorothy is heavy on my mind. I leave a message for her at Tabby's, one of the places we use as an answering service. Lately we're having trouble hooking up.

Later that evening I'm alone, half-drunk, fearing the night, when she calls. Her usual bell-toned gaiety is gone from her voice. She speaks in a windy rush.

"Johnnie, I must see you."

"When? Shit I can never find you."

"I heard your Liberty recording with Timi Yuro."

"And?"

"She sounded like Dinah Washington on speed." A small laugh. "Matter of fact, so did you."

"That good, eh?"

No laughter, no nothing on the line.

"What's wrong, baby?"

"Johnnie, I've got to talk to you. You're the only one I feel safe with."

"When?"

"When I get back. I'm going to California to meet Mark Lane."

"The guy with the book on JFK's assasination?" I'm thinking oh, no.

"Yes." She swallows something with ice in it. "I'm making progress on my book, too, the Kennedy stuff."

I don't know what to day to that. It makes me shiver under my skin. I reach for my glass, find it empty when I tip it up.

After a pause, she says, "Did you hear Malcolm X was shot down?"

I hadn't. I'm not sure who the cat is. "Maybe we can get together on the West Coast."

"You'll be there?"

"We'll compare dates."

"Take me to the beach, first thing." Her voice is dragging like a record losing its spin.

Mine must be as bad. "Come up for a nightcap, baby."

"Can't. I just chased a goodbye."

A goodbye. Her pet name for Seconal.

"Be careful," I tell her, trying to beat the click of her hang-up.

In front of my long windows, I look out at the night. Same lights, same moving line of traffic.

Same, only different.

twenty-eight

 Dorothy

Her head ached. The light from a blaze of candles hurt her eyes. She stared at the leather sofa, the too-silly drum table of the Black Room. Why was she here? Where was Johnnie? The phone rang. She grabbed it. "Johnnie?"

"Dorothy, it's me, Clara."

"Be careful what you say."

"You sound terrible, dear. Have you been ill?"

"Yes, ill." Clara wouldn't say anything incriminating. She wouldn't have to worry what those monitoring her phone heard now.

"I was just wondering. You missed our party for Sophia's new film last night."

The party, damn.

"Sorry. I'd written it down. This book has taken all of my time."

"Still, one has to think of one's friends."

"I think of you."

"Roland was hurt."

"Without me, you wouldn't know Sophia or anyone else. And you're concerned about one party?"

"Parties, plural. And it isn't the first time. I can't count on you anymore, Dorothy."

She closed her eyes trying to lock out the high whine of Clara's voice. Everyone wanted something from her. The station had wanted too much. *What's My Line* wanted too much. Her paper. Jack Ruby. Dick. The government.

"Clara, I'm not some piece of jewelry to be trotted out anytime you want to impress a guest. I'm not just writing a book on my career. I'm working on the biggest story of my life."

"Of course, dear. The JFK conspiracy."

"It is a conspiracy, and everyone involved in it is dropping dead left and right. Marilyn's death may even be part of it. My own life could be in danger." Oh, God, she thought. They were listening to every word she said. "I must go. I can't talk anymore."

"Very well. You clearly have more important things in your life than my parties. If you should need anything—"

"Goodbye, Clara. I'll talk to you later."

She slammed down the receiver before Clara could say another word. She'd be damned if she ever talked to her again. What the hell was she going to do? She couldn't use her home phone, couldn't trust what she might inadvertently say. From now on, she'd rely on public phones. It was the only safe way.

The pearls around her neck felt as if they were choking her. She needed another drink. She went to the bar to make it, then realized she was holding one. She drained the glass.

A man surprised her at the door. She shook her head to clear her vision. It was Babe Pascoe.

"Jesus, I didn't recognize you in that suit, Babe. Where's Johnnie?"

"He's in California, remember? Sorry to give you such a start. Your man let me in. He was right here. I thought you saw us."

"Oh, that's right." She felt confused. When had she argued with Clara? Where were she and Babe supposed to be going? He seemed to sense the confusion, answered the question for her.

"Rosehelen is waiting downstairs. Remember we had tickets for *Funny Girl?* Don't have to go, though, if it's a hassle."

"No, I want to." Now, she remembered. She wanted to see Barbra Streisand, the young singer for whom everyone had such high expectations. And she needed to get out of here, away from the eavesdroppers on her phone.

"I'm ready."

"All right," he said. "Here, we'd better zip your dress, though."

That's what they were doing to her. Making her absentminded, forgetful. "You must think I'm terrible going around unzipped."

"Hey, I can see how it must be hard to hang the way they got you going."

She tried to zip the dress, got it part of the way, couldn't budge the zipper.

"Damn. Would you mind?"

"No sweat." He stepped behind her, moved the zipper easily.

"It's this story I'm working on," she said. "They're bugging my phones, Babe. I don't know who's on my side and who isn't."

"Well," he said, taking her arm. "I'm on your side. You can count on that. And Rosehelen, too, always."

"And Johnnie?"

"He's on your side too."

"I know." Counting the people who cared for her made her feel better. She took a deep breath. "I have a new source, Babe. He's tied into the government, knows a lot about what did and didn't happen in Dallas that day."

"I'd be careful with everyone right now," Babe said. "You don't need to take any chances. Ready to split?"

"Of course," she said, impatient with his scrutiny and his solicitous manner. "What are you waiting for?"

He looked at her right hand so pointedly that she followed his gaze. She still held the tumbler as if it were part of her attire. "Oh this," she said, slamming it down on the drum table.

She nodded toward the phone and whispered as they left. "CIA. They listen to all of my conversations. Can't talk in here anymore. Not ever."

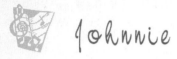 ## Johnnie

We hit L.A. a week before my first engagement. I'm booked off Sunset in a club I've never heard of. It's a whole new game out here. The action is moving to the Strip again—kids everywhere on the street, marijuana in the night air.

"Lotta boo," I say to Phillip. He's tooling a rental, looking out the window. I'm slumped down with jet lag.

"Boo," Phillip says, laughing. "Tomorrow is Halloween."

The sky is a lustrous dome ahead of the car. Phillip takes his time. Cars honk along our procession.

"Where's the San Fernando Valley?"

He jerks a thumb at the iridescent night. "Over the hill."

"My sister Elma remarried, came out here couple years ago. I've got to see her."

"You will," Phillip says. "Tomorrow night at the Halloween party."

That throws me. "What?"

"I've rented Vic Damone's old place in West Hollywood, given her the number."

In a trance I feel the car turn off Sunset Strip. I hear Damone's sweet voice, indulge a memory of Dorothy's small hand in mine as he crooned *An Affair to Remember.*

"You going to be all right?" Phillip's hand squeezes my shoulder.

"She might be here tomorrow."

"Dorothy?"

"Yeah."

"I know. I gave her the number too."

I can't believe the night. All this and Halloween coming up.

Next day we meet in Saul Rosen's office. It's typical old Hollywood, lot of blond wood, beachy furniture. Saul and Morrie are waiting when Saul's secretary escorts Phillip and me in. We all watch her ass when she departs to her front desk. Like most women aware of my career, she seems a bit awed by me. These types, admittedly, have become scarce.

Four men at a desk. Suits not too dark—lots of heliotrope or pastel in shirts, ties, socks and in Morrie's hanky. Cigar smoke hangs above the desk, which means Morrie's been here a while.

All is friendly at first, and I can tell Morrie is thankful I'm still alive. Saul's always proven himself a straight shooter, so I'm glad when he becomes serious.

Serious as a chancre.

"Johnnie, there's only one way to say this. You're broke."

First one I look at is Morrie. I expected this to be bad, but Jesus. Sunset and Vine clash softly outside. A rude opulence laughs from the room's corners.

Saul reads my mind. "Costs keep escalating. I've sent you warnings. You're like always one step ahead of the storm."

Phillip stands. "Johnnie's been taking less and less percentage."

"True," Saul says. He looks pale, a century old.

"Why didn't you cut back everyone else?" Phillip stares down Morrie. "Everybody but Johnnie keeps eating high on the hog."

Morrie waves his arms like he's trying to escape a strait jacket. "Goddammit, I ain't taking the rap over here. Every time I want to discuss finances, Johnnie is smashed or laid up in a fucking hospital."

"No one but Johnnie could have survived his schedule," Phillip says, pointing at me. "He's been your meal ticket. It's time he's treated with respect."

Right now, don't ask what I'd do for a drink. "How broke is broke?" I say.

233

Saul don't move a muscle.

I snap my fingers. "Tap city?"

Saul covers his face with vein-lined hands. "That's a correct assessment, thanks to the IRS."

"And just how bad are they on my ass?"

"I should be able to fend them off," Saul says, "but, Johnnie, they might lien your folks' farm. It's still in your name."

"Jesus, I can't have that happen."

Saul starts mumbling, looking for some papers. I'm shaky, but I get to my feet, lean across the desk on my knuckles. "Look at me, Saul."

A crack splits his brow. Genuine sympathy shines in his eyes. Some fright, too.

"Okay." My voice trembles. "You've always been a friend to me, Saul, and I'm going to trust you with some requests."

Phillip places a hand on my elbow.

"It's okay," I say to him. Then to Saul, "I want you to fire everyone on the payroll except you and Phillip."

"Everyone." He repeats the word and looks smack at Morrie. "What about Mr. Lane's contract?"

I turn so Morrie can see my face. "Mr. Lane's always said if it ever came to a point we weren't compatible, if the contract wasn't working, he'd tear it up." I almost choke, but I manage to keep my voice level. "So, fish it out of your files, and we'll make confetti out of the motherfucker."

Outside the office I catch up with Morrie. He seems to have lost his car or is searching the streets for a ride.

"Can Phillip and I drop you anywheres?" Christ, I don't know how to talk to him. Maybe I never did.

"No," he says, shading his eyes. "Gladys is picking me up for lunch."

We stand on the corner. Memories swarm like bees between us. I feel I can't let loose of the guy but can think of no gesture or speech that will give rise to anything kindred.

"You know, Johnnie," he says, finally. "I was nothing but a song-plugger when I found you. A stupid, fucking song-plugger."

"Well."

"But I knew what I had."

"Ah, shit, Morrie."

"I've always known what I had with you. I saw things in you all the smart sonsabitches missed." He holds out his hand. I shake it. "The trouble was, Johnnie, you must not of seen it, or you wouldn't have been so hell bent to throw it away."

"I got some left, Morrie. I know I do."

His grip tightens. I sway. He pulls me upright. "I see it too, kid. Let's just hope someone else does."

We part, and he stumbles backward. I murmur so long, and he gives me a bewildered grin.

"Meeting the wife," he says. "Think that's her waiting up there at the wrong corner."

Like she don't know Hollywood and Vine. Like he can see that far, pick out his wife's car in all that traffic.

twenty-nine

 Johnnie

Damone's place on St. Ive's Drive is the most. A view of all L.A. hits you outside the sliding glass doors. A white piano sits on orange carpet in a perfect party room.

Guests start arriving for our Halloween bash—tanned smoothies from Phillip's world, a few old ghosts from mine like Chip O'Hara and Marcy the stripper. She's the blond Dorothy still steams about from that long-ago New Year's Eve.

My sister Elma and her husband arrive. Seeing her lifts my spirit. We make plans for a reunion with the folks. I promise myself to save Dad's farm from the IRS.

Phillip appears fresh after a hard day. The guy's a rock. First the meeting at Saul's office, then he called on half the booking agents in L.A.

Everyone is in some degree of costume. Phillip wears a paisley mask to match his psychedelic Peter Max flared trousers. I've put on a tangerine pirate shirt the same shade as the carpet and a hoop earring that clips onto my so-called "good" ear.

Don't ask what blond Marcy is wearing. Ain't enough there to tell.

We're clinking glasses, telling lies, yuk-yuking when another couple flounces in. Cornshucks and Babe Pascoe.

Phillip watches my face beam. I figure this is more of his doing.

"We're in 'Frisco," Babe says, pumping my hand. "Johnny Otis calls us for his review tonight. Shit, we don't open there 'til next week, so I ball the jack, and we're here in seven hours."

Cornshucks is slinky, radiant. Her hair springs from her scalp like steel wool dyed the color of my pirate shirt.

"My, my," I say, appraising her trimmed figure, wigless dome.

"Just a shadow of my former self," she says, making a full turn for me.

We jive ass a bit, me thinking of Otis's review tonight, feeling a pang, that old trooper's wish to be there.

She pulls me into the kitchen. "Johnnie, I got a show primed for the Latin Quarter, late December. I mentioned it to Phil on the phone."

"Jesus," I say. "I'm happy for you."

She grips my shoulder. "Listen, Bluebeard—"

"Blackbeard, if you're talking buccaneers."

"I'm talking cotton, fool," she says. She flicks my earring with a carmine fingernail. "Listen."

"I'm listening."

"I want your skinny ass up on that stage with me."

"If I'm in New York, I'll drop by to see your show. You know that."

"See my show? Shee-it. You in it, sharing my billing."

My knees feel that one. "Ah, Shucker, that's nice, but the last time I shared that stage was with the fucking Harmonicats."

"What's wrong with that?" Her grand smile sparkles. "You play a little blues harp yourself."

Later, when I know I won't break out in tears, I act cool in conversation with her, Babe and Phillip.

Alone with Babe, I tell him how much I've missed him. "No one can match your beat."

"There's drummers every corner."

"There's drummers and there's musicians like you," I tell him. "By the way, how's married life?"

"Like Korea, 1951," he says, grinning.

First time I've ever heard him make light of his war. "Vietnam going to be another one of those?"

"Worse."

"How's the Shucker's little brother?"

"Let's just say Carlton never made the Yankees." Then that tough Hell's Kitchen face softens under his road whiskers. "Best we run, Johnnie."

"I love you, Babe."

"Love you too, J.R." he lays his rough cheek against mine. "We go back a ways, pal."

"Yep."

"Me and Rosehelen, we don't forget."

"I was out of it, but I know you came to see me in that Bronx hospital."

"Yeah." He pulls up his coat sleeve, checks his watch. "Phil said Dorothy might drop in."

"Maybe, if she makes connections."

"Give her our love."

"Will do."

"Last time I saw her, Johnnie, she didn't look good."

"She's trying to solve JFK's death all by herself," I say. Pondering, I add, "It's like she's fighting to salvage her career."

Cornshucks comes up behind me. "Sometime we look for salvation in all the wrong places."

"You can bet I did," I say, but she and Babe are leaving, carrying their music and their wisdom with them.

Dorothy shows up late. A few diehards still listen as I pound the piano, impersonating Damone's young movie star wife, Pier Angeli, her role in some awful bible flick.

Thank God blond Marcy has split with some guy looks like Johnny Weissmuller's younger brother.

Dorothy is stiff but polite. It's plain she's waiting to get me alone. We steal away to a study, toss back shots of vodka. She relaxes some, sits in a leather chair. She's in a black suit, pearls woven into her upswept hair.

"Who are you supposed to be?" she asks. "Errol Flynn?"

"I could be, we go into a bedroom."

She smiles. "I checked into a Ramada Inn between Venice and Santa Monica." She slaps her hips. "Should have changed clothes."

The room is stuffy, warm. The last thing we need is another drink. I pour us more anyway. She drinks and takes a deep breath. It's plain to me she's trying to hold herself together.

"I shouldn't be out like this," she says.

I'm confused. "Like what?"

My question goes by her.

"You promised to take me to the beach," she says.

I drive the rented Oldsmobile. Behind the wheel, I'm no A.J. Foyt, but I find a fissured strip of asphalt so close to the moonlit beach, so full of ocean smell that I relax, rid my ears of metal.

Dorothy jumps out of the car, and I follow. We join up on the sand. The air hasn't lost all its summer. Fires burn in the distance, and Halloween screams are faint against my naked ears.

Southward, a boardwalk displays paint-worn structures to the sea, their pastels reflecting a trio of night rummagers searching under boardwalk lamps.

Dorothy runs shoeless to the waves. A phosphorescent glow brightens the pearls in her hair. I give chase until our hands meet. Cold froth breaks against her dress. I try to stand firm against the undertow, but I'm too weak. We pull one another in opposite directions.

"Dotty."

"No."

"It's sweeping us out."

We go under. I see the orange of my pirate shirt, her pale face in the black water. I taste the sea and feel its ever-living force. It yields for a millisecond, and I break the churning surface.

"Johnnie."

I flail my arms, hook her slender neck in my right bicep. We ride the sea as it slides toward the beach, and I fear I'll splinter her neck to stay afloat a crest. I loosen her as the current carries us ashore.

My face against hers, I feel her gasps. A cloud obscures the moon, makes an equinox. After a time, I feel strong enough to urge her, and we crawl like wayward toddlers to dry sand.

"My God," I say. "What the fuck are we doing?"

She shrugs, then shouts. "My pearls."

I touch them in her wet hair, and they cascade into my palm. "Luck," I say.

"Of the Irish," she says.

At the car, I dig wallet and keys out of my wet pants. I'm about to open the car door when a police prowler grinds onto the strip and swings its spotlight on the two of us.

We freeze. I wrap an arm around her wet back. A tremor plays her body like a tune, and I fear she'll break into pieces.

"Late to be taking a dip." He's left his spotlight on, stands soaked in its beam with us.

"Officer." Somehow I've found a voice. "You'll have to speak up. I'm Johnnie Ray, and my hearing aid is on the front seat."

He slowly moves toward the car's window. He's in a larger-than-life looking uniform, and in a funny thought, I think what if he's an imposter in costume? The ominous patrol car emits static and radio words that blow that thought. His leather squeaks as he puts one hand on his holster.

He looks from me to the car's interior, then back to Dorothy. "What's your name, Miss?"

I know she answers, but I don't hear it. A chilling wind has broken free along the beach.

"This your car, Mr. Ray?" Flat tones but decibels higher now.

"Rental," I say. I get a good look at him. He's older than at first sight, face an outbreak of fine lines.

"Open containers," he says, moving his eyes for a second to the car again.

Now I feel the fear. Dorothy must be terrified. "What?"

His uniform glints as he shifts his weight. "Them itty bitty kind the airline give out."

"Miss Kilgallen flew in today," I say. "She collects them."

"She collect them empty or full?"

"They been empty for hours."

"You really Johnnie Ray?"

"Yes. But please don't ask me to cry."

An actual chuckle is what I hear. "Know what I almost said when you told me who you are?"

Silence from me, and then I feel Dorothy's hand pull away from me. Her voice is hard on this desolate strip.

"You almost said, 'Yeah, and I'm Little Richard,'" she says. "Right?"

"Well, I'll be goddamned."

The man gives a little one-finger salute and hustles to his car. He ignores his radio, eases into his seat, pulls the prowler so close I can smell its interior.

"Where's home tonight, Mr. Ray?"

"Washington Street, not far," Dorothy answers.

"I'll see you get away here okay."

I hear that. "We're a little shaky, sir. Both been hospitalized recently."

"Oh?" He's looking up and down the beach. His stare is cold as the night. "You folks got no call to be out here like this. Now ease that Olds on out of here."

"I'm a tad rusty behind the wheel, but I'll do my best."

"I know you will, Johnnie," he says. Then he's barking in his radio, pulling out in a low screech.

Next to me, Dorothy says something I can almost hear about having to pee, but I can tell the encounter with the cop has left her terrified.

Salt and sea on our lips, we fuck like there's no tomorrow, desperately, lost in the getaway of it, lost in the our-song of it. Lost, lost, lost. Finally, mercifully, we fall into a sensationless limbo. Then in the faint dawn light, we trip over our pile of wet clothes, find light switches, and I guide her into the bathroom.

Standing under steaming water, I massage her shoulders, press my persistent cock against her soapy ass. In the brightness, I notice her body's changes. Jesus, it's been so very long since we've been naked together. The drum tightness is gone from her flesh, not as much rosiness—small bruises, a large, mean one staining her arm above and below her right elbow.

She turns and in her eyes, there's that hard, cold blueness, more deep set than I remember.

"You examining me?" she asks, water flying from her lips. Before I answer, she's moved away to turn off the water.

"Christ, Dotty," I say. "You look great compared to me." True. "I'm a cadaver with half a hard-on."

She sweeps the shower curtain out of her way and nearly falls stepping over the tub's edge. She flings a towel into my chest.

My face in the towel, I mumble how young she still looks. Her hand reaches in, begins masturbating me. My knees buckle. She releases me with a flourish.

"I think you've had enough."

"Never," I lie.

Our eyes meet when we're dry, standing naked against the night fears. We swallow Seconals and seek the driest part of the tangled bed.

"Here come the killing hour," I say.

Her face is stoic. I swear I can hear her body buzzing like she's plugged into a socket.

"Still scared?" I ask. She'd been convinced during our wet drive from the beach we'd be intercepted, killed as fugitives.

"Think I'm paranoid, like everyone else does?"

I don't answer soon enough.

"Don't pretend you can't hear me."

"I always hear your voice, Dorothy," I say. It's true. For some reason, I'm tuned to her like no other voice or sound.

"Johnnie, listen to me." Her breasts spill lightly against my side. "I know more facts than any reporter about the assassination. And I'm the only one willing to publicly attack the Warren Report."

"I know that."

"Johnnie, our president's head was blown away, and the government is lying about where the shot came from. Don't you care?"

"Yes," I say, "but different theories—"

"When the back of a man's skull and brains are blown into a goddamned phoenix behind him, and nearly every witness agrees the kill shot came from ahead of the motorcade, should I clam up about what I know and merely report the next Broadway flop?"

"What do you know?"

"I know Oswald was a pawn. I know Ruby killed him, and I know, in a matter of time, Ruby and others will be killed."

"Ruby? He's locked up." I get out of bed, stand rocking back and forth. I'm sick, wishing the pillskies will kick in. She sits up, dark hair against a propped pillow.

"Melvin Belli won't let the state kill him, but Ruby will be killed."

"By someone higher up?"

"You talked about someone higher up when you were violated in that Detroit alley."

"That happens out there amongst 'em. I told you about the sins of night after we ran with Lenny Bruce."

"After Detroit, you talked Sinatra plus the Mob, plus the law."

I rub my face. My mouth is so dry I can hardly reply. "A triangle."

"Well, try the Mob, the CIA and the FBI," she says. "When I return from New Orleans, I should know more. I'm meeting with a D.A. there who's investigating the conspiracy."

For a short moment, I believe she wants me to offer to go with her. I head into the bathroom, return with more water. We drink with trembling fingers, spilling half on the bed.

"We're a triangle," I say low like a child, hoping not to be heard. "You, me and Phillip."

"No. If there's a triangle, Phil and I are in the same corner."

"One corner will always be yours," I say. I sit on the bed. She leans into my lap. I feel her kiss on my penis. "You've always been the one, Dotty. That's the only thing I know for sure."

"Oh, God," she says, raising her mouth to kiss my lips.

"Equilateral," I say from a lost childhood school lesson.

"Oh, God," she says again.

"Impressed?"

"Yes."

"Means indestructible. Three equal angles—you, me, our careers."

"No, Johnnie," she says. "It was you, me and Dick."

Fever rages along my skin. I knew a word, for Christ's sake. *Equilateral.* A fucking word.

"You and your damn parlor games."

"Equilateral," she whispers, and the word rushes me as if she's screamed it. "Means indestructible, yes. It also means tomb."

"One, two, three, wham," I say. Ellington's metronome.

I walk from the bed to the window. The motel is California style, two stories wrapped around a pool. I gaze down at vehicles, hear their echoes as they race for the Pacific. L.A. madmen, crazy women, on the same paths since the first studios, the first unreal, imaginary, play-acting, lying sun-up.

"Come back," she calls. "Hold me."

My outline must look whittled too thin, brittle in the window's rectangle. I run the one question I've wanted answered all night over my tongue.

"You doing this investigation just to stay on top?"

"What would you do to stay on top?"

"I'd risk only so much."

"Me too." She moves across the bed on her hands and knees, a white cat. "Now tell me, what would you do if you'd lost it, wanted to get back on top again?"

"Anything," I say, feeling chilled.

"There's your answer."

I start another question, let it fade into the room's blue shadows.

"What were you going to ask?" she says.

"Nothing."

The white cat turns her tail to me. "Then stick it to me, Johnnie Ray, before the *goodbyes* knock us out."

thirty

Dorothy

Everyone was afraid of what she knew, even other reporters. No one wanted to talk about the fact that The Warren Report was concealing the truth, for whatever reason, about the assassination. Even *Nightlife* backed off after inviting her as a guest. When she showed up with her file bulging with notes, she was greeted by a producer in her dressing room and asked not to discuss the subject or her book.

"Too controversial," she was told. "Don't even bring it up."

"Then why did you invite me?" she countered. "You know it was to discuss the conspiracy. What changed your mind?"

The producer shrugged. "This is television," he said, as if that should explain it all.

She lost interest in her *Voice of Broadway* column. Who cared if Elizabeth Taylor and Richard Burton reserved an extra hotel room just for Elizabeth's wardrobe? She could barely muster the malicious energy to report Ava Gardner's costly little tantrum at the Regency, involving spaghetti sauce and broken furniture. Tired of gossip and bored with stars, she needed time to work without interruption on *Murder One*.

November had begun with snow flurries. Her trip to California was a blur of furious action, full of panic and recklessness. Had

Johnnie felt in their night together how much she needed his support? Did he remember all the times she'd been in his corner?

On November 7, the snow stopped. Dorothy chose a black gown with bat-wing sleeves for *What's My Line?* The dress was cut so low that she needed more foundation to cover her décolleté than her face. In the dressing room, she sat before the mirror as Marie applied her false eyelashes piece by piece.

"Makes them look more natural this way," Marie said. "The way the British models do. No more shaggy look for you."

Dorothy chewed her lip as she regarded her haggard appearance in the mirror. "Maybe I could use a little shaggy."

"Nonsense. You've got your sparkle back, you do. Must have been your trip to the West Coast."

Little did she know, Dorothy thought. "It was quite a trip."

Marie dusted a fluffy powder puff over her face, against her closed eyes. "More work on the JFK story?"

"Yes, very cloak and daggerish."

"Tell me."

She couldn't of course. She'd told all she dared to tell. Now it was time to stack up all she knew, go through it page by page, gather her courage to fill in the gaps. "I'll not give up."

"You'll get to the bottom of it if anybody can."

She met Marie's dark eyes in the mirror, brushed the powdery residue from her cheeks. "If it's the last thing I do, I'm going to break this case."

"Well, you just be careful. Here." She pressed a tissue against Dorothy's lips. "You really do look beautiful, like a star yourself."

Dorothy's vision blurred. Why did she feel so close to tears? The woman was just being kind. Damn, she shouldn't have had that last martini. She couldn't go before the camera a blubbering mess.

"There are those," she said, "who think I bear a resemblance to Sophia Loren."

Marie drew back, studied her reflection with an expression Dorothy couldn't begin to read. Slowly, she nodded. "I can see that."

"You can? You can really see it?"

"Oh, my yes," Marie bounced back. "There's certainly a resemblance, all right. The eyes, I think. Yes, the eyes."

"I don't really see it myself," Dorothy said, but she had to bite her lip and look away to hold back tears.

She ran into Bennett Cerf in the hall. He was a gentle, monochromatic man—suit, hair, glasses, voice all the same tone. He never pushed her, although she'd owed him *Murder One* for more than four years now. Away from the show, he was her editor at Random House, but on the show, he treated her like a colleague. Two weeks ago, he'd walked in to find her sobbing about her poor job of guesswork that night.

"It's just a game," he'd told her.

It wasn't a game to Mr. T. though. He gave her a friendly wave as she and Bennett filed past. She'd show him tonight.

"I read the chapters you gave me last week," Bennett said. "I like it."

"Wait until you see the rest."

"The Kennedy part?"

She nodded. "I have a stack of files this thick." She showed him with her hands, then noticed they were shaking.

"You're okay?" Bennett asked. "You're safe and all?"

She couldn't think about that right now. She needed only to keep a clear head for the show. "As safe as any reporter," she said.

On the show, she was as quick as she'd ever been, besting Arlene, Bennett and Tony Randall by identifying, with damn few clues, a woman who sold dynamite for a living.

"You're on tonight," Bennett whispered.

Joey Heatherton, blond and breathy, was the mystery guest, on her way to entertain troops in Vietnam, she said.

Then the Kool commercial. Then another guest. At the end of the show, with just moments remaining, Dorothy identified a woman sports writer in record time.

"Good heavens," John Daly exclaimed.

Take that, Mr. T, Dorothy thought as she flashed what she hoped was a gracious smile. The panel exchanged rapid goodbyes as the show wound up.

"Goodnight, Dorothy Kilgallen," Daly said.

"Goodnight," she mouthed.

In her dressing room, Marie handed her the phone.

"He insisted on waiting," she said, holding her hand over the mouthpiece. "Said his name is August."

Taking the phone, she tried for her stage voice. "Yes, this is Dorothy Kilgallen."

His soft voice came to her ear swiftly. "Your shrimp got cold, so I came to you."

She made a quick getaway from the studio. At P.J. Clarke's, she picked out a table deep within the tavern and ordered two vodka martinis.

"Someone's joining me," she explained.

True, but not for an hour. This would give her time to think, to drink both cocktails before August arrived. She felt a surge of excitement lift her as she drank. Was this corner dark enough for such a meeting with this strange, enigmatic man?

How fascinating he was, how game, to lead her to the truth, no matter the price. A fearless man, a man unlike any she'd met. At first he had flirted, made subtle advances, but sex was too soft for this hard man, and it was certainly not what she wanted. Sex was never and would never be the way it had been with Johnnie.

Johnnie. She'd call him here, from a pay phone. J. Edgar Hoover himself couldn't eavesdrop. But first, she'd order another round. "Make them doubles," she requested.

She found the pay phone she'd used so many times before and dialed the Hollywood number. Music mixed with Johnnie's voice as he answered.

"Hi, Johnnie," she said. "This is Esther Williams."

Not fooled, he laughed into the phone. "Dotty, I don't believe it. I just finished watching you."

"Was I good?"

"The best. Are you okay, baby? You sound funny. Did you catch cold from your swim in the ocean?"

"It's the phone. I'm at P.J. Clarke's. Can't use the ones at home. I told you, they're bugged."

"If you say so."

"They are, Johnnie. This is not something I made up. I'm meeting someone tonight, a government official who I think will fill in some gaps. He insists on meeting with me before I go to New Orleans."

"Can you trust him?"

Good question, one she hadn't been able to answer herself. "Trust? You're the only one I ever trusted."

"I never betrayed you, baby. I just couldn't let you walk out on your family, not for a guy like me."

"I miss the love, Johnnie."

"You got all of it, Dotty. You always will have."

A click sounded on the phone.

"What's that?" she said. "Is that on your end?"

"Nobody here," he said. "I'm spinning Cornshucks' latest record. Can you hear her?"

Cornshucks' LP played in the background. She could make out, *At Last,* the Etta James hit. "Barely, but she sounds great."

"Top of the charts without compromising her sound or her soul. Can't imagine how that would feel. Look, Dotty. You sound shaky."

"I'm okay. I told you."

"I'm afraid for you, getting into this conspiracy thing so deep. It's so unreal, so spooky. But do you really think you're being followed, that people are listening into your conversations?"

"Yes, goddamn it. I thought after being with me again you'd understand."

"I'm trying, baby, but you're on a fucking public phone. J. Edgar Hoover can't hear you now."

"I don't know. Maybe they're bugging your line."

"We'll talk about it when I see you." She could hear the finality in his tone. He was not convinced, thought she was going off the deep end. No point in a long-distance argument, especially since someone might be listening in.

"I need to see you again," she said. "I'll show you the notes for the book, the stuff no one's seen. This is the story of the century."

"Okay. I was planning on coming out for Thanksgiving, but I'll come next week. We'll meet someplace private, talk about it."

"All right," she said, although it wasn't. It just wasn't enough. "I love you, Johnnie Ray."

"I love you, Miss Kilgallen."

She couldn't remember how long she'd been holding the phone like this, her forehead pressed against the wall. She glanced at her hand, wrapped tight around the empty glass, thought of Jack Ruby's stub of a finger. The rose quartz glowed as if lit from within. Tiny hands. Cute feet. What had Johnnie said about her feet?

A hand gripped her arm from behind. With a start, she whirled around. August stood smiling in his same navy suit, the same American flag in his lapel.

"Here you are," he said, his drawl soft and low.

"You needn't grab me like that."

"You weren't at the table. I came looking."

"Looking. We're both looking."

"Seek and ye shall find. Let's have a drink, talk."

He helped her back to the corner table, where two fresh martinis stood. She couldn't remember ordering them, didn't know how long she'd been on the phone with Johnnie. She had been on the phone with Johnnie, hadn't she?

"He's flying out next week," she said, lifting her glass to August.

"Who's flying out?"

"Johnnie Ray. He doesn't believe me, about the phones and the FBI." Why was she going on like this? She couldn't seem to shut up.

"No one believes until they've been through it," he said. "I saw your show tonight. You were brilliant. Lovely."

The compliment felt impersonal, an observation made by a stranger, which this tall, quiet man really was. He happened to be a nice-looking stranger, one who wore too many navy suits, probably because some woman once told him they matched his eyes. His short blond hair, shorter than the trend even for government officials, made him look more conservative than he was. They were two people devoted to the same cause, nothing more. They would never be anything more.

"Better than my show last month. I was terrible, broke down and wept after the show. Bennett saved me."

"From what?"

"Humiliation."

"You should never feel humiliated. You have more right guesses than anyone else on the show."

"That's what my make-up woman says, but she's been with me from the start. How do you know?"

"I'm interested."

Dorothy tried to read his features, his dark blue eyes. "What's your real interest?"

"You, of course."

"We both know better than that. Why are you risking everything to help me?"

"Risk is what I handle best."

"You do want the truth to get out?"

"The truth demands the ultimate risk."

"I must have the truth. That's what I handle best."

"Maybe you should be careful whose truth you handle."

In the game of Maybe, he was the winner. She reached for her glass, couldn't quite navigate. He helped lift it to her lips.

Music came from somewhere. *Hang On Sloopy*. The closest thing to a love song today, Cornshucks aside.

"He's flying out in a week," she said. "Johnnie Ray."

More music. Beatles and Byrds and Rolling Stones. Loving feelings and yesterdays and turn, turn, turn. *Get Off Of My Cloud, Eight Days A Week, Mr. Tambourine Man*. Music pressed into her pores, the way Marie had pressed the powder. She managed to walk, leaning on his arm, managed to lift glass after glass. Important to sit straight in the chair, to sit like a lady, Dorothy Mae. Always sit like a lady.

"We fell in a doorway once, Johnnie and I. Babe found us there, picked clean as chickens."

Had she said it aloud, or was it a stray thought drifting through her brain? No, she could see the blur of his face, the sympathetic nod.

"Those things happen, even to people like you."

"He nearly died. Babe took us to emergency, Sinai." She chuckled as the next thought fluttered past. The curtain around the bed, her skirt up around her waist, their laughter. This time she didn't speak. Why tell anything to this stranger who stared into her thoughts?

"Here. Have some more," he said.

"That's better," she said. At least his voice was warm, the Texas drawl urging her to the safety of a drink.

Shadows lunged at her from the hall like the man who had grabbed her arm in the dream. Not a hall, a tunnel with a narrow circle of light at its end. The ladies room must be there. Shadows loomed out again like bats. She'd had too much vodka. Couldn't trust it anymore. She saw apparitions that weren't there, edited existing scenes to surreal blurs.

More shadows, larger. She tried to dodge them, stumbled. "Hang onto me," a voice said. "Let me help you."

She needed bed, sleep, a pill to sleep, to push back the morning, give her time to catch up. The elevator creaked with its load. Had to get it fixed. Just spend the money and do it.

It was old and ugly, but she loved this elevator. Dorothy pressed her cheek against its cold wall, closed her eyes and sailed straight up.

Now, it was just bed. She twisted under the pressure of the covers. How did she get here? Something wasn't right.

"What's wrong?" She raised her head, felt warm fingers on the back of her neck. "Hold me there until I find a dream."

"Be still. You'll find it. Everything is as you like it."

"But the bed. It's Dick's, not mine."

She twisted in the darkness, heavy, so heavy was the weight on her chest. Not her bed anymore, this room of clocks. This was the master bedroom, not her retreat on the fifth floor. And her eyelashes, those tiny fragments of glued-on human hair. She must remove them. Dorothy Kilgallen never slept in her false eyelashes.

The Valium was right there, offered on an imaginary tray. Her fingers fumbled, then pressed the tablets into her mouth. Thick fingers. Were they really hers? She saw movies of Ruby's hands, her hands, her arm of bruises.

"How can a dream leave a bruise?" she asked.

A chuckle answered her, then more tablets. She tried to argue, to ask questions, but the night fell over her like a blanket. No more fight left. Fingers at her lips. She went ahead, swallowed them like pills, like pillskies, Johnnie would say.

"Johnnie, why aren't you here? Johnnie, I'm so afraid."

thirty-one

 Johnnie

She's dead.

She died in her sleep. News of it above the fold of the *L.A. Times* stops my hand mid-way to my mouth. I lose my grip on the piece of what Morrie used to call grease toast, and it falls slowly in distorted time. I feel it land lightly and think, shit, on my blue pants, part of a suit she liked so much.

I know I'm in The Pantry, corner of Figueroa and Olympic, not far from where we last loved so hard that Halloween dawn. I know the printed words mean she's gone. I know that I'm alone. I see my hand still in front of me, feel the warmth of the sourdough toast in my lap, hear the clatter of plates, the clinkle of utensils. The clatter, the clinkle, the music of morning patter drops like musical notes. Drops sharp and bright, full of light and life.

Drops like music.

But I can't move, haven't since I read those words.

"I need a hand over here."

There's one of the ancient waiters. "They sign up for life in this jernt," Morrie used to say. The waiter is a kindly man in a tuxedo shirt, bow tie, waist-to-shoes apron. His hands are firm, helpful.

Musical notes dropping, and I can't move.

"Whom do you wish we call, Mr. Ray?"

"I don't know," I say.

Someone says 10,000 people have come. Clara says the lady looked beautiful before they closed the coffin at the funeral home across the street. "All cream and gold, her gown is, a pearl rosary in her small, perfect hands."

Julian urges Dorothy's three kids along protectively.

Anonymous mourners move in slow motion like extras in a movie. One little shit quotes Sinatra to a reporter. "Guess I'll have to revise my act."

Her decorator, the big guy who helped her with my apartment, sits with other arty types and wipes his eyes with a large white handkerchief.

Stars of film, television, world affairs twinkle twinkle in the ugly beauty of daylight, not once interrupting the dirge, the promise from the church of St. Vincent Ferrer that behind our dark glasses, we're known to God, and our day too will come.

Phillip helps me.

Babe and Cornshucks help me.

I see Dick Kollmar, and I feel a rush of pity until his stare meets mine. In the time it takes for the look between us to connect and fade, I swear to call on him.

Today, every time I hear the question, "How did she die?" and every time I hear the answer, "No one knows," I vow to face him again.

Soon.

I stop to let my eyes adjust to the smoke-stained, dark-wooded dimness of the bar. He is here, waiting. An apparition, his edges bleed into the gloom. He's dark-suited, guarding a glass, its contents as dark as the dark bar he sits hunched over.

"You're early," he says. He pours into his glass from an amber bottle, pours into another, sets the bottle down, shoves the extra drink a stool away. "I see you," he says.

A step, and I focus on the glass.

"Chivas," he says. "No ice." He chuckles. "Ice maker's on the fritz."

In the wicked light, he looks haggard, tragic. I wonder how I must look to him. This thought makes me lift his offering, drink half of it.

"That's the way, friend," he says.

"I'm not your friend," I say.

"No," he says. "You're not."

His voice is resonant, a radio voice like one I remember, its dial's glow soft and intimate against my white pillow, my mind spellbound, wondering why no voice in real life sounded like that.

I squeeze the glass, swallow hard, screw my gaze into his. Fear strikes, but not the sort I felt when he threatened to kill me months before.

"Another?" He doesn't wait for my answer, pours. The sound of the liquid is enormous in the stillness. He could murder me now, and not a living soul would know.

"What killed her, Kollmar?"

"I killed her."

Jesus. I don't say a word, but my face, even in this light, must be a scream mask.

"And so did you," he adds. "I kept her nightstand plied with dope. You started her on the shit. We all three drink enough of this—" he raises his glass—"to sail the fucking Atlantic and Pacific, three in a boat."

"Triangle," I mumble. I set my glass down with a vengeance.

"Another?" he asks.

"Yes." I sit on a stool he's pushed out with his foot. He ducks my glance. I raise my voice. "You're hiding something."

"Bullshit."

"Her files, Kollmar. What happened to her files?"

He pulls in his chin, thickening his neck. Hell, he ain't saying anything.

"You motherfucker," I say, shame running into my own blood. "I didn't believe her at first either. But goddammit, we can't give up on her now. She was too tough, too professional."

Without raising his eyes, he says, "I destroyed her files, burned every fucking note."

I kick the stool out of my way. "You son of a bitch! All her stuff on the cover-up should be turned over."

"Turned over?" He is plenty drunk, but his voice comes to me with conviction. "Who the fuck do you think it should have been handed to?"

I'm silent, trying to read him correctly. I still can't believe he'd destroy the words she'd risked her life for.

He swings his feet to the dark carpet. His arms hang ape-like. "I loved her." He jabs a hand out between us. "Not like you think you loved her. You kept her around, hoping she'd make you look like a man."

He falls to his knees. I reach for him. He swings his clinched fist through the air, watches it drop like a stone.

"Her coffin," he says. "I saw she got one of beautiful African mahogany."

I turn from him, search for a trail back through the sad-colored dining area. I see shadows of Dotty and me touching under a table, daring the big man at the bar to catch us in our lust.

He must be remembering too. His sobs rip at the club's interior. His words, stage-trained as they may be, aren't discernable, but as I start to leave, I feel his baritone voice vibrate through me like Babe Pascoe's drums.

It sounds like he's crying out desperately for me to return, have another drink with him.

I look away from a mirror that doesn't lie to me. I pour a stiff drink, let it sit on the dressing table. Cornshucks comes in and looks at the drink too.

She makes a thing out of busying herself with her gown.

"An hour to go," she tells me. "Meantime, you can relax on the cot in my room."

"I'll be okay here."

"We can go right to your medley. I'll be by your side, throwing in some funk."

"That okay with Babe?"

"We'll be wich ya."

"I'll try not to parody myself, escape before they eat me." I study my drink. "Then you can give 'em what they paid to see."

"Don't deal that fool hand." Her fingers caress my cheek. Her full lips make a kissing sound, then the glorious aura of her is gone.

The drink watches me. I watch it.

Babe opens the door a crack like he doesn't want to bug me. Our eyes meet in the mirror.

Something about his look jabs me.

"What?"

"Dick Kollmar died."

The triangle. You, me and Dick, Dorothy had said.

"You sure, Babe?"

"Yes."

"How?"

In the mirror, he nods at my drink. "That and the pharmacy. They're saying suicide."

"Jesus."

"You want we should cancel your numbers? Rosehelen and me are cool with that."

"No."

"Want to be alone?"

"Yep."

January, the bitch, comes cold and sharp through cracks in the tiny room, from under the door as Babe closes it.

I draw a triangle in my mind—equal angles for perfect strength. Equilateral. I picture me in one of its corners, for some reason lower right—crouched, alive, poised to escape.

Tomb, she'd said.

"Fuck it."

I spring from my chair, leave the room without touching the drink.

In the narrow hall, I walk fast toward the sound of musicians getting ready.

"Taste, J.R.?" Alto man offers a half-pint from his case.

I don't break stride.

Behind my back, I hear him say, "That's a first."

Check out these other fine titles by
Durban House at your local book store.

EXCEPTIONAL BOOKS
BY
EXCEPTIONAL WRITERS

Current Titles

BASHA   John Hamilton Lewis

DEADLY ILLUMINATION   Serena Stier

DEATH OF A HEALER   Paul Henry Young

HOUR OF THE WOLVES   Stephane Daimlen-Völs

A HOUSTON WEEKEND   Orville Palmer

JOHNNIE RAY & MISS KILGALLEN   Bonnie Hearn Hill & Larry Hill

THE MEDUSA STRAIN   Chris Holmes

MR. IRRELEVANT   Jerry Marshall

OPAL EYE DEVIL   John Hamilton Lewis

PRIVATE JUSTICE   Richard Sand

ROADHOUSE BLUES   Baron Birtcher

RUBY TUESDAY   Baron Birtcher

THE SERIAL KILLER'S DIET BOOK   Kevin Mark Postupack

THE STREET OF FOUR WINDS   Andrew Lazarus

TUNNEL RUNNER   Richard Sand

WHAT GOES AROUND   Don Goldman

Nonfiction

MIDDLE ESSENCE—WOMEN OF WONDER YEARS   Landy Reed

PROTOCOL   Mary Jane McCaffree & Pauline Innis
    For 25 years, the bible for public relations firms, corporations, embassies, governments and individuals seeking to do business with the Federal government.

BASHA   JOHN HAMILTON LEWIS
Set in the world of elite professional tennis and rooted in ancient Middle East hatreds of identity and blood loyalties, Basha is charged with the fiercely competitive nature of professional sports and the dangers of terrorism. An already simmering Middle East begins to boil and CIA Station Chief Grant Corbet must track down the highly successful terrorist, Basha. In a deadly race against time, Grant hunts the illusive killer only to see his worst nightmare realized.

DEADLY ILLUMINATION   SERENA STIER
It's summer 1890 in New York City. Florence Tod, an ebullient young woman, must challenge financier, John Pierpont Morgan, to solve a possible murder. J.P.'s librarian has ingested poison embedded in an illumination of a unique Hildegard van Bingen manuscript. Florence and her cousin, Isabella Stewart Gardner, discover the corpse. When Isabella secretly removes a gold tablet from the scene of the crime, she sets off a chain of events that will involve Florence and her in a dangerous conspiracy.

DEATH OF A HEALER   PAUL HENRY YOUNG
Diehard romanticist and surgeon extraordinaire, Jake Gibson, struggles to preserve his professional oath against the avarice and abuse of power so prevalent in present-day America. Jake's personal quest is at direct odds with a group of sinister medical and legal practitioners who plot to eliminate patient groups in order to improve the bottom line. With the lives of his family on the line, Jake must expose the darker side of the medical world.

HOUR OF THE WOLVES   STEPHANE DAIMLEN-VÖLS
After more than three centuries, the *Poisons Affair* remains one of history's great, unsolved mysteries. The worst impulses of human nature—sordid sexual perversion, murderous intrigues, witchcraft, Satanic cults—thrive within the shadows of the Sun King's absolutism and will culminate in the darkest secret of his reign: the infamous *Poisons Affair,* a remarkably complex web of horror, masked by Baroque splendor, luxury and refinement.

A HOUSTON WEEKEND   ORVILLE PALMER
Professor Edward Randa11, not-yet-forty, divorced and separated from his daughters, is leading a solitary, cheerless existence in a university town. At a conference in Houston he runs into his childhood sweetheart. Then she was poverty-stricken, neglected and American Indian. Now she's elegantly attired, driving an expensive Italian car and lives in a millionaires enclave. Will their fortuitous encounter grow into anything meaningful?

JOHNNIE RAY & MISS KILGALLEN   BONNIE HEARN HILL & LARRY HILL
Johnnie Ray was a sexually conflicted wild man out of control; Dorothy Kilgallen, fifteen years his senior, was the picture of decorum as a Broadway columnist and TV personality. The last thing they needed was to fall in love—with each other. Sex, betrayal, money, drugs, drink and more drink. Together they descended into a nightmare of assassination conspiracies, bizarre suicides and government enemy lists until Dorothy dies...mysteriously. Was it suicide...or murder?

THE MEDUSA STRAIN CHRIS HOLMES

A gripping tale of bio-terrorism that stunningly portrays the dangers of chemical warfare in ways nonfiction never could. When an Iraqi scientist full of hatred for America breeds a deadly form of anthrax and a diabolical means to initiate an epidemic, not even the First Family is immune. Will America's premier anthrax researcher devise a bio-weapon in time to save the U.S. from extinction?

MR. IRRELEVANT JERRY MARSHALL

Sports writer Paul Tenkiller and pro-football player Chesty Hake have been roommates for eight seasons. Paul's Choctaw background and his sports gambling, and Chesty's memories of his mother's killing are the dark forces that will ensnare Tenkiller in Hake's slide into a murderous paranoia—but Paul is behind the curve that is spinning Chesty out of his control.

OPAL EYE DEVIL JOHN HAMILTON LEWIS

From the teeming wharves of Shanghai to the stately offices of New York and London, Robber Barons lie, steal, cheat, and kill in their quest for power. Eric Gradek will rise from the *Northern Star's* dark cargo hold to the pinnacle of high stakes gambling for unrivaled riches. Aided by his beautiful wife, Katheryn, and the devoted Tong-Po, Eric fights for his dream and for revenge against the man who left him for dead aboard *Northern Star.*

PRIVATE JUSTICE RICHARD SAND

After taking brutal revenge for the murder of his twin brother, Lucas Rook leaves the NYPD to work for others who crave justice outside the law when the system fails them. Rook's dark journey takes him on a race to find a killer whose appetite is growing. A little girl turns up dead. And then another and another. The nightmare is on him fast. The piano player has monstrous hands; the Medical Examiner is a goulish dwarf; an investigator kills himself. Betrayal and intrigue is added to the deadly mix as the story careens toward its startling end.

ROADHOUSE BLUES BARON BIRTCHER

Newly retired Homicide detective Mike Travis is torn from the comfort of his chartered yacht business into the dark, bizarre underbelly of LA's music scene by a grisly string of murders. A handsome, drug-addled psychopath has reemerged from an ancient Dionysian cult, leaving a bloody trail of seemingly unrelated victims in his wake.

RUBY TUESDAY BARON BIRTCHER

Mike Travis sails his yacht to Kona, Hawaii expecting to put LA Homicide behind him: to let the warm emerald sea wash years of blood from his hands. Instead, he finds his family's home ravaged by shotgun blasts, littered with bodies and trashed with drugs. Then things get worse. A rock star involved in a Wall Street deal masterminded by Travis's brother is one of the victims. Another victim is Ruby, Travis's childhood sweetheart. How was she involved?

THE SERIAL KILLER'S DIET BOOK   KEVIN MARK POSTUPACK

Fred Orbis is fat—very fat—but will soon discover the ultimate diet. Devon DeGroot is on the trail of a homicidal maniac who prowls Manhattan with meatballs, bologna and egg salad—taunting him about the body count in *Finnegans Wakean*. Darby Montana, one of the world's richest women, wants a new set of genes to alter a face and body so homely not even plastic surgery could help. Mr. Monde is the Devil in the market for a soul or two. It's a Faustian satire on God and the Devil, Heaven and Hell, beauty and the best-seller list.

THE STREET OF FOUR WINDS   ANDREW LAZARUS

Paris—just after World War II. On the Left Bank, Americans seek a way to express their dreams, delights and disappointments in a way very different from pre-war ex-patriots. Tom Cortell is a tough, intellectual journalist disarmed by three women-French, British and American. Along with him is a gallery of international characters who lead a merry and sometimes desperate chase between Pairs, Switzerland and Spain to a final, liberating and often tragic end of their European wanderings in search of themselves.

TUNNEL RUNNER   RICHARD SAND

Ashman is a denizen of a dark world where murder is committed and no one is brought to account; where loyalties exist side-by-side with lies and extreme violence. One morning he awakens to find himself paralyzed in a mental hospital. He escapes and seeks vengeance, confronting old friends, the Pentagon, the Mafia, and a mysterious general who is covering up the attack on TWA Flight 800.

WHAT GOES AROUND   DON GOLDMAN

Ten years ago, Ray Banno was vice president of a California bank when his boss, Andre Rhodes, framed him for bank fraud. Now, he has his new identity, a new face and a new life in medical research. He's on the verge of finding a cure for a deadly disease when he's chosen as a juror in the bank fraud trial of Andre Rhodes. Should he take revenge? Meanwhile, Rhodes is about to gain financial control of Banno's laboratory in order to destroy Banno's work

Nonfiction

MIDDLE ESSENCE—WOMEN OF WONDER YEARS   LANDY REED

Here is a roadmap and a companion to what can be the most profoundly significant and richest years of a woman's life. For every woman approaching, at, or beyond midlife, this guide is rich with stories of real women in real circumstances who find they have a second chance-a time when women blossom rather than fade. Gain a new understanding of how to move beyond myths of aging; address midlife transitions head on; discover new power and potential; and emerge with a stronger sense of self

OCT   2002